EX LIBRIS

GIFT OF

SIMI VALLEY FRIENDS
OF THE LIBRARY

BY BARBARA NEIL

A Man with His Back to the East

Someone Wonderful

The Possession of Delia Sutherland

A History of Silence

A HISTORY OF *Silence*

NAN A. TALESE

D O U B L E D A Y

New York   London   Toronto   Sydney   Auckland

A HISTORY OF Silence

A Novel

BARBARA NEIL

PUBLISHED BY NAN A. TALESE
an imprint of Doubleday
a division of Bantam Doubleday Dell Publishing Group, Inc.
1540 Broadway, New York, New York 10036

DOUBLEDAY is a trademark of Doubleday, a division of
Bantam Doubleday Dell Publishing Group, Inc.
First published in the United Kingdom by Macmillan Publishers
Ltd., London.

"STROLLING" Words and Music by Ralph Reader
© 1959 Reproduced by permission of Keith Prowse Pub Co Ltd,
London WC2H 0EA
"JAMBALAYA (ON THE BAYOU)" Words and Music by Hank Williams
© Copyright 1952 renewed 1980 Hiriam Music & Acuff-Rose Music
Incorporated, USA. Acuff-Rose Music Limited, London W1
Used by permission of Music Sales Ltd. All rights reserved.
International Copyright secured.
"HOW DO YOU DO MR. RIGHT" Words and Music by Vivian Ellis CBE
Copyright 1938 Chappell Music Ltd, London
"MUSIC MAESTRO PLEASE" Music by Allie Wrobel, Words
by Herbet Magidson
Copyright 1937 Bourne Co. USA Warner/Chappell Music Ltd, London
Reproduced by permission of International Music Publications Ltd

Library of Congress Cataloging-in-Publication Data
Neil, Barbara.
A history of silence: a novel / Barbara Neil.
p. cm.
I. Title.
PR6064.E426H57 1998
823'.914—dc21 98-14335
CIP

I wish to express my profound gratitude to the following people for their advice and encouragement throughout the writing of this book: Alexandra Pringle and Andrew Christie-Miller, as well as to my two dear "A" type friends.

My thanks as well to Jenny Thompson, MCSP, for sharing with me her expertise, and to Humphrey Wakefield and Julie and Parker LeCorgne for their unfailing generosity.

Barbara Neil, 1997

M U R R A Y

(1947–1994)

Either the Darkness alters —

Or something in the sight

Adjusts itself to Midnight

And Life steps almost straight.

—EMILY DICKINSON

CONTENTS

I / *Snapshots* 1

II / *Something Had Woken Me* 23

III / *There Are Places* 61

IV / *Teddy and Marie* 101

V / *'Specting Company* 131

VI / *Back Again* 177

VII / *All the Joy* 197

VIII / *Esther* 237

IX / *The Woman Jane* 265

X / *We Don't Do Teatime Anymore* 287

XI / *Freedom Fields* 305

XII / *You Can't Get to Heaven Without Passing Through Atlanta* 329

XIII / *Snapshot* 333

A HISTORY OF Silence

SNAPSHOTS

Laura was my sister, alive those four years before
I was born—born not to protect her, although I made the
mistake of thinking so, but to witness the show of her
survival. Unkindness was not in her. Cruelty, yes. My
failures could always be softened by her humor, and
none of my achievements felt confirmed until I had
shared them with her. It was also true that she could pass
through my life and some element of vitality could ad-
here itself to her presence, go with her, and I would be
left thinking, Life went that way.

I know the most valuable communication between
people is made without words but I'll write about Laura
because there is a commotion in my brain. Images press
there. They arrive unsummoned in their own precise order, nine snapshots dredged from the silt of the past. I'll

lay them down here, brief scenes, to study, and understand, and be free. Two of them are not even my own
memories but those of Esther, our mother. The last
comes, I believe, from thin future air.

In this first one, I, Robbie, am sitting alone:

JANVIER, BAYOU PAYS BAS, LOUISIANA

It's cooler outside on the verandah now the sun is low
over where the bayou ends, towards Pointe Coupee. Re-
cumbent in the swing chair, maintaining momentum
with one foot to the floor, I shut my eyes to marry the
textures of wood and the rattan pressing into the back of
my neck, down the side of my body. There's the smell of
creosote but faint, faint, its usefulness long gone, and
Theresa's stew cooking over in the dependency. The closest sounds are the intimate creak of that rattan and the
chair that suspends the seat grinding in hooks fixed to
the rafters way above. The voices of the children reach
me from further off, from down on the levee where
they've been all afternoon lolling and bathing, livelier
with the coming of evening.

I bend forward to view down the steps and see the four
of them returning, led by their shadows over the grass.
Will is bumping his old guitar behind him like always.
Marie makes believe she has a ball to tease Miss Moley,
who's jumping, excited, walking backwards on her hind
legs. Gauging direction from the circling arm, she runs
off barking, seeking, then stands forlorn and confused in
her failure, watching the figures, drawn close and talking, walking away from her towards the house.

I call, "Miss Moley, poor Miss Moley. Come on, Baby, are they teasing you?"

My call arrests the four. They are halted in a line, their eyes directed towards me. I have not moved. My hand is still raised in a wave to where the dog had been, although she has trotted right up to me.

"Do that again, Robbie?" Marie takes the steps in twos. I still hadn't moved, had stayed just that way, hand up. "You sounded exactly like Granny Esther."

"That was the darnedest thing," Teddy says, his arm sticky with sun oil around my shoulders.

They cluster, amused, interested, smelling of bubble gum, sneaked cigarettes, and the uncomplicated sweat of youth.

"Did you mean to, Aunt Robbie?" Will's brown eyes roam mine. "Or not?"—with the trace of a frown. I shake my head. He knew it. "So say something else. Speak to us again, please," his soft voice urges. The others become differently attentive.

I feel as if I've been asked to sing, which I couldn't, had never been able to.

"Please," Will whispers, and the others murmur it too, *"Please," "Please."*

I open my mouth not knowing, not trying for anything to happen. "Helloo Babies, there we are then." Esther's voice from my mouth.

"Esther," they say, the four of them, "Grandma," "Granny Esther," "The GrandEst," as if in greeting, charmed, uncertain, embarrassed. They settle close to me, behind, beside, at my feet, touching a knee, a hand, an ankle. Miss Moley's there too and we stay, content to be that way, not speaking anymore until the descending night is complete.

IN LONDON WHEN ESTHER, MY MOTHER,

WAS VERY YOUNG

Esther strains, seeking her reflection in a mirror framed with pastel glass flowers. On the lace-tiered table at her eye level are silver-backed brushes, ivory buttonhooks, paper packets printed with "Windemere, Human Hair, Price 6d." Purple ostrich plumes are tucked between the tendrils of the glass flowers and a cock-feather cloche hat nods on a stand, beckoning to be worn. Perched on a stool, lace-tiered to match the table, she searches among the enamel boxes and china pots. There is a gold case she knows about. She has been here before. Finding it, Esther removes the lid, unwinds the tongue of red grease, licks it over her lips and cheeks. From under a crystal lid she removes a swan's-down pad and smothers her face with sweet-smelling beige powder. Now she is balanced precariously and reaching, reaching for that gleaming green-black hat. Her fingertips are brushing the gloss of it when her wrist is grabbed, she is swung around, and a hand crashes across the side of her head. Then she's let go and plumps to the floor without a sound because, above all, she knows she must not do that, make any noise in here of all places where she has no business to be.

Her vision clears. There is a dizzy back-view of her mother's ankles brushed by the hem of her black dress, the white bow of her apron, the tails of her cap resting between her shoulders. From the open ends of knitted mittens those dextcrous fingers restore the dressing table to order. When she does turn her face is flushed and her mouth is moving rapidly but Esther cannot hear what her mother is saying. But she knows she should have remained where she spends every evening after school, down in the servant's hall, which is not a hall at all but a low-ceilinged room where she makes jigsaw puzzles, eavesdrops on conversations she does not understand, and dozes sometimes until long after midnight when her mother is free to go home—when they will walk up Pont Street, around to Sloane Square, which is lit by electric, to Chelsea Bridge Road and on to the Embankment, which is still in gaslight, and all the while fear is transmitted to Esther through her mother's grip, fear of an encounter with what she refers to as "one of those poor young devils" who roam the streets out of work, out of step, mad and forgotten, their minds still embattled in a war that ended four years ago—but now, now sitting on the deep-pile rug, there is only singing and whining in Esther's head. Her hearing is gone. Then her mother hoists her onto her hip and pauses to listen before passing brisk but cautious along the passage. They stop to peer over a polished rail, Esther's mouth covered by the rough-skinned fingers. She clings on tight, rolling her eyes up to see night through the oval skylight from where a pipe of blue velvet hangs between the unbroken treacle-ribbon of bannister and is lost at the end in the blaze of a chandelier. Below the light, to the left, is a line of people, heads then feet on a black and white floor, their bodies lost in perspective.

They rush on, Esther in her mother's arms, to the end of the passage where they shoulder through a green cloth door and descend a coffin of stairs.

Inside Esther's head there is a sucking and a roar, a wave rising and smashing on shingle. It subsides and returns repeatedly, bringing back each time some fragment of other sound, real sound: her mother's feet on the stone, the swish of her skirts, some of her words, words of a familiar litany: *Stupid goose—lose my job—starve— you keep out of sight—shhh, shh, shh.* Only it is all coming differently, echoing in surf with velvet gaps of silence where sense is being lost. But *out of sight,* she hears that and knows the part very well. The Family must not see Esther. She must stay in the basement.

Finally she is set down in the dark on the top step of the flight leading to that basement. Her mother pulls the mittens from her hands and drops them into her own lap, shakes her apron, touches her hair, and, opening it as little as need be, slips through a door into the bright, bright hall. Esther rubs her face in the mittens, they smell of that pinkish powder her mother uses to polish the blades of the dinner knives. Through a crack in the door she can see the line of feet again, and now black-stockinged ankles brushed by black hems, the white bows of aprons, the streamers falling from white caps. Esther cannot tell anymore which one is Mother.

Swinging in front of all of those skirts come two wooden sticks with one trousered leg between them, a cream spat and polished shoe at the end of it. She knows who it belongs to, this leg. It's his. The one who lost his other leg in France during a battle against the final German offensive. The same battle at which, as this man's batman, Esther's father had lost his life.

Esther told me that to comfort herself in the weeks before I was born she would cradle her belly and say, *It's you and me, just you and me alone,* although Laura was already there, four years old. But she sensed leaving would soon be forced on her, had been watching the signals for months, so perhaps she was simply confiding in the companion best placed for flight.

The Healing Room is a calm place with long, freestanding mirrors on casters, a treatment couch, wooden blocks to support the knees, the neck, the small of the back. There is a cupboard containing a skeleton called George who slides out on a runner when the door is opened. The paintings on the walls are by young artists who can't afford the fee. And he is sitting there by the window, Matthew, my father, the faith healer, with his limbs immaculately arranged, palm up on either knee, torso in perfect alignment, so wholly relaxed that gravity appears to have lost its hold.

The woman Jane had found Esther preparing supper in the basement and asked her to, please, come upstairs because they wanted to talk to her, no, later wouldn't do. Right away. Please. Now the woman Jane is standing by the window, looking out, while Esther curls and twists on the hard chair to find the particular angle that numbs the prenatal ache.

"Esther, Esther, look at you." Matthew approaches,

crouches next to her with his hands poised, unable to resist correcting his wife's posture, release tension, have her sit just so. "Laura was carrying on again all afternoon. It's very distressing for our patients." Matthew and Jane's patients.

"She doesn't like being made to stay downstairs. She never used to, did she? And she doesn't understand why she can't be in her old nursery. Nor do I."

"I've told you I can't work with her under my feet. Nor can Jane. We've discussed it before, Esther, haven't we?" Matthew walks away from her to say that, towards the woman Jane. Esther watches them. He turns. "Well, haven't I?"

"What?"

"Told you?"

"Told me what?"

Still facing out the window, the woman Jane crosses her arms and her ivory bangles clack.

"Esther, you're being provocative," Matthew says. "Come now." He returns to place his hands on her shoulders. "Jane and I can't work with children running around."

"One little girl. Your daughter. I'm not having the nursery in the basement, so don't ask me again. Isn't that why we searched London for a big enough place at the right price? To have room for both family and practice?"

"I didn't think I'd be taking on a partner so soon."

"We've waited so long to start our family. Now we've got our baby at last and you want to hide her in a damp basement. No, Matthew, she stays upstairs in the sunshine, and when the next one arrives that will too. Take your patients to the basement. I'm going to read to Laura now, it's her bedtime. Are you coming to say goodnight to her?"

The ivory bangles clack again. Matthew moves towards the woman Jane, stopping midway between her and Esther. The woman Jane comes close to him. He speaks to Esther, only he looks at the woman Jane. "In that case, Esther, in that case Jane and I feel it's time you found somewhere else to live. I'll pay for it and I'll come to see you there, of course. Laura can visit here at the weekends and holidays. And when the new baby is old enough they can visit together. Esther, think of it this way: Jane and I are doing important work here, unselfish work healing sick people when they've nowhere else to turn. We need a tranquil atmosphere. I know you understand."

Matthew is still holding his eyes on the woman Jane—who is wearing a pair of his own trousers pulled tight on her thin waist, her shirt, too, is his. She toys with those ivory bangles on her wrist. The sound seems to encourage him. He turns to Esther. "So? What do you say?"

"What about?"

He sinks his face in his hands. The woman Jane tells her, "It's time for you to go, Esther. And take the child with you. We'll help you find somewhere."

Esther stares at her husband, waits, asks finally, "Matthew? I don't understand what *you* really want."

Head back, elbows high in the air, face still hidden, he whines, "*I* don't know, *I* don't know, do I? I want peace. We need peace and quiet to work. I thought I'd been very clear about that."

Esther leans forward. "Did you say 'clear,' Matthew?" He uncovers his face. "I can't cope with any more of this."

The next morning Esther left with Laura and me. Me unborn inside her.

IT IS DARK IN HIS ROOM WHERE WE SLEEP

Laura and I are staying with our father. It is night, dark in his room where we sleep alongside his bed in two army cots, a scoop of canvas across an iron frame. He is not there. The door opens and I wake enough to know the outline, slick curls lapping her head, lean shoulders. It is the woman Jane. She comes close and I feel her looking at me, hear her turning away, movement in the air, she is bending low, a noise in her throat, involuntary, coming with the effort of lifting. The sounds recede, her breathing, her steps, all heavier, fuller. I open my eyes. She is leaving the room, her back to me. Hanging down on one side of her are Laura's arms limp in sleep and on the other are her dangling feet. The woman Jane maneuvers awkwardly to shut the door without knocking the child in her arms. She does not see me sitting up. I listen to hear the lavatory flushing in the bathroom between here and the passage. But there is no more noise after she has crossed the marbled green linoleum in there. I touch Laura's sheet to know if she has wet it. She still does that, often. Eight is too old to do that, she is told. She minds. Everyone minds. Especially the woman Jane.

Laura's bed is dry. I wait, sitting on the side of the cot, carefully, not to have it tip over. At the window, open a few inches, my nose is high enough to breathe in the summer air. There is laughter way off down the street and a muddled group of footsteps coming nearer, passing, going away. Then the crying starts, instantaneous, no working up to the mood of it. It is a Matthew-signaling cry, the one to let everyone know, or someone, *the* one, to make Mummy come and have everything be all right again. I know the kind. I have used it. Then the sound of it changes. A different signal. After that it stops but goes on in my head because it has been Laura crying.

Across the brown carpet, on over marbled green linoleum into the high funnel of passage, I go to sit on the lowest of the narrow stairs beside The Healing Room, which is opposite the room where we are not allowed to go, the one they say was Laura's nursery when she was a baby. I sit and bite my nails, bite them to the quick to taste the blood and tug at the slivers with my teeth until they come free and I chew them. It stops me thinking about her and it hurts me the way Laura is being hurt somewhere without me to look after her. There is no sound anymore, not from anywhere.

We had been told tenants lived in the top-floor rooms. The woman Jane had told us. We didn't know what tenants were and decided they must be animals, someone's pets, or wild, like birds or rats. We had never seen one and wondered who looked after them, cleaned them out. We would have liked a tenant of our own to keep at home but "no large pets," Mummy told us, she said it was written in the lease. We knew what a lease was because she'd told us. We drew pictures of what a tenant might look like. Mine was like a donkey, Laura's was more like an ostrich. She said she had heard them moving and it did not sound like four legs.

I sit tasting my bleeding fingertips, sucking them to numb the sting and thinking about tenants, when the door at the top of the stairs opens, the door that seals off that upper floor. The woman Jane's moccasined feet and the flapping hems of her trousers move down towards me. Laura is saddled upright on her elbow, not trying to hold on although she is awake. Not trying to hold on although it looks like she could fall just like that. Then she sees me, the woman Jane. She's never caught me waiting for Laura before. "So it's prying little you, is it? Very well then, miss." She leans down, hoists me to my feet, and Laura keels backwards, does nothing to stop herself, her head bangs the wall, she does not cry though. She is suspended only by her knees between the arm and body of the woman Jane, who has released me long enough to pluck Laura upright by the neck of her nightie and grab my wrist again to drag me, arm-stretched, toe-brushing, to the top of the stairs.

We are through the door at the top and she closes us into the darkness of a passage smaller, lower, than any other in the house. She lets go of me, sets Laura on her feet, but Laura will not, cannot, stand, bumps to the floor. When the woman Jane opens a door I see from the light in there that Laura is sitting straight-backed, staring ahead the way she had been up on the woman Jane's arm and fell back and was righted again. The door is pushed shut. I hear voices from there, not the words, but voices serious as though they could argue but would not let themselves. A laugh rattles, ceases, and the voices stop, begin again, more serious than before. I stand near to Laura. I want to hold her hand but don't dare because she is so strange and different and it might be my fault, whatever it is that has happened.

A man comes to the door to look at us, his bulk blocks the light. He leaves and comes back and out of the room to me. I do not look up at him, only at his cracked brown brogues spattered with white paint. He takes my hand, not roughly but hopeless of release, and leads me into the room where I know Laura was, and from where she cried and came out not crying but stiff and quiet and not seeing with her eyes wide open. I pull away but am dragged forward.

The woman Jane pushes past, the cloth of her trousers presses into my face and her hand pushes my head aside like it's the knob on the banister, and I feel the momentum of her passing. The door shuts and the only thing I have is this hand, these fingers splayed fast around my fist. This is all there is. There is no more world outside this room. It has all fallen away, everything is gone and will never come back. Not Laura, not Mummy, not our nursery with Battersea power station at night, not Great-Aunt Violet who looks after us when Mummy is at the office and who wears three hair-nets all at once, and lots of bloomers that reach right down to her knees. All that is left are these hard, dry fingers trapping me, but they've come with me into this, so I work my fist into a hand to hold them with, to not let go.

A cough, low voices, very low, one, another, two to-

gether; furniture moving, a chair or something, the ringing of glass on glass, delicate in the gross quiet. If I don't
look they won't see me, won't know I'm here. They do
know. The lines of their sight are piercing me. Someone
takes off my nightie. Strong smells are making me feel
sick. Pipe smoke and other smoke from those oval cigarettes that make people pick their tongues when they
smoke them; another smell too, sharp like the sea, a bit,
but not.

I want to see if there is a tenant. Maybe I could sit
with it. They might let me hold it and I will look into its
eyes and find that quality in an animal's eyes that makes
you feel happy. So I look: a thin man with dark skin,
black beard, and a boat-shaped cloth on his head. He
looks away. A woman in a bright dress is sitting in the
corner. Her eyes are laughing at me. There are some
other people too but I can't see a tenant so I squeeze my
eyes shut to make it all go away and it does and it stays
away because then something soft covers my head. I can
breathe but I can't see. But I do know there's someone
else there and the reason I haven't seen him is because
he's behind me, at the back of the room. I want to call to
him and go to him but I'm frightened because maybe I
shouldn't. Maybe he is cross with me and that is why he
hasn't called me, come to me, spanned the distance to
where I'm alone.

LAURA IS SINGING IN THE DARK

Great-Aunt Violet has put us to bed, Laura and me. She
is nine, I am five. Laura is singing something into the

darkness. We get out of bed and stand in our nighties on the window seat, gripping the high sill to see the sheen of London night and the distant, looming chimneys of Battersea power station. Then we hear from downstairs what we have been waiting for, a key in the latch and the front door opening and slamming comfortably shut. We storm back to bed, giggling. Mummy is home from the office. Feigning sleep, we wait for ti-tip-tip-tip on a quick rising note as she ascends the single flight of stairs. "Hellooo Babies." That voice, warm, broken, light. She stands in the doorway filling our room with the scent of outdoors and night. Rain glistens on her round black-velvet hat with the tiny silk balls dancing around the crown and rain glistens too on her skin. She pretends to believe we are asleep, that she will turn and leave us. "Oh dear, I'm too late. They're fast asleep." "Booo." Laura jumps, bounces on her bed. Mummy crosses the nursery to settle her and whisper things I cannot hear, just as, in a minute, she will whisper things to me that Laura will not hear. "So what about you then?" She glides over to me, my bed gives to her weight as she reaches for my hand. I tell her all the things I have saved to tell and then some more to prevent her from leaving, and as I speak I watch her features flowing from inter-ested, amused, indulgent, towards the sensation she has been fighting—is always fighting: exhaustion. She leans to kiss me. Her cheek smells so deliciously of the ele-ments she has brought with her, of outdoors, of mystery, of the night and of her face powder, that I draw my tongue from her jaw to cheekbone. She pulls back, her face stiff with horror, then her hand, from nowhere, sears the side of my face, slams me into my pillow. I hear nothing but a high-pitched note deep inside my head until her voice seeps through. "I know where you learn that filth and you're not bringing that smut into my home."

IN MATTHEW'S GARDEN

There are wooden seed boxes nearby, and bright-colored packets, a sieve caked in soil, and, at the edge of my field of vision, a rake stands jabbed into a half-tilled flower bed. My hair, falling around my face, breaks up the sunlight, encloses my world. Close to my face are his hands—square, neat, very large—cupped around a flowerpot, shirt cuffs rolled above his wrists. "Can you manage?" he asks. "Lower, Daddy," I order him as he crouches next to me while I dig with a trowel, almost too heavy for me to hold, and fill the pot with earth. "Where's my dandelion?" "I have it safe here, see, Robbie?" He nods to the pocket on the front of his shirt and there it is, golden and wilting. "Are you sure you want to plant this one? It hasn't got any roots. I don't think it'll live long." But that's the one I want to plant. "Cover the stem gently then, now press the earth around it. That's the way. Clever girl. Now shall we plant another one? One with roots this time and perhaps a daisy or two with it? After that you can help me if you like. Come on, we'll start off by—"

"Matthew? Matthew? Would you come here, please?" The woman Jane's voice.

I don't look. He gets up and leaves me.

MIMOSA HEAPED ON THE FLOOR

The mimosa, heaped on the floor, is set in a fall of sunlight, crossed by the shadow of glazing bars. I open the
window, French windows, glass doors, and step onto the
balcony, gripping, leaning over the wrought-iron rail to
watch for the mushroom-colored Ford Anglia to turn out
of the Old Brompton Road into our street. From behind
the house a bank of cloud advances on the sun, which is
slipping into the west, stretching its light further across
the red carpet inside, sliding it to the left, leaving the
mimosa out of frame. The car is still not in sight. I go in,
close the window behind me, and relay, yet again, the
scores of fronds in the new oblong of sunlight, setting
each one with such care that not a green stem shows,
only a mass of yellow flower, the filaments on each
round head responding to an unfelt draught so the whole
is minutely quivering, seeming to breathe.

I am nine. It is March and Esther's birthday. For an
hour and a half I have been ready, moving the flowers
with the sun. The manner of the giving is as essential as
it being her favorite flower. If she does not arrive soon
those clouds will cover the sun, then it will set behind
them and leave my offering pointless. Now she is coming. I can hear her outside the room managing packages
so as to reach for the door handle and I watch it dip
down. I stand with arms wide open on the far side of my
flag of mimosa. It *is* still framed in sunlight. Even more
brilliant than it has been all afternoon.

Esther emerges halfway around the door, her hair,

frizzed from an unattended perm, pushing out from under a head scarf. She is holding a new Squeezy mop wrapped in cellophane and a pedal bin that is also sealed. Some of her purchases from an afternoon in Selfridge's household department.

There is no lapse between her entry and her greeting, nothing estimable, but I do register her private face. The face that is hers when she is alone, the one she wears unconsciously in shops, in the street among strangers. The corners of her mouth dip with exhaustion, disillusion weighs on the lids of her eyes. I feel the trampled cast of her thought, how it has been, is, through the day without Laura and me to pretend for. This is why the mimosa. To give back something I know she has lost, and lost before ever I was born. This is why the attention to time and light and scent and those things you cannot touch but know just the same. It is to make up for her lost things despite not knowing what but suspecting them to be magic and hope. Mostly magic.

She beams, not at the mimosa, she has not taken that in yet, it is still only seconds. She is beaming at me. "Helloooo Darling" in that way she always does. I just stay, arms wide, smiling, not moving to make her notice, to make her see. And she does.

"Oh look"—setting the mop, the bucket aside to sit neatly, feet together, hands clasped in her lap, reverently on the sofa. Her eyes do not move from the hump of glowing gold. She shuts them to inhale. "Oh look." It is all she is able to say and the wonder in it is enough. "Oh look," like it is nothing to do with me and I might not have seen it. So I squat down where I am on the far side of the mimosa and honor it in silence just as she is, lifting my eyes to her and back, to her and back.

She stares, dreaming and drawing deep breaths. She is very far away from me. We stay that way until the sun is gone. Then she looks at me and remembers that it is I who have done this for her, arranged it all, made it right. "Robbie, you clever little girl, did it take all your money?" "Yes," I boast. She comes swiftly to hug me, hide me against her, away from her face in case I should see in it what I already have, the baffled regret. It was all so right, so right. The right gesture from the wrong one.

ON THE STAIRS IN MATTHEW'S HOUSE

It is morning on the day of my eleventh birthday. We are sitting on the bottom of that last narrow flight in Matthew's house, Laura and I. Esther is there too, for the first time since they turned her out, Matthew and the woman Jane. Esther is inside his bedroom where he is lying dead. At dawn that day the telephone rang and rang and, when she answered, someone told Esther that Matthew had died of a heart attack. She had to come because she was, after all, still his wife. We had to go with her, Esther said, she couldn't possibly go alone, she said. Laura didn't want to but Esther was crying and crying and so was I. Laura hasn't cried at all and isn't crying now.

Strangers pass us on their way to and from his bedroom. Laura leaves me, opens the door. "I want to look at him," and her voice is cold, as if she's angry. "No, Laura, stay out." I can't see Esther but I hear her voice. "The deathbed is no place for children. It's not right."

Laura returns to me. My fingers have reached my mouth, I'm chewing my nails and don't even know it. Laura pulls my hand away. "Where's the woman Jane?" I whisper. "He turned her out a while back, didn't I tell you?" "No." Her arm encircles my shoulders. "Listen to this: 'When you and I are couched in our porphyry tombs and the last trumpet sounds I shall turn to you and say, "Robbie, Robbie, let's pretend we don't hear it." 'Now who said that?"

I'm rubbing a sliver of nail between my teeth, frowning at her and fighting my longing to chew on a fresh one. "You did."

"Silly. Oscar Wilde said that to a friend of his called Robbie, like you. So now I'm saying it to you." Laura is quiet for a long time until she says, "No more being woken in the night." Again she stays quiet and I am fidgeting. "Let's make a promise, shall we, Robs? If I ever find you sleeping, I swear I won't wake you. I'll watch over you but I'll never wake you. And you'll never wake me. Shall we have that promise?"

"What if I have something to say?"

"Keep it till I wake."

"Okay."

Esther, surrounded by those strangers, passes us, doesn't appear to see us. From over the banister we watch her descend the broader stairs to the ground floor, then Laura turns towards Matthew's room. I follow. It's odd in there without the army cots. He is all alone, lying very tidy, arms straight on either side on top of the blankets, a pillow under his chin. The wrong place for a pillow, it seems to me, and I go to move it. "Don't," Laura says. "His mouth'll drop open." She studies his face with her arms crossed, head on one side. I kneel beside him, frightened to touch his coldish hand but touching it anyway and remembering that hand holding the flowerpot while I filled it with earth to plant my dandelion. Laura's foot comes past my shoulder and prods his shoulder twice, like she doesn't believe he's dead. I brush off the dust left by her shoe and we leave.

JANVIER, LOUISIANA, AGAIN

It won't always hurt like this. Time will pass and it'll be different and you will still be here with all of us. With me. I know it and you don't—Patrick is telling Robbie, telling it without speaking—*You would know it too if only you looked at me for long enough*—making this known although her face is averted to where Miss Moley is pressed against the screen door, following the passage of moths on the other side with her paw, like a shortsighted person reading small print. Darkness surrounds their two faces, candlelit at the supper table. The children have left them for the cool of the verandah steps. The heavy air brings back the sound of their talk and Will's guitar from lower down on the bottom step. It is a composite picture of how their lives have been for a few months now, and of how they could be for all time if only she would look and see what he is telling her, and cover his hands, resting together before him on the table, cover them with her own.

11

SOMETHING HAD WOKEN ME

Something had woken me. I lay mentally touring the darkness of my flat, home for three years now. It was clean, that was certain because my routine was scrupulous. Bedroom: clothes folded on the chair, fresh uniform hanging in the cupboard over there, window shut, secured, door the same. Across the hall in the kitchen, the gas stove off, supper things washed; in the bathroom, the taps turned tight. The front door, then, was that cause of my waking? Mustn't get up. I walked about too much in the night, checking and checking and checking. Think harder: Are the chains on the door? They are. And that window in the kitchen, fastened too? Yes. I had returned twice to be sure. So what was the matter? Because something remained, waiting to be recalled, preventing sleep.

The studio room: Was my treatment couch covered with its dust sheet? Of course. The files in the cabinet were orderly, all those files on my patients. Ex-patients. Ah, there, of course: I was leaving, wasn't I?

Then I heard the reason for leaving shouting my name from the street. The bell rang and continued to ring until I pressed the intercom. "Let me in, Robs, quick." Two flights down, the street door clattered. I switched on lights and when I opened my own door Laura was leaning against the jamb wrapped to the ankles in a black shawl with Will, white-blond hair luminous, fast asleep in the well of her arms. She rolled to finish against the inside wall with her back to me, reached over her shoulder and touched my cheek in a familiar benediction. I followed her through to the studio where, still cradling Will and wrapped in her shawl, she began to pace and hum one plaintive phrase, interrupting herself to ask me, "What is that, Robs? Where's it from? It's driving me nuts."

"I don't know."

"You know it though, don't you?"

"Yes." Although I couldn't say why, and I didn't like hearing it. Laura named the notes as she sang, hesitating to identify each accurately, "B-C-D-D-D-C-D-E-FLAT-D-C."

"I hate it when you do that. You know it means nothing to me. Now let me take Will, he's too big to carry around. You'll hurt your back."

"But what's the tune, Robs? You do know it, don't you?" Keeping her face averted.

"It doesn't matter."

"It does,"—clasping Will tight, holding him from me as I reached out. "Listen again. I think it's Schubert."

"Don't. I don't like it, whatever it is. Give me your shawl, it's soaked. I didn't know it was raining."

"Pouring. Couldn't you hear it? And couldn't you hear me calling? I was calling you for ages." She twisted to assist in removing her shawl.

"I'll put this in the dryer."

When I returned she was crouched over Will nested in cushions on the sofa. One of his arms flailed. She caught it and eased his fingertips between her lips, infusing his sleep with security until the tiny limb relaxed and she tidied it to his face where his thumb, still glistening from her mouth, burrowed into his own.

"He'll be four in a couple of hours," she said.

"Two hours and"—I checked my watch—"thirty-three minutes. His card's over there. Forgot to post it. I was going to bring it along this afternoon."

Laura lit a cigarette and delicately parted the curtains an inch or two while I found an ashtray. "London rain. City rain. It's different from any other kind. You can only see it shining, not falling. It's a good time to get born, the early hours, the world you're coming into resting, ready to wake you. A good time to die too. They execute at dawn, don't they? Do you think it's so the soul's released into a new day rather than night? It could get lost in the night, couldn't it, not knowing its way around, unused to being free? Do you think that's it, Robs?" With her head tipped back and teeth clenched, she prepared to reveal her face. "What do you think?"

A cut under her left eye swam into the swollen cheekbone, a deepening. Another wedge of blood at the opposite edge of her mouth balanced the wounds. She remained by the window, allowing me to stare before gathering the things I needed. She didn't flinch when I bathed the cuts or try to stop me. When she did pull away it was to say, "God, I've just thought: Are you alone?"

"If I wasn't?" I waited long enough for her to cross the room, reach for Will. "I am, Laura. Let him be. You know very well I'm alone. Were you at the club?"

"Yup."

"Same club? Same songs?"

"Same old crap they love: 'My Way,' 'These Foolish Things.' "

"You love them too. Keep still, mouth shut. That's it."

I was applying a plaster when the telephone rang. We watched each other listening first to my voice on the machine, then to Sam's. "Robbie, it's me. Is she there? Laura, are you there? Pick up. Please Robbie? Laura?" He repeated our names continuously, the silences between more plangent than his voice, and he would continue until the tape ran out. He had before. So I picked up. "She's with you, isn't she? Is she all right? Did she tell you what happened?"

I held the receiver towards Laura as though she could have heard those questions, and she approached slowly, eased it from my hand. Sam must have known the transfer had happened because Laura just stood listening, nodding her face to the ceiling—such a long neck, thin, her larynx so defined. You would not have thought such a voice as hers could come from it, strong and rich with a river of sorrow through the words of even the most light-hearted song. "Don't Put Your Daughter on the Stage Mrs. Worthington," say, she could sing that and make you think twice.

Laura pressed the receiver hard against her ear, eyes squeezed shut, and drew her mouth in such a way that revived the bleeding, which did not appear to hurt her as much as whatever Sam was saying.

"I don't know, Sam, I don't know. It's my fault. Sorry. Sorry."

She joined me in the kitchen, slid into a chair, hooked her heels onto the sink opposite, lit another cigarette while I fetched the ashtray from the studio, placed it beside her. She caressed her cheeks, this side, that side, against the steam rising from a mug of coffee. It was a moment before I realized it was because she couldn't control her mouth enough to drink. There were straws in the drawer there bought on a previous occasion such as this.

"Robs?"

I washed my mug, folded a tea cloth, screwed the top on the coffee jar.

"*Robbie?*"

"Don't ask me, Laura. Couldn't you stay with Esther?"

"The Witneys are home. There's no way Will and I could be there and them not know. Esther would lose the job. Me alone, maybe. But not both of us. Will's the problem. He's the problem here too, isn't he? You think he'd disturb your patients."

"He would. Remember last time?" We stayed without talking, remembering last time. When eventually she allowed our eyes to meet I indicated her face and she sheltered behind a weak salute. "So what happened this time?" I pressed as though it could have had some bearing on whether or not she could stay.

"Sam came to the club to collect me after work. Didn't say he was going to. He came to my dressing room. I wasn't alone. There it is." She shrugged while behind the wounds her face collapsed under something more brutal than a beating. "There it is."

"How *not alone* were you?"

"Very not alone."

"Did Sam hit you?"

"Don't be stupid. He wouldn't. Ever."

No point in asking why. It was how she was, had been since possibly longer than even I knew. There was always a someone like Sam, and behind the someone there would be shadows.

"Can we stay? Will and me?"

Only two weeks more and my flat was to be hers anyway. She, Will, and Sam were to have moved from their dim dwelling into my place for however long I stayed away. Two more weeks with each day precisely planned to wind up my life in England leaving a tranquil path behind me, a tidy path as I'd tried to have my life be and failed. Failed because of Laura's messy life tangling with mine.

Dawn in the kitchen of my flat. Laura almost asleep where she was slumped. Will in the other room chuckling through his dreams the way he often did. And now there was I: angry, guilty, cornered.

"Come on, Laura, get some sleep before Will wakes." I

raised her as I had been trained, walked her to my bed, removed her boots, covered her. Already she was away in something more than sleep, a dedicated unconsciousness, her limbs flexed, forming the shape of a query, her fists lined defensively before her profile on the pillow. The wounds on her face no longer so apparent. She was thirty-four but did not look so different from when she was fifteen. The age she'd been when Matthew had died and when she'd taken nail scissors to her mass of thick dark hair and went on clipping until it ended in the zigzag crop of angles she had never allowed to grow since. The line of her fine black brows dominated her face. The bridge of her nose was another line and her long, narrow-lipped mouth yet another. That was Laura's face and I'm not saying it was beautiful, just a collection of lines with almost too much space between. Nothing much in repose. Her eyes, light brown and spangled with green, were not hard but neither was there any wonder in their expression. What they contained was an animation that made her whole face exceptional. And should she have opened them just then it would have been impossible to sum up her features, or anything else about her.

As I rose to leave she grasped my arm without waking, searching down to my wrist, my hand, and drew it with both of hers to cover that face I had been studying so hard. Awkwardly poised, I pictured how she had leaned over Will, imbuing his sleep with something, and I waited for the signal of her limp arm. It wasn't going to come. In truth Laura never slept, not as others do. I detached myself and her frown intensified. I re-covered her and left.

When the park gates were opened I walked between the formal flower beds through to the wilder part and wandered there until the morning lost its vulnerability and became, with its common light and common noise, a plain day as robust as any other. It was probably still raining, I cannot remember, but two unrelated incidents do remain with me from that morning. The first happened when I was walking with my head down and crashed into a black woman, taller than me and I'm not short. She was very thin and her dress flapped around her calves as she flailed the air with a white cane. "I need help. I need to get there. How'll I do that without help? Is there no one? I'm in shadow here." I clasped her arm and she turned two milky eyes on me. *"Who are you?"*

"I'll help you cross the road."

"It's not the road, it's the river, the river of life. I need a cab," then added with no attempt to free her arm from my guiding hand, "You hold me that way, that way."

"What way?"

"Like they do. You one of them?"

"I'm a physiotherapist."

"No good for eyes, then. You don't do eyes."

Her cane bowed under her weight as she waited, staring haughtily into her world. A cab drew up. Moorfields Eye Hospital in the Marylebone Road was where she wanted to go. I told the driver and helped her enter, only she managed to draw me in with her and smacked the glass with her cane. "Let's go." So I traveled with her to the Marylebone Road while she raged on about the dark and there being no one out there. The driver stopped at last and reached around outside to open the door. The woman walked towards the hospital steps. "Hey," I called, "I don't have enough change," only by then the steps were empty and the swing doors at the top had stuttered to a halt.

The driver sighed, "Bad start for both of us, eh?" and cruised into the rush-hour jam, leaving me far from where I wanted to be.

The second incident happened nearer home. Ahead, through the crowd, a little girl in a yellow skirt, five, maybe six years old, stood uniquely still amidst the daytime hubbub with her head on one side apparently engrossed in my appearance. Her face was so familiar yet I couldn't think from where and wanted to ask her. For each of my steps she took one back away from me. A compulsion to reach her forced me into a run and I knocked people aside, was shouted at. Then she turned and ran too, that little girl, right into the traffic without looking, into the lorries and taxis and cars. I lurched to the curb, straining for sight of her, at last glimpsed her yellow skirt way across on the far side of Ladbroke Grove. She'd made it and was waving. Waving at me. A container truck blocked her from view and when it had passed she'd vanished.

A visit to the bank to collect traveller's cheques, the American embassy for my passport stamped with a visitor's visa, back to the dry cleaner's, shoe mender's, Safeway. Such errands kept me away long enough, I hoped, to give Laura time to wake, make her plans, and leave.

The street door slammed behind me. The scent of her

cigarettes had penetrated the stairwell. So did her voice as I turned my key in the latch. Perhaps I was relieved that irritation was an option rather than the certain shame I'd have felt had I found her gone. I tripped over Will's miniature suitcase in the hall, spilling pajamas, picture books, and grubby, grubby Teddy Fred. I froze in the doorway to the studio, my treatment room. Three tables stood draped in bright cloths and streamers and were laden with crackers and every kind of party food including a turreted castle in green icing. A rocking horse, wooden tricycle, and stuffed toys littered the floor. Countless balloons clustered the ceiling and there was Will strutting beneath them, chuckling as the strings tickled his upturned face. Laura was doubled over a helium gas cylinder, inflating, knotting, and passing more of the balloons to Esther on the sofa, who, squinting through half-moon glasses, was attaching the candy-colored tails before setting them free. Esther.

"Esther" to us for so long now, ever since—when I could have been no more than four and Laura eight— Laura had dared me to call her that, just once, instead of Mummy. She didn't react, appeared not even to have noticed. Next it was Laura's turn to call her Esther. Then the two of us tried it on together, Esther this and Esther that. We played the game until the day I wanted her to be who she really was again and I called her Mummy. Too late. She blinked at me, didn't answer, not until I called her Esther. So it was Esther ever after.

She was surely comfortable that afternoon on my sofa, being useful without having to move the hips that gave her so much pain. In her youth she had been more slender, taller, as dark as Laura and I were then. Sometimes a hologram of that vivacious girl from a time before we knew her was fused with the familiar Esther, there in the carriage of her shoulders, a gesture of her hands, in her laugh—unconsciously moving her upper lip to hide the gap between her front teeth. Or when her notional bun slipped free and revealed that swathe of black hair wrapped up in the gray. But there was no hologram that day in the chaos of my studio. It occurred to me that I was seeing her for the first time as others did, as, simply, an old lady. Little old lady, dear old lady, sweet old lady. Esther was sixty-nine then and gravity had the upper hand. It had rounded her, loosened her. The arthritis that plagued her hips was in her fingers too and her face was puffy from drugs prescribed for Crohn's disease—the name of it distressed her as much as the symptoms. We weren't allowed to mention it. Her effort to overcome slight deafness since childhood had set her features in an almost invariable expression: expectant, intent, eyebrows raised, and lips on the way to a smile. Yet she could still check us, chasten Laura and me. A sharp turn of her head to a certain angle, chin raised, lips pursed. It was enough. We were mere children again. What would always remain unchanged was also her greatest asset: her voice. Her yeasty, her brown and broken voice. Seeing me then in the doorway, she said, "Hellooo Darling. Now don't look like that. We're having a party for Will. Come in and help, there's plenty to do."

The image of their faces turned towards me is an icon in my memory, my mother and my sister. Esther with her expectant expression, Laura surprised, and both of them apprehensive. Esther patted the sofa. "Come and sit down"—stifling a grunt of discomfort as she made space among string and paper chains. "Here's a string and here's a balloon. All you have to do is—"

"What is this? What about my patients? What if one was due here and now? And is that my treatment couch stacked up there against the wall? You collapsed it without asking?"

"Robbie, Dear, you told me yourself only yesterday that you'd canceled all work until you leave. You haven't said happy birthday to Will yet, have you?"

It was true. Now he was clinging to my legs to make me fall, our favorite game. I was the Giant and he was Jack. I was Goliath and he was David. The rules were the same, unless it looked like he was losing and then he'd announce a new one. "Who am I today, Will?"

"You're a Borg, Aunt Bob. I'm a Tron."

"Lovely." Then I lost concentration and was over. We scrabbled on the floor until I sent him to fetch any pictures he'd painted at play-school. There was a screen in my bedroom on which Will and I had pasted all of his work collected since he could first lift a brush, a pencil. When it was full we would varnish it. "So they'll be forever, Aunt Bob? And will you let your patients see?"

"I do already. I charge them."

While he was out of the room, I asked, "And where does all this clutter come from?"

Laura approached me, fingers linked, thumbs circling. "Please, Robs. It's not clutter, it's toys for the party. Say it's all right, Robs. You don't mind, really, do you?" Her face had settled into precise areas of bruise and damage.

"What's wrong with your place?"

"You know I can't go there. And we've rung everybody now."

"It's not *Please Robs* at all, is it? I mean you've done it. It's all arranged. What about Esther's, why can't his party be there?" Knowing perfectly well why it couldn't be.

Will returned with a clutch of paintings but Laura collected him up, drew his head against her, and covering the side of it with her hand, left the room, closing the door behind her.

Esther clicked disapproval and heaved herself up to inspect the tea things, touching here and there, heightening effects only visible to her. "The Witneys told me today they don't want a caretaker anymore and that I'm free to leave. Of course they need one but I think they want someone younger, more agile. *Free to leave.* What they really mean is for me to be out by the end of this week. But that's all right because Laura says she'd like me to take care of Will. And with you going there'll be room so it'll all work out very well."

It had happened before. It always happened this way. Laura's uneasy requests for shelter in my home—or any space in the world I'd made for myself—becoming sanctioned and granted by the appearance of Esther. Nothing was ever really said or settled, the replayed scene just rolled into place. Only this time I had the mean sense they were doing it purposely to punish me for leaving, for going so far away and not saying for how long. I left Esther among the balloon strings to find Will, standing on my bed, with Laura pulling up his trousers, buttoning the bibfront, saying to me over her shoulder, "Sorry, sorry. We've nearly finished."

"Can we stick on my paintings now, Aunt Bob?"

"No, Will," Laura answered for me. "Robs is tired right now. After the party, maybe. Okay?" Again she bundled him into her arms to back apologetically from the room.

I flung myself facedown on the bed—into a pair of wet trainer pants.

A couple of hours later I woke, intending to stay put, only a persistent banging drew me out. The flat door was jammed open with an upright piano halfway through it, a Rastafarian pulling from the inside and Sam's polished egghead intermittently visible from the other end as it was eased forward. Sam's bongos—I had never seen him without them, Laura said he slept with them—slid up and down the top of the piano secured by their strap under the lid. Sulky and astonished, I watched my home fill with two dozen self-assured little people the same age as Will, experienced party-goers. Esther handed cups of tea to their adult charges. Sam played ragtime for musical chairs. The Rasta settled himself on my filing cabinet, peaceably smoking a joint. Back in my bedroom two mothers, feet up on the bed, were breast-feeding infants. There was only the kitchen left.

Sam blundered in and must have seen something in my expression he couldn't associate with himself because he glanced back over his shoulder. "What's the matter?"

"Nothing. The noise."

"I like a party. What is it, Robbie?"

I had been glad about Sam and Laura, had even been

thinking, At last. He was big and kind. They were always happy whenever I'd seen them together. They had plans as a team, him on the piano, Laura singing the songs he'd written for her.

"You didn't do it, did you, Sam?"

Gripping the side of the table, he lowered himself to a chair as if years were being heaped on him and he couldn't take the weight. I could not watch, continued clearing the mess left by Esther, but it was a small space and in the end I had to turn. He grabbed my wrist. "Hit her? Did she say I did?"

"No. Only who did?"

"Don't know. Never do, do I? But she says she won't come back this time."

"Do you really want her to? Unfaithful as she is?"

"Yeah. I do. And it's not *unfaithful*. Unfaithful's when you give your head, your heart, feeling. Right? She gives her body to get it beaten up. I suppose her instinct susses out the types who'll do that sort of thing. It's a sickness, I know that. *Me* hit her? Are you mad? When she left for the club yesterday evening we were happy and now it's all over and I don't understand, Robbie. She let me come for the party, make it fun. She knows I love him like he's mine. Can you make her come back? Talk to her?"

Someone pushed on the kitchen door. I leaned against it. Esther's voice carried from the other side. "You in there, Robbie? Can I have the bridge rolls? They're on the side under a damp cloth."

"Hungry?"

"Yeah." Sam sniffed, stuffed one in his mouth while I handed the plate on through.

When we joined the party Laura was holding hands in a circle of children while Esther tottered in the center, blindfolded, failing to grab a tiny boy ducking all about her and tweaking her skirt. One of the mothers stood behind Laura to feed her a series of Esther's miniature sandwiches until Laura, chewing, swallowing, laughing, shook her head and the woman gave her shoulders a hug. Such warmth in the gesture. All of the women there gave Laura a special kind of attention, more like protection. It was hard to know why they treated her this way. She was just one of them, wasn't she? Just a young mother no worse off than they were?

Laura's gaiety faltered when she saw us, fear replaced it. I could see nothing in Sam's face to cause that— because it was to him, if anywhere, she was directed. He watched her with tenderness. Tenderness, that's all. She squeezed her eyes shut, using all the muscles of her cheeks, jaws, forehead, and somehow, in this substitute solitude, she found her other, calmer self again. Even before she opened her eyes she was dissolving in fresh laughter with everyone else because Esther had at last fastened onto the boy, feeling around the back of his head for his face.

"Make it all right, Robbie, please," Sam whispered. "You could if you wanted to." Without waiting for me to tell him he was wrong he leapfrogged onto the piano stool. "Okeydoke, kiddies, 'Honky Tonk Train Blues.' "

When the party was over—three balloons up there stringless, unreachable, against the ceiling—Sam and his friend stayed to lend a hand. He must have seen what I had seen in Laura's face because he was careful to look elsewhere whenever he spoke to her. She was gentle with him, and not cold at all, and it must have hurt very much having her be that way, the way she really was, the way that made him love her. Because she would not be going back to him. There was already a pattern to her life. I knew it and I believe Sam did too. Once the piano was on the pavement outside he rushed on up again to say good-bye to Will, only we couldn't find him. Busy clearing, we had forgotten him. And now he wasn't there. As Laura frantically searched, pulling aside the sofa, checking behind doors, she breathed that phrase again, the one she'd sung in the early hours of that morning, the Schubert, only staccato this time, driving the notes out of herself. Then I understood I was hearing her pain made into sound. It couldn't have been ten minutes before Sam found Will curled up asleep in the bottom of my wardrobe, where I kept fresh linen. When Laura crouched to lift him, Sam said, "Let him be, Love. He looks so comfy. I'll give him a little kiss, there, like that. I'd choose that spot if I were him. Nice place to sleep." He chuckled a bit in that way he did, and smacked the top of his head, then he reached his arm around her. "Come back," he said. "Let me help. I love you, Laura. Everything'll be all right if we stay together. You see."

She wrenched away from him, head buried in her tangled arms. *"I can't, I can't, I can't"*—the words running into each other, and she wasn't talking to him really, not answering him exactly.

"No, don't, Love. Laura, don't."

"*I can't I can't I can't I can't.*"

"Shh, Darling, I'm going now. Shh there, feel, that's Will's hand. Take Will's hand. There, that's right. Sam's going, okay?"

She let him curl her hand around Will's, and gradually she leaned past Sam down to Will. Sam laid his head between her shoulders for a moment before he staggered up, pushed his way to the front door. It slammed behind him. Laura stroked Will's head and quietly half-hummed, half-sang:

"*Mm-mm, skip to my Lou,*

Mm-mm, skip to my Lou,

Mm-mm, skip my Lou,

Skip to my Lou my darlin'—"

Esther was in the kitchen with the radio playing. She must have known what was happening but chose to stay there collecting the leftover party food, reheating and re-presenting it with that knack she had. Sam had been part of her life too. He'd called her Angel Face and flirted with her the way dutiful young men do with the mothers of their girlfriends. And she had liked it, flirted back, a little rusty maybe for the want of practice.

The three of us ate supper at the kitchen table while Will slept on. "We've landed up in the kitchen again," Esther said, as she always did, and she was right, only it had never been the same kitchen for very long.

"So what *did* happen to your face?" I asked because I was not Sam and afraid of losing her. Nor was I Esther and afraid of the truth. But why I did ask I don't know and shouldn't have because I had seen her when she finally came out of my bedroom, tired and vanquished and vacant.

"Fine. Fine thanks. Doesn't hurt at all."

"Good, Dear. I must say it looks much better. Sausage roll, Robbie? They're still warm."

"I didn't ask *how* it was. I asked what happened. You see, I thought Sam had done it." Laura drew her shoulders, turned away. "I think I just assumed it was jealousy or something because he caught you at it. And that's never happened before, has it? I mean he's never actually caught you?"

"I *told* you he didn't do it," she whispered.

Esther eased around us out of the kitchen. "Where are you going?" I shouted.

"I think I heard Will"—her voice from just outside the door.

Laura lit a cigarette, retreated to the window, rubbing one forearm then the other. "Why are you being this way, Robs?" She was composed, without anger.

"I'm sorry for Sam, that's why. He doesn't mind what happened last night, only that you were hurt again. Why does he have to pay by losing you? If you could only explain, that's all, so we could understand, Sam and me and Esther too. She'd like to understand although she'd never say so. We were all so happy yesterday evening, weren't we? Content, at least, in our various places. Now all this. It's so messy. Messy and sordid."

She slid down the wall to the floor, hands draped on her bent knees, and gazed around the kitchen as if selecting details to remember. "Neat and tidy *in our various places.* That's how you like it best, I know. Not *messy and sordid* in your nice clean flat. But we're only people, Robs, doing what people do when they live and love and fight and get together and part"—and I was thinking, No, it's not only that, there's something else with us here when we're all together this way—"and after all, wasn't it a lot of fun with the children this afternoon? And Esther was happy, wasn't she, pretending to be the only thing she's ever really wanted to be: a regular granny with her bridge rolls and tea? And Sam? Sam? Didn't he play well? Didn't the children love him?"

"Do you?"

"Of *course.*" It didn't sound right, though. It didn't sound the way you'd want it to sound if someone asked the one you loved whether or not he loved you.

"So go back to him."

"It's not like that."

"So explain."

"I can't, don't you see? I *can't I can't I can't.*" Unable to pass those words. Without crossing to her I said the same thing Sam had, I said, "Shh, it's all right, Laura."

She cradled herself, covered her head with her hands, then lifted it and pointed a finger, screwing it into the corner of her mouth. "And, hey, listen, what happened to that friend of mine who was so keen on you? Eh? Did you ever see him after that first time? Did you?"—drew on her cigarette, eyes narrowed against her own exhaled smoke.

"You know very well I didn't."

She came to me, held me. "Sorry, Robs. I was bad to say that. Bad, bad. Hug me back, won't you?" And I was doing my best with my face all muffled into her black sweater saying, "Sorry too," when Esther returned.

"So you girls have made up again, have you? I don't know. You've always been the same ever since you were little. Loggerheads. One day I'll knock them together. I've always said I would. Now what's left of supper?" She dished out a sherry trifle neither of us could face. "By the way, Robbie, I told Mr. Witney today that you were off to Georgia."

"Louisiana."

"Well, anyway, *he* said it's very dangerous down there. Race troubles and things and it's not a place for a girl like you."

"Mr. Witney's never met me."

"No, but he knows the sort of daughter I'd have."

"Oh yeah?" Squinting, cigarette glued between pouting lips, Laura bared a shoulder that Esther patted approvingly before covering it and ruffling her hair.

"Well then, the sort of daughter I'd like him to think I have. Not the mad ones I've really got."

"No, no, we're not mad, *you're* mad. We got it from you," we said together because we always said that together.

"Then we're all mad," Esther said, which was the cue for the three of us to say all together, as we did, "All mad, quite mad, mad, mad, mad," with Laura and me dancing around twisting fingers into our cheeks. I smile every time I think of Sam's expression the first time he saw us do that.

I was ready for what would come next. It always did come. Why didn't I have a man in my life? Get married? Settle down? I should be thinking of having children. "Why, Laura was your age, weren't you Dear, by the time she had Will." Esther overlooked that Laura was unmarried, that she either didn't know—or pretended not to—who Will's father was, because to know and not to tell Esther would be unforgivable. She never referred to any of that, and if either of us did her deafness became more acute. And now Esther had something else to goad me with: Why was I leaving England anyway? What was wrong with England?

She opened with, "You're too set in your ways, Robbie Dear. A pleasant occasion like a children's party shouldn't throw you as it did, not at your age. You should be more outgoing. And I don't mean by going halfway across the world." Laura had been tapping her nose, miming Esther's words as she spoke them. That is how often we had covered this ground. "You say it's a challenging job, Dear. Aren't your patients here challenging enough?"

"This is something different. I'll learn a lot, things I couldn't pick up here. It's very demanding. They have equipment and techniques I want to study. I'll be better placed when I return, far broader in my approach." A speech we all knew backwards by then.

"Well, I wouldn't know about any of that because you never discuss your patients, do you? I've no real idea of who they are, what sort of people."

"They're ill people, most of them. That's all they have in common. Bad chests and things."

"It's always chests with you, isn't it?"

"I like chests. They're interesting."

"You *like chests*. Is that what I'm supposed to tell people like the Witneys when they kindly inquire if you specialize? *Robbie likes chests.*"

"Why not?"

Esther was tired, drifting between bursts of talk. Her lids falling, falling over eyes focused elsewhere—nothing to do with us, there, as we were. Her expression was sad, resigned. I believe at those moments she was watching scenes long gone, searching for that other path she might have chosen, which could have led to something more satisfactory than this, this: the three of us here in yet another kitchen.

She grew aware of Laura and me watching, reached for my hand. "Go wherever you want to, Dear," adding, as she always did, "You must do what you think's best."

And I, as I always did, felt disowned.

Esther shifted her chair, planted her feet wide so her dress draped between her knees, and leaned forward to ruffle Laura's hair again—we all liked doing that, its short, resilient thickness was irresistible. Laura told me once that a stranger behind her in a queue had done so, reached out and ruffled her hair. Imagine. Esther traced without touching the damage on her daughter's face. "Look at my baby," she murmured to herself. "Look at my baby. What have they done to her? There, there then, Dear. What have they done?"

With each word Laura was drawn to Esther until she was kneeling on the floor, her head pressed into Esther's lap—"Mummy, Mummy"—and Esther rocked her and rocked her and I left the kitchen to make up the sofa in the studio.

It was after midnight when I walked, with Esther resting heavily on my arm, towards Ladbroke Grove. She stopped, turned back to examine the name of the side street we had just crossed. "Well, fancy," her voice, though not raised, unfurled around the deserted street, "three years you've been here and I've never thought about it before. That woman, the woman Jane, she took a place down that way"—circling an index finger. "Let's see, one, two, then there would be the crescent with the church, then four, five roads down, I guess. A ground-floor flat in a corner house, someone told me. It sounded so pleasant. More than I was ever able to afford. She bewitched him. That's what. He was a weak man with women, couldn't have done it without her, turned me out like that. Her there with her arms crossed, those blessed bangles clacking. Her giving him courage to turn us out, little Laura and me."

"Esther?"

Only she was back there in the Healing Room. "I'm not hiding my baby in a basement."

"Esther? Come on. Everything's all right now."

"Robbie? Robbie, Dear. You do know your father had a powerful gift—"

"I know. You've often said."

"*Healing hands,* they call it, and make it sound so simple. Well, it's rare. People came from all over. *His* gift was rare. Pity was: He didn't have the strength of personality to go with it. *She* had that but couldn't heal. Didn't stop her pretending. Bewitch. That's all she could do. It was enough. Robbie? Don't be cross anymore, will you?"

"Who with?"

"Laura. Coming in with you. I'm sure it's for the best. Wasn't Will a darling with his little friends? Keep an eye on her and I'll be along tomorrow when I can. Do you think the tube's still running?" But she allowed me to settle her in a taxi, pulled the window down. "You're a good girl, Robbie."

It's you and me, just you and me alone. Could my rudimentary ears have heard Esther say that? I wasn't her unborn baby. I was her confidante who lived on inside her because she lived on and there was nothing she could do about either. My status as youngest was never removed, it was simply never to be. Laura was the baby born, the one who cried and was cuddled. Laura was the one who had made Esther a mother when she still wanted to be one, when she still shared hopes with our father. I was the internal witness to her humiliation. When they told her, my father and his mistress, the woman Jane, "We can't work with you here. You must find somewhere else for yourself and the baby——" Esther didn't have to lift me or hold me or cover my ears or shelter me the way Laura did with Will in moments of distress. As with our two lives, it was yet another thing she could do nothing about. If it is so that strong emotions produce substances in the body, then I was born with the taste of her humiliation, her fear, which must have surged through Esther and into my fetal system. And her subsequent courage and determination too. So when, at last, I did plunge into the world and Esther gazed into my unfocusing eyes, possibly she saw it all there, all her knowledge. I would always remain too much part of what had happened to her, and not her baby at all.

"*Esther had one of those turns.* You know. Talked about the woman Jane again."

"Mmm? Just tired, I expect, after the party." Laura was standing beside the filing cabinet in the studio, an open file in her right hand, a blue air-mail letter in her left. I tried to snatch it from her but she swung away to read facetiously, "*There is no point my creating a false impression of our life here.*"

"Give it to me."

"*Which is a very quiet rural existence. Someone as highly trained as yourself might find the position undemanding.* Oh, *un*demanding, I thought I heard you say *demanding*, right."

"It's none of your business, Laura."

"*My uncle, Mr. Patout, is seventy-two years of age. The polio he suffered in his early twenties impaired his walking but until now he has never resorted to a wheelchair. Please refer to the notes I've hastily gathered and included here.*"

Laura glanced in the file that I pulled from her, but holding the letter high, she continued to read, "*He has no will to regain even his previous mobility since his stroke last month, although he could have done so by now. I am advised of this by experts over here. He does not like the idea of a resident physical therapist—physical therapist,* is that what you're called over there?—*and I believe his insistence on an English person has been, in truth, obstruction on his part.* This is *so* interesting, Robs. *It is I, Miss Heath, who cannot accept his resignation to immobility and the inevitable consequences that will follow in too short a time.* Where's the bit about techniques and equipment, is that here? Let's see what else he says. *I write this way, not to deter the enthusiasm you expressed during our last telephone conversation, but to avoid any disappointment or misunderstanding on either part. Yours sincerely, P. Janvier.* Some old bugger who doesn't even want to live, let alone want your expertise? Is that what you call broadening your experience? Why did you lie?"

"It was all I could find with pay and accommodation."

"You mean over there?"

"Yes. It's just an informal arrangement. I haven't got a green card or anything."

"So why?" Forgetting the bruises, she rubbed her face, winced, sat herself as far as she could from me. "What if I went away first thing tomorrow. Would you change your mind?"

"No. It's nothing to do with you being here this time."

"*This* time."

"I didn't mean it like that. I want something different for a while, that's all. And it'll give you somewhere, a base. Esther too."

"No, she'll be fine. She'll have a new job in no time. Caretaking, another job with a flat. There's plenty of those about."

"Don't you look at her? Can't you see she's ill and old?"

"Stop it."

"She's worn-out, Laura."

"I said don't. Why can't everything just stay the same? Give us time. Everyone's always changing places and growing up and old and there's no peace anywhere."

"I wonder if Sam's asking the same."

"Oh thank you, Robs. Very nice." She left the room,

and from the bedroom I heard the wardrobe door creak. "Sam's right"—Laura returned with her dressing gown on her shoulder—"the wardrobe's a good place to choose. Fantastic how he sleeps, isn't it? Wish I could." She drew close, gripped me, hid her face against my collarbone. "Well done, Robs, about the job, making the break. You're very strong. You've always been stronger than me. Maybe I'm just jealous." She released me to poke a finger in her cigarette packet, crush it, throw it across the room.

"Can I just ask you—don't get upset, okay?—about last night and other times when—"

"I *can't.*"

"No. Don't. Listen. I need to know for me, to help *me.*"

"Why help you?"

"Could I get that way?"

A smile imminent, I could feel her joke forming, knew the line it would take until she saw my face properly, then she held me again. "I'd never let you, Darling. You're safe."

"Please, Laura, just some little light on what goes on in your head?"

"For you?"—recoiling, stroking, checking points on her neck, shoulders, arms. "Jesus, I wish I had a cigarette. Nothing, is the answer. A vicious disquiet and when that falls away everything is gone, won't ever come back. Not Will or you or Esther or Sam. There are no more touchstones, there's nothing to value. There's only this worthless, dirty bitch. And it's me. Can we leave it there, *please?* Hey listen, I'll take the couch, okay? Meanwhile I'm off to get more cigarettes. Won't be long."

She was long. She returned at four. I heard her approach and smelled the flowers she laid by the sofa where I was wrapped in blankets, eyes tight shut.

One evening I accompanied Laura to the club where she had been singing two nights a week. I hadn't seen her performing in public since the Notting Hill Carnival a couple of years before. The club, sad and sleazy, was on Beak Street. We pushed through the bored and tawdry crowd that was ignoring a fat Scotsman under a spotlight bawling jokes and insults at them, and on through a door, across a passage into a windowless room. Laura kicked aside a suitcase spewing trousers, trainers, and shaving kit, and changed out of her jeans, sweater, shawl—black, black, black—into a T-shirt and floral pinafore dress. She exchanged her long-toed boots for heavy walking shoes, then exhaled with a kind of hopeless impatience at her reflection in the mirror. Once her lips were smeared with lipstick and her eyes smudged with black, she announced, "There," and banged down the eye brush, crossed her arms.

"Is that it?" I'd half-imagined sequins and false-fronted dresses.

"Yup."

"You look like some kid who's been at her mother's makeup."

"Yup."

"Do they like it, you looking like that?"

"Don't care if they don't."

There had been so many chances in Laura's career,

talk of recording contracts and tours and managers who were going to change her life. How many times had she said, "All I needed was a break and this is it"? It never was it. I never asked why or what happened about this or that, what became of so-and-so. Perhaps this perverse nonchalance was the reason.

As she was sirening and intoning phrases to loosen her throat, the comedian burst in, cursing to himself. "Aw, sorry, you on now? They're buggers tonight, I'll tell you that. Mind if I use the lavvy there?"

He gushed behind a screen like an old horse and Laura shouted, "But they were roaring. They thought you were really funny. Couldn't you hear? Maybe not. I get that. Adrenaline deafens me. You were brilliant. We thought so, didn't we Robs?" She winked at me, grinned, but the expression in her eyes had altered.

He reemerged making big show of zipping his fly. "Really? You think so? What about the granny joke, did that work? It's new, you see. Real dirty."

"The best thing, really. Very original."

"Ta very much then. They might have me back, you think?"

"They're mad if they don't"—elbowing me from the room.

"You the singer? Will I see you later?"

"Really brilliant," she shouted from the passage. I had to loosen her grip from around my wrist, rub where her nails had dug in.

Laura greeted the slouched pianist whose few strands of hair were snatched into a pigtail. She knew him, didn't like him, and had told me once that she would have liked that job for Sam. After riffling through sheet music, she slotted some on the carrier. Sustaining a tune with one hand, he shrugged and reached for a glass on the keyboard ledge. Laura leaned against the piano pulling her lip, picking her nails. Then the melody slid from one thing to another and she was into "Careless Love," like that, for me. My favorite song. "What do *you* know anyway," she used to ask me, "about careless love?" No one stopped talking, they didn't even lower their voices. Some raised them. After "Careless Love" she gave them "The Shadow of Your Smile" then "Yesterday," the dog-eared ballads we both loved. Not anymore, though. I couldn't hear those songs now. Wouldn't listen.

The after-theater crowd arrived, equally indifferent to her songs, hardly listened as she sang "Ne Me Quitte Pas." She did not care, didn't even notice. Nor did the pianist, who was now inclining towards her as he played, shutting his eyes, rolling his shoulders, mouthing the words. When I saw Sam he was over by the entrance. If I hadn't recognized him by the back of his head it would have been by the bongos slung under his arm. He was tiptoeing to catch sight of Laura, who was closing her act. When they finished, the pianist gave Laura a brusque, one-armed hug before threading a path to the bar. No one applauded and she stood there, coming to, as it were, realizing, possibly, that she'd sung alone, to almost no one. I raised my hand to remind her there was me but now her eyes were filling, drowning with panic as she backed to the wall. She could not have seen Sam from where she was, although I could see them both now, quite clearly. She shut her eyes, and keeping them shut, she jumped with both feet and landed, bang, like that. Of all the noises in that cramped space, this one created a fraction of silence. Then, eyes open this time, she stamped one foot hard, paused, stamped again and again, faster each time. She had created complete silence. Each time she slammed down her foot an answering rap came from the bongos on the far side of the room. Hidden from each other, a channel of energy was running between Laura and Sam, magnetizing interest. Everyone was uncertain and excited, craning this way and that to see where the two sounds were coming from. Then Laura's unaccompanied voice peeled the air, quite different from before, untutored, loud, furious:

> *I'm gonna jump down, turn aroun'*
> *Pick a bail a cotton*
> *Gonna jump down, turn aroun'*
> *Pick a bail a hay, whoop . . .*

All attention was riveted on the skinny childlike figure, gauche, as she stamped, jumped, turning out the nonsense verses.

> *I saw a skeeter sittin' on ma head,*
> *Blinked his eye and he was dead.*
> *Gonna jump down . . ."*
> *Lil' Jo jump down,*
> *Lil' Mary jump down.*

After every verse she let out a shattering *"Whoa"* and the audience yelled back, *"Whoa."*

She ceased as abruptly as she had begun. Reedy voices trailed on while she sank into a pantomime curtsy, arms wide, plucking the hem of her pinafore, then she vanished, leaving everyone applauding and calling, "More, more."

She was already in her jeans when I reached the dressing room, stuffing a canvas bag with her belongings. "Arseholes, they're all arseholes. I'm never coming back. Let's get out of here. I want to see Will."

Following Will's birthday, Esther had made daily visits to my flat, depositing more of her possessions on every trip. Only I never saw her do it. I even believed she must have been ringing Laura to discover when I would be out. The smell of cigarette smoke, the full ashtrays, the disarray—I had tempered myself to handle all of that. The accessories of Will's toddlerhood—potties, noisy toys, loads of dirty clothes—I suffered all this too because I loved him so much—that much since he slithered bloody and white-greasy from between Laura's thighs, behind a curtain on the floor of a men's ward in St. Stephen's hospital. We'd raced there in a taxi, she on the floor screaming, me leaning over her from the jump seat going, *Breathe, breathe like I taught you.* He was a month premature. At the hospital they thought she'd make it through to maternity, walking, I ask you. But Will had had enough and wanted out and, as I say, made his debut on the floor of the men's ward. He was very quick. The first thing Laura said, stroking her lips over his unwashed head, mostly covered with a blue-striped

Handi Wipe, was, "God, Robs, that was incredible. I want lots of these." No, what did exasperate me was Esther's amassed belongings.

You would think a woman of sixty-nine who for the past thirty years had had no place of her own for more than five minutes would have little in the way of possessions. You would think, too, that considering her peripatetic existence she would have preferred to travel light. I couldn't help wondering how some of those she worked for as caretaker-housekeeper viewed her arrival in their homes as she dragged in the kind of stuff she was bringing to mine: bursting suitcases tied with string, plastic shopping bags stuffed with tights and underwear, five cardboard boxes containing over a hundred back issues of a magazine called *Panorama*—a subscription arranged years before from South Africa by her late brother—a forty-year-old Raleigh bicycle, some saucepans tied together with string, more cardboard boxes containing unmatched crockery.

The gathering began discreetly in the studio behind the sofa, which after a day or two was pushed forward, making space for a second line. When the sofa had almost reached the middle of the room, the collection spread self-consciously unlocated like evacuee children on a railway station. It must not matter. I was leaving. I managed, even, not to refer to a motorcar tire leaning against the leg of my treatment couch or the mahogany lavatory seat that was set on the couch itself. Finally two tall stools were placed, not in the studio—no more space there—but in the hall. They finished me, those shabby stools with their original blue-and-white striped seats covered and re-covered and covered again with stick-on plastic all filthy, cracking, peeling to expose the layer beneath. It was my last evening in England and they were what greeted me when I returned home, posted either side of my kitchen door.

Esther and Laura were giving Will his tea. They must have heard my key, the door shutting, and their faces were towards me as I entered. Again, I see them so clearly. So clearly I could reach and touch them.

"Hi, Rob."

"Hellooo Dear?"

"Bob Bob Bob's home."

"What's all this stuff outside here?"

Esther leaned into the washing up. "What stuff?"

"This stuff we've been pretending isn't here?"

"They're Esther's things, Robs. You know that. Don't be unkind."

"Sorry, forget it. Doesn't matter. But, actually, why old saucepans? What possible use are they?"

"For when I retire and make a home for myself. When I settle. It's all for that. You'll be glad to find I'm not dependent, that I have my own things."

"And that's when the tire'll come in handy?"

"Its from the Ford Anglia."

"But you sold it years ago."

"Nineteen-sixty-three. And I didn't sell it. The garage bill was too much for me so those rogues just kept it. That was the spare and I didn't see why they should have it too. In any case, Robbie, you've become too"— hesitating at this point to examine the accuracy of her word—"too tidy-minded. Yes. You didn't used to be like that."

"That's not true. I've always liked my things to be—"

"She has, Esther. Robs is naturally tidy."

"Oh, no." Esther raised her finger. "You see I recall more than you. Laura wasn't well—remember the time, Laura?"

"Don't let's talk about that now. Have you seen Will's picture of you, Robs? Let's find it, it's in his satchel, I think."

Laura held my arm to draw me from the kitchen, compel me to follow.

"Just a minute, girls. I want to finish on this because I'm right. *You* weren't well one weekend and so Robbie went alone to stay with her father—no, let me finish. Now, Laura, you were eleven so she would have been—"

"She was seven. She was only seven. Please don't, let's."

"Don't get silly, Laura. It turned out you had the mumps so Robbie stayed on until you were better. And I'm only saying—"

"*It's not important.*" Laura snatched the tea towel from where it was tucked around Esther's waist, snatched it and struck the table with it.

"Now what did you do that for? Robbie's not cross, are you? No. My point is simply that before that stay Robbie was messier than you, Laura. And that's saying something. The change in her was marked."

"You do so *have to* be right, don't you, Esther? Robs? Robs? Come on, come and see the picture."

Will spread pieces of newspaper daubed with poster paint over the floor. Laura pointed to a blue circle surrounded by a mass of black. "That's you, Robs." She stood at the window with her back to us, hands—all but two fingers pinching a cigarette—pushed into her hip pockets.

I sat on my bed, turning his pictures over, delivering thoughtless praise. "Laura?"

Will pulled my ear against his mouth to whisper, "Can we pin them on?"

I knelt in front of the screen with him on my lap. Together we pressed in the thumbtacks. Laura hadn't moved from the window. "Laura?" She didn't turn. "She's right though, isn't she, Laura? Because when—"

"We won't go over it, Robs, okay?"

Esther was sipping tea in the kitchen. "We could sit in the studio," I suggested, knowing very well we wouldn't.

"Hang on there a second." Laura left us—ruffling Will's hair on her way—and returned dragging the two stools with her.

"I have to say, Esther, that I agree with Robbie about these." The corners of her mouth were twisting that way they did when she was trying not to laugh. "These nasty stools *do* need explanation."

Esther yanked the stools from her and Laura whisked Will to the floor with her as she collapsed spread-eagled and giggling.

Esther embraced the low backs of the stools on either side of her. "These aren't any old stools. *These* stools belonged to Bud Flanagan."

"Who's Bud Flanagan?"

But Laura jumped up. "Not *the* Bud Flanagan?"

"Who's Bud Flanagan?"

"You remember when Uncle Frank died he remembered me in his will and I bought the short lease on that flat in Dolphin Square? Well, I bought it from Bud Flanagan, along with his carpets and his kitchen stools. I met him. I shook his hand. And his wife's."

"No, wait. You met him? You've touched his hand and you never told me? How could you not? Let's see your hand." Laura stroked Esther's right palm over and over. "Is it really true?"

"Of course."

"Who for pity's sake is Bud Flanagan?"

"He's a singer, Robs. You must have heard of him. Flanagan and Allen. Brilliant. I know 'Strolling,' right Esther?"

"All right, Dear." They linked arms to step from side to side, singing:

> *"Strolling, just strolling*
> *In the cool of the evening air.*
> *I don't envy the rich in their automobiles,*
> *A motorcar is phony,*
> *I'd rather have shankses' pony."*

So I scooped Will into my arms and we sailed around the only spot left in the kitchen. And that's what we did on my last night in England. We sang. And we danced. Esther, Laura, and me.

III

THERE ARE PLACES

"Laura? Did I wake you?"

"Robs? Is it you?"

"Yes. Just to say hello."

"You *woke* me. You okay?"

"Yes, I think. All right, anyway. Laura?"

"What?"

"What are the cigarettes with the particular smell? You know the ones I mean. Not hash. Something else."

Hollow pounding of the pillows, sighs of the bedclothes as she arranged herself. "Turkish? Someone smoking Turkish, Robs? Hello? Hello, you still there?"

"Yes."

"Forget it, okay? They're just cigarettes. And a cigarette's a cigarette. You hate the smell of all of them. You always have and don't I know it, blimey."

"These are different. They remind me of things."

"Like what?"

"I don't know. Feelings, something."

"Leave it, okay? Don't look back. Keep going on. Push all that stuff out of your head."

"What is the stuff? Why's it there now?"

"I don't know why now. How should I know why now? Push it all out, hear me? You know you can do it. I want to go back to sleep now, all right? So 'night, Robs. Please? Goodnight?"

There are places memory distills in a certain light, one that may have been fleeting, nonexistent even. Reality has nothing to do with it. Janvier on Bayou Pays Bas, Louisiana, is such a place, and sunshine is the light.

It remains today as I saw it then: the plantation house with its delicate architecture and infinite tones of white, fanlights above every door, green shutters beside the windows, and the whole encircled by a first-floor verandah screened by fine mesh. There is a bridge that leads across from the main house to a red-brick building behind it, called the dependency, where the kitchen and laundry are located. Wide steps descend from the verandah to grass that runs down to the river—the Mississippi—hidden from view by the rise of the levee. Set on the grass, close to the house, are four clapboard cabins, two to the left and two to the right, each with a stoop, shingled roof, and stack chimney. They were slave quarters once, these cabins. Also on that broad swathe of green are twin pigeonniers, octagonal, white-painted, with slate roofs and finials like the house, and pigeons live inside them. And all of it, all of it, is shaded by ancient oaks and cedars that themselves are shaded—no, blinded—by moss so long and gray and sharp to touch, suffocating not only the trees but the light all around them.

It was to one of those old slave cabins I was shown on arriving at Janvier, my quarters now—restored with a kitchen and bathroom. A letter was propped against a lamp on the table there:

Dear Miss Heath,

I am vacationing in Europe at present but please make yourself comfortable in your cabin. Theresa— wife of Charles, who met you at the airport—I trust he did—will keep it stocked with food as you require. My uncle is expecting you and has indicated some willingness for treatment. I only ask you should be patient and await his request for you to go up to the house. Meanwhile, please take pleasure in my home, ask Theresa for anything you may need, and thank you for your assistance and understanding.

Yours kindly,
P. Janvier

And Charles Bizet had met me, after a fashion. An eight-hour flight, a four-hour delay in Atlanta, another short flight, and I landed at New Orleans stiff and disoriented. The crowd behind swept me so swiftly into the hall I couldn't be sure my name had not been waved on one of the many papers, crayoned on a torn piece of cardboard confronting the arrivals. I watched the world greet the world and depart before I leaned around the barrier again to study the remaining placards held lower now, with less enthusiasm. Nothing there resembled *Heath.* When I found the telephones there was a tall black man languidly parading before them, his attention fixed on the floor. He was wearing a dark, double-breasted suit, electric blue necktie—knotted so tight it gathered his collar—and he balanced a broom handle across his right shoulder, secured there with his forearm, which left his hand and fingers free to key a rhythm in the air. I approached that nonchalant pacer and caught hold of the limp paper napkin pinned to the end of the broom handle. There was my name pressed in faint ballpoint. I touched his elbow and he swung around smiling, patting his gray hair. "Miss Heath? Figured you'd come by the phones sooner or later."

I unpacked and arranged my things—photographs of Laura and Will and Esther, some books—then I walked from the cabin past the great bank of magnolia growing on the far side of, and as high as, the house, the quiet house, the ground beneath littered deep with the cadavers of its leaves. I passed through camellia and honeysuckle and jasmine, all of it left to be itself. Behind a stand of pines I found where the bayou runs almost to the river then veers away, as if declining an invitation to mingle its own viscid water with any other. And from the bank I watched a man poling a flat-bottomed boat, the load inside it covered with a tarpaulin. He faced the other way when he saw me. Through gaps between the silvered boards of a boathouse half-set in the bayou, half on the bank, I made out the shapes of three craft tied up and bumping companionably. Between my cabin and the house was an oak grove where that light-absorbing moss made it hard to see at first. A red tricycle had been left there, fallen on its side—as though some little boy like Will had just run off—and there was a swing hanging from way, way up in the branches, and a knotted rope to climb.

Later on that day, the day of my arrival, in a profoundly violet twilight, I saw Charles and Theresa Bizet walking from the house, their arms loose at their sides but linked by his left hand covering the back of her right one. They matched each other, these two black, narrow-bodied people, easy-moving, tall, although she appeared far younger than her husband. They talked low, ceaselessly together, as if newly acquainted. Near my cabin Charles stopped to unbutton the cloth jacket he wore on duty, slung it over his shoulder. I said, "Good evening," and he inclined towards me. "Uh-huh, it sure is." They passed on by the cabins to the pigeonniers. She climbed the steps of one, hesitated until he encouraged, "Go on, Honey. I wait. You know I always wait."

She pulled the door towards her, leaned around it to croon inside, "Come on now birdies, here birdy-birdy-birdies. You all c'mon to Treesa now."

A brewing and kerfuffle within was followed by the pigeons emerging in an unlikely fashion to take their evening meal, which she threw to them from a battered saucepan. Charles stood and laughed and laughed, slapping his thigh and throwing a getaway hand and calling, "Honey, I ain't never seen the like of that before, never." I learned he had seen the like before because the same scene was played most evenings, and most evenings he said the same, he said, "Honey, I ain't never seen the like of that," and would walk off scanning the pines before the bayou to remark, "Ol' fox'll get 'em, see if he don't swim on over 'n' snap 'em up," loud enough for her to hear no more than a word or two. Then Theresa would run to catch him and have his free arm flung around her shoulders while she touched her hair, her chin modestly drawn, her mouth working at being closed over protruding teeth.

Once they had stepped up to their cabin opposite mine, each lifted a hand, palm out towards me. " 'Night, there." " 'Night." Later on from behind the closed door their voices reached me with words I couldn't make out, the pitch rising and rising. I waited for the crash of something thrown but the climax was laughter coming out of there, clattering laughter followed by a stillness that filled the night.

I woke early on my first day, hardly light yet but that came fast. I saw that man again, the one with the loaded boat out on the bayou. When he saw me he tugged the tarpaulin, which this time didn't fully conceal the pile of dead alligators underneath. Way down in the direction of Pointe Coupee fishermen were throwing nets, spinning them high in the air where they flowered and faltered before descending to the water. Later on they'd pole on back, calling to one another about their catch. They called to me too, "Woo there, lady, fine day, huh?" And they waved. They waved.

I heard the Bizets talking and the noise of a television as I passed their cabin and continued down the side of the house where that magnolia grew so high. At the end of a path between beech trees I was confronted by a cathedral of a barn. It was the inside of this I drew as my first picture for Will. I tried to capture the air loaded with the scents of leather and manure and oats, and how the awesome calm was unsettled only by the shifting of five gangle-legged mules in their stalls—each with a back hoof fancifully resting like a line of gays at a bar— and the panting dogs camouflaged among the sacking and shadows, all keeping a one-eyed watch on me and the hunting cats.

I approached the house from the back where the resinous scent of newly cut pine bit the air, emanating from a ramp that ran down from the verandah alongside the back staircase. Planed to the sheen of pearls, dovetailed and dowelled, with stilts underneath to create the gentlest gradient, it had clearly never been used. At right angles to the ramp was the dependency—and Theresa was up there in the kitchen now, humming and shooing out a cat. In the oak grove I set the red tricycle upright and knelt in the sandpit to brush off the dolls' cups and plates and line them on the side of it. I remained in there long enough that my eyes were dazzled by the light when I emerged with the Spanish moss trailing over my shoulders. By pulling it free of the branches I made a cloak and spun around and around so it flew out behind me.

And there I was spinning when from inside my dizziness I caught sight of a low shadow up at the rail of the verandah, more substantial than anything else behind the screen. I staggered to a halt and it moved away towards the steps, passing smoothly, not like someone up and walking. Only I knew it was a living being who had been watching me. "Mr. Patout? Good morning." I added my name, too loud, misjudging the distance and the habit of sound in that place. From the bottom step I repeated the greeting even though my previous call seemed still to be vibrating. The indistinct figure neared the screen doors at the top of the steps. I remained silent, heard the sawing of his breath, allowing myself to be seen. To be seen without seeing and hating it.

A shadow swayed, then one of the doors slid aside. With his right hand resting on the arm of his wheelchair—jeweled rings, an oval cigarette caught between index and middle fingers—and his left hand abandoned, palm up, in his lap, Raoul Patout stared down at me. Needlepoint pupils penetrated beyond the rigmarole of my features. His mouth would have been full, sensuous once—too much so to make a good mouth on an old man. His nose was spread by age. Black, over-black hair was slicked back to brush the neck of the caftan that enveloped his enormous body. He was wearing the same kind of nylon slippers I'd been given on the flight over. I lifted my arm to indicate his feet and was going to say, *I've got some like that.* Damned silly. And I didn't anyway because he leveled his eyes on my hand, relocating my attention onto myself. Then I heard the huff of the wheels of his motorized chair and stepped up in time to see him passing to the back of the verandah. He reached for the handle of the French windows and was swallowed within the obscurity of the house, leaving behind the scent of his cigarette.

The scent of his cigarette. I sat down where I was and it was no longer a Louisiana spring morning but the inside of a house on a different stair with Laura next to me and she said, "I shall turn to you and say, 'Robbie, Robbie, let's pretend we don't hear it,' " that day, the day Matthew died and before the nail scissors so her hair was still full and black like mine. Other, less uncertain, memories flickered on a life before even then, flickered on me alone on that stair, "Someone smoking Turkish, Robs?" "Promise you'll never wake me?"

Don't think about these things. Now is the only reality. Think about your patient. What did you see?

It was his left hand that rested immobile. A left-sided hemiplegia. He was slumped in his chair. Noisy breathing. I knew from the notes that his intercostal muscles had been permanently affected by the polio. He had reached across with his right hand to open the door, an easy rotatory movement requiring both sides of his trunk muscles working in unison. Good. Good. So there had been a degree of recovery since the hemiplegia, which was two months ago. There was no vigor about him but an aura of latent power. Nothing weak or failing in his presence. On the contrary. The skin of his feet was shiny and they were already swollen at this hour of the morning. Could be heart. He was a bad color, very gray. Except, of course, for that hair. How old? Seventy-two, according, again, to the notes. Yes. Hard to tell which leg was affected by the polio, neither appeared flaccid or spastic. But they can be placed and balanced when seated.

Two weeks passed without Patout requesting treatment. I walked, I read, I waited and wrote, wrote, wrote back home with dozens of drawings for Will, received no letters in return. I was content enough to note the passage of daylight, how fragile it was in the mornings with mounting brilliance on those days when the sun burned away the mist. The year was still young, the weather still soft, and the nights were glossed with stars. I knew about the nights because dreams had begun to shred my sleep, and rather than risk returning to those places, small spaces and the hands and the eyes and the choking choking smoke and sweat and rough clothing pressed against my skin, I lay untrapped outside on my stoop.

Toward the end of the second week I entered the barn as part of my usual morning tour. What I thought was an injured rat scrabbled in the middle of the earth floor. Close to I saw it was a puppy, too young for more than a few steps without dropping. Its body in my hand was a tight, tepid sack of liquid as I searched every dim corner for the litter, pushing aside bails, scattering invisible creatures, affronting the ordered tranquillity. By then I knew the dogs by sight, the rough-furred black one, the squat fellow with a bulldog head—the only ones around that morning—unreliable, cringing creatures, always ready to duck from a stone. They were sufficiently curious to let me approach, first one, then the other, offering the puppy at arm's length. Their responses were the same. After some tentative sniffing, each turned its head, ears flattened, eyes half-shut, then, after a few backwards steps, deferential, embarrassed, they trotted away. I made

a nest of straw in a corner among rotting bags of corn—
blades of grass sprouting through the burlap—with a
dripping water-stand close by. I tried to leave her there
but that grubby ginger rag-ball kept on coming after me,
feebly whining. On my third trip back with her,
Lenny—the stable hand, the carpenter, the fix-all—
emerged from a tack room in a corner of the barn, with a
saddle under his arm. He wiped his nose, collected sweat
from face and neck, and out of a jar held in the hand
supporting the saddle he scooped a glob of grease and
stood caressing it into the leather. "Been watching you.
Saw you pick the puppy. Come back from drowning the
rest not a half hour gone. Dropped that one, I guess.
Bitch died. Okay, Lenny, I say to myself, leave it be. You
done 'nuff killin' for one day. Saw you showing it all
'round to the animaux."

"I'll just put it down here then." Because he wasn't
going to free a hand to take it from me.

It spread-eagled on the floor. At the door I turned and
it was coming on after me yet again, was still there behind and whining even as I neared the house. So I picked
her up, held her high. Her paws paddled the air. Theresa
called from the bridge where she was hanging dishcloths
on the rail, "You want that puppy?"

"No."

"Well you done it now, uh-huh. You done it. You
shouldn't pick it you don't wanna keep it. You wanna
keep it?"

"No. I don't really like dogs." But there it was and
Charles gave me a hutch and it spent the night in that on
my stoop to whine through my dreams. My dreams.

The following afternoon I bathed her and Charles

showed me how to remove the ticks embedded in her skin without leaving the heads to grow another body and swell pink and fat on her blood.

"You pull 'im this way, see? Just a tweak, uh-huh, see that critter wrigglin'. You knows you got it when you sees those feet wrigglin'." He struck a match, lit the tick, and flicked it, fizzing, into the sky. Then Theresa called him and he was gone, left me alone to douse the puppy in flea powder.

"What the devil you doing to that poor dog?"

"I'm getting rid of the fleas, Mr. Patout."

"Yours or his? Huh."

"She's a she."

"A bitch. Well a dog with no fleas is no dog. It's the host, you understand. A link in the chain of living things. E-cology, Miss Roberta Heath, MCSP, SRP, and, oh my, BSc. We mustn't forget that little *c* there must we?"

That evening I walked the puppy in the oak grove where the lonely toys were. She shook a rag doll I'd retrieved from the sand. Unable to chase after when I threw it, she plumped down and yelped.

"What's the palaver down in there?"

"It's me. I'm playing with the dog."

"You not named it yet?"

"She's not mine so I won't name her."

"You picked her."

"Maybe but not like that. I was just being kind for a bit."

"That's a good thing to know, Miss MCQPD Tiddly-tiddly. Your kindness comes in bits. I'll remember that."

I parted the branches. He was up there again, screened away on the verandah. "That mutt house-trained?"

"Of course not."

"Bring it on up. It'll piss on my feet but never mind, warm 'em up a bit."

I climbed the stairs into the fume of his cigarettes, more pungent with every step, it penetrated my eyes, crawled through my nostrils down my throat.

"You scared of me, Miss Heath? I scare you, that it? Come on in now. That's better. Let's socialize, why don't we?"

At the back of the verandah a black woman was arranged on a rattan swing with earphones clamped to her head, her legs stoutly parted under a cotton dress. A trail of knitting flowed from her fingers to her lap to the floor. Her blank eyes were milky white and as she spoke she stroked her features against the place where sight used to be. "Who's there? Someone there? Raoul child? Someone there?"

From his place behind a small table set with a glass, a bottle of whiskey, tub of ice, and a mess of playing cards, Patout answered, "S'okay, Allie. It's the English party come to make me move. A certain Miss Heath.

"Miss Heath, Miss Alice Wine. My nurse the day I was born, been by me ever since. Blind now." I lowered the puppy to the floor, preparing to greet Miss Wine. "Don't waste your time. Pretty well deaf too but I talk anyway. No one else to talk to, so why not, I say."

Alice Wine cried out, "Who? Why I know who. It's the Supremes, that's who. I could get the prize. Raoul child, where's the phone? I wanna call in and get the prize."

"Game shows on the radio, Miss Heath. Pay no attention to her. That's what she lives for. Good a thing as any when you're ninety-eight. So, what you doing here, then?"

"You know the answer to that."

He stirred the cards with his right hand. "I mean why here of all places on God's earth? What you running from?"

Night was down, came down when my back was turned. There was nothing beyond the rail anymore, no grass, no cabins, the pigeonniers, all gone. Just the three of us now in the light of oil lamps hung from the beams. "Nothing."

"Nothing, eh? Run all you like, can't get away from that."

He was resting on both elbows to contemplate the cards, so there had to have been some recovery in the shoulder girdle, shoulder and elbow. But, so far as I could see, not in that disowned left hand.

"Is it two months now since your stroke?"

"You tell me. You got notes."

"It's two months. The longer you remain immobile the harder—"

"Puppy's whining, wants holding. Pick it up."

"I don't want it to become dependent."

"Saw you hold it tight enough just now, top of the stairs there, fixin' to squeeze it to death."

"Its mother died. Lenny drowned the rest of the litter."

He let his left arm fall towards the floor, very little control in the movement. "Here puppy-puppy." The puppy licked his hand. "You a lucky puppy? Come from above, maybe? Sent on down to us to save our souls? That it, little critter? Hear me say that, Allie? I say we got a holy puppy among us. Huh."

"What's that, my fine young man? You call my name?"

"Listen to your radio Allie, everything's all right. Why won't you look at me, Miss Heath, don't you like my features? There now. That's all right then. How do you like Janvier?"

"It's beautiful."

"You a married lady?"

"No."

"Divorced?"

"No."

"Uh-huh"—as though understanding more than I'd told him. "Uh-huh. My great-nephew—great-nephew, you see—told you, I guess, that I discharged myself from Oschner. That's the place they put me. The hospital, you know. And he told you too, no doubt, that I don't want anyone messing with my limbs."

"He did. He also said I should come anyway and he left a letter in my cabin telling me you're now willing to have treatment."

"Is that so?"

"Yes. Aren't you?"

"Tell me why I should be. I'm sixty-eight years old. Been a cripple since I was twenty-five. Nothing's come out like I figured it would. I'd just like to drift off peacefully with dignity. Give me a reason why I should trouble myself to live on?"

I stared out over the rail towards things I knew were there and could not see.

"Well, miss. Do you have a reason for me?"

"The reason's your business. But you do want to recover."

"How's that?"

"People who are tired of living don't bother to lie about their age or dye their hair."

He dropped the cards collected in his right hand, slumped back in his chair laughing. "Huh. Allie? Allie? Hear that? Hear what the young lady said to me?"

"Getoudahere man, you're a liar, you're a thief. You don't get my vote. No way."

"We're electing a mayor and Miss Alice Wine here, well she's a Democrat. Staunch. Have a drink." He pushed the bottle towards me.

"No thank you."

"I said have a drink. There's a glass on the table by the chiffonier inside the door there." I opened the French doors into the unlit house, lifeless as a room set in a museum. Such furniture as I could make out appeared gilded, unwelcoming, precious. Reflections from the lamps were caught in ceiling-high mirrors in ornate frames hanging forward from every wall. There were bottles and glasses on a tray at the far side of the room.

Outside I poured some whiskey and Patout said, "See the mirrors back in there?"

"Yes. Impressive."

"Backed with diamond dust, you know. Diamond dust. Brought over from Paris in 1757 by the first Janvier bride to come out here. Seventeen years old was all she was. So, tell me about yourself. Got family back home?"

"Yes."

"Go on."

"There's my mother and my sister."

"Your daddy?"

"He's dead. Laura, my sister, she has a little boy called Will. My mother's name is Esther"—glad to be speaking their names. "They're all staying in my flat while I'm away. And she's a singer, my sister, that is, and they're, they're—I don't know what else to tell you. I miss them very much."

"Shouldn't have left then, should you?"

For a while there was only the night with its sounds: the moist clicking of the puppy's tongue, the creaking of the swing, the moths batting, igniting with minute gasps against the lamp funnels, Allie murmuring, "Yes, sir. Mmm, mmm, speak on, ain't that the truth," and the plak-plak-plak of the playing cards.

"You can go now."

My eyes bored anger and—worse for him—determination into his gray roots as he perused the cards, until he lifted his head and stared back. At the same time he drew a tortoiseshell cigarette case across the table with his right hand, sprung it open, laid it down to remove one, placed it between his lips, and lit it. He dragged deep then leaned forward to release the smoke in my face. "I said you can go now. You may come to me at six a.m. tomorrow morning."

The puppy was sleeping in his lap. "Shall I leave her with you?"

"She's your puppy. You picked her." I reached to gather her. He touched her head lightly with the tips of his fingers and "No need to be afraid" is what I thought he said.

I was down below, halfway across the grass, when—as

if all the noises of the night had pressed back to make way for one alone—I heard him clear his throat. There he was, up there in the pale light, chair side-on to the stairs, head resting against the doorframe. I walked on again until his voice came down again between that cordon of sound. "Goodnight, Miss Heath."

"Hi. It's me."

"Is that you, Dear?"

"Are you busy?"

"No. Laura's out. Will's asleep. We love your letters. And the drawings."

"Where is Laura?"

"She's found something new or, rather, we *hope* she has. Something better. A better class of audience."

"It's a good line, Esther, you don't have to shout. Can you hear me?"

"What?"

"Can you hear me?"

"Yes, Dear. Just as if you're in the next room. Where are you ringing from?"

"My cabin. There's a telephone here."

"But *should* you?"

"I miss you."

"We miss you too, Dear, but never mind. You'll make a big success of it. Nice people, are they? I said *nice people?* Only you haven't mentioned the people in your letters. What a lot of letters. I expect it's hot with you. We've painted the studio yellow."

"For God's sake."

"No, *yellow.* Brightens the place up. I lost the keys to the flat in Ladbroke Grove. I'm sure it was there because I'd been to collect Will from play group. So we changed the locks in case someone saw and followed me home. Will's having violin lessons. It's a Japanese thing. I think he's a bit young but there you are. Where are you ringing from?"

"I told you, my cabin."

"It must be costing an awful lot, Robbie. Had we better go now?"

"We could talk some more."

"I don't think it's right, Dear. Not if you're not paying. You don't want to lose the job. I'll post a letter tomorrow."

"Esther?"

"All right then, Dear. Bye-bye. Big hug."

Esther continued to listen, not in case I should say more but in case something of what I'd already said was still arriving down the wires and it would be indiscreet to leave it. I heard her murmuring to herself, making noisy arrangements to replace the receiver, and when she did, I knew I was far away. Farther than I'd ever been. And I was left with only an afterimage of Esther: Esther in my flat, in the studio room, Will asleep in his cot, unwashed dishes in the kitchen, the tumble dryer groaning with Will's unending laundry. Esther sits down again—because she would have been standing to speak on the telephone, she always stood to speak on the telephone—but from her seat she remains watching it, remembering me. It wouldn't be the me who spoke to her just now she was remembering, but the me of a long time ago, before

I was silent or independent or angry. A time before I could provide for her and be resentful, or resented, for doing so. She would be remembering a young me who didn't take patience to love. Then she rubs her hands, Esther does, amalgamating her memories with the present and goes to the kitchen to make a cup of tea.

No matter how hard I tried I couldn't make Laura blow into that far-off room. Void of even so much as the sound of her voice, it was filled, filled, with her absence.

The following morning I climbed the steps to the verandah, opened the unlocked French doors in search of Raoul Patout's bedroom. The formal drawing room I had seen the previous night led into a sitting room where toys were scattered on the floor. This room led, in turn, to a dining room. I passed through that out into the hall, which ran from front to back of the house. The only bedroom I found was clearly unoccupied. It appeared that the living quarters were all centered on this floor, but rather than blunder further I found Theresa, already at work in the dependency. Without accompanying me there she indicated Patout's room in the back corner of the house. I knocked on the door, tried the handle, found it locked, pressed my ear to the rosewood panel, and waited, breathing in the stagnant scent of his cigarettes. Remote but succinct, I heard the unmistakable sound of a drink being poured. I knocked again, called his name. From inside came the tap of a heavy-bottomed glass being set down. I returned to my cabin.

He remained out of sight for the rest of the day, the

rest of the week. Every morning at six I presented myself at his door. He made no pretense of being asleep on the other side of it, and no attempt to respond to me.

"May I talk to you, Charles?"

He had been sharpening knives outside the dependency and stopped what he was doing to check nervously up at Patout's window before answering, "Uh-huh."

"You help Mr. Patout into bed at night, am I right?"

"When he wants that, I do"—nodding at the window up there, assuring the unseen Patout of his loyalty.

"And when he doesn't want that?"

"I don't know 'cause I ain't there."

"He has missed several treatments this week because his door is always locked so I can't get in, you see. But he did ask me to come. What if something were to happen to him? It's very likely, do you know that? Because he's not well. He's not getting better like he should. And he won't unless we help him. He won't unless I can start with his treatments. What can I do, Charles, if he's always asleep when I go there? I don't know what I'd say to Mr. Janvier if anything happened to his uncle and it was only you and me here taking care of him."

"There could be a key, maybe."

"Where?"

"I can't say that, uh-uh. Nope," and repeated to the corner window up at the back of the veranda, "I can't say that," shaking his head hard.

The next morning I arrived at his door again. This time no sound at all came from within. I intended to fetch Charles and bully him into bringing a key but as I turned in the confined lobby outside Patout's room I saw one lying conspicuously on top of a book pulled a few inches forward from the rest on a shelf to the side of his door.

Inside, the curtains were drawn across two windows, the third was open and sunlight penetrated the shutters. Clutter overwhelmed the room. Giant papier-mâché cobras reared from the corners of a canopied bed, which was draped with red silk, a Chinese lantern hanging from its inner dome. Dried sago palm fronds erupted from brass sconces on either side of the open door, where I remained unwilling to shut it and close myself in there. A vast gilded mirror hung forward from the wall reflecting a life-size statue of the Virgin Mary on the floor in front; her blue painted robes had been scorched by fires in the marble grate behind. Her head was modestly averted from the direction indicated by her left hand. And in that direction, backed into the meeting point of two book-lined walls—past tables bearing photographs in elaborate frames, a grand piano, an upright ladder with a stuffed alligator nailed to it—was Raoul Patout slumped in his wheelchair, an empty whiskey bottle on a table to his right, and in his lap, along with his left hand, was a glass and playing cards.

I had heard his breathing, that sawing and burbling, as soon as I entered. To judge by its rhythm, he was asleep. I knelt close to make use of the time before he woke. Fingers badly swollen, the rings cutting into them, the skin of his left hand was tight, translucent, and I touched it to feel how damp it was. He didn't wake. His feet were the same though the skin was drier, flaking. I shut my eyes to concentrate on those sounds from his chest.

"What you doing down there?"

"Listening. Good morning."

"Charming. A man opens his eyes to find a woman at his knee. Guess I should flatter myself." I stood up, crossed my arms. "Guess not," he added. "Huh. Well, you're late. I've been waiting. Been waiting over a week now." He motored across the floorboards, negotiating a rocking chair, a marble table, the piano. "Come on. Get on with whatever it is you're going to do to me."

I studied his transfer from chair to bed, a procedure he appeared to be accustomed to, and yet, "Do you always get in and out of bed unaided?"

"Oftentimes there's Charles."

An old-fashioned iron brace for his right leg—this was apparent now—was propped against the wall between the bed and a mahogany commode. Curious he didn't use a modern lightweight one in molded plastic.

"If you like I could show you how you can do the same only without such strain."

Not even the caftan could disguise his 259 pounds as he lay there, and knowing this, he was self-conscious, without bravura, his frightened eyes fixed on the silk folds above him.

"Mr. Patout?"

"Uh-huh."

"Relax. I'm not going to hurt you."

"Uh-huh."

"Now, allow me to take your left arm, so." I eased the sleeve to his shoulder. "Are you comfortable at night?"

"Why? Planning on joining me?"

"Can you please just tell me if you're comfortable at night, do you have any pain?"

"But for the cramps, no."

"Can you describe the cramps?"

"Guess I can," and he did so while I raised his arm, gently raised it until I felt his resistance and heard the catch of his breath. I fetched a towel from the adjoining bathroom.

"I'll examine your legs now, if I may?" I reached for the hem of his caftan.

"Got no shorts on."

"It's of no significance."

"Ain't that the truth. Ah, there now, nice laugh you have."

I covered his left leg and groin with the towel while I discovered the degree of flaccid paralysis in his right one from the polio.

I have some notes I made back in my cabin after that initial examination—which had lasted maybe an hour— as well as some others from our first wordless encounter. I confirmed the polio had affected his right lower leg, leaving the anterior tibials quite badly affected, causing the foot to drag unless supported by a brace. The intercostals were weakened and, being of such height and weight, the pressure of his slumped shoulders on his heart and lungs had to be immense. Not to mention the damage he was doing to himself with the smoking. The hemiplegia had been of medium density or he'd never have been able to discharge himself from the hospital in the first place. He had come home, refused further treatment, eaten quantities of heavy food, not to mention the whiskey, and taken no exercise. He didn't have to tell me he rarely slept in his bed, nor that he slaughtered a bottle of whiskey most nights. This explained the early-

morning swelling of his feet. The cramps weren't cramps
but stress from Charles's inexperienced handling. I would
teach him the correct method of lifting and supporting,
although I suspected Charles himself was no longer
strong enough, young enough, for this task. Because the
polio had affected his right side and then the hemiplegia—the stroke—his left, Patout had lost confidence to
stand upright, much less walk. With physiotherapy, exercise, diet, and cooperation from him, I hoped that a virtu-
ally complete recovery to his antehemiplegic state could
be made. I wouldn't tell him that. I'd save that. Have
him find out for himself.

Docile, like a child, Raoul Patout allowed me to learn
all I could from his limbs, his skin, the sounds in his
chest. "There, then," on an emphatic note, was how I
indicated I'd finished his treatment that first morning,
and from then on always would. I've found it's best to
have a signal to show the treatment is over without actually saying so. Different signals for different patients, the
right one always presented itself. "There, then" was the
signal for Raoul, together with my hands placed quite
still for a long moment on his shoulders or lower spine.
"There, then, Raoul."

"Your voice changes when you're working. All brisk
and sure. And your hands are cold."

They couldn't have been. I was meticulous about that.
I snatched them back. "I had no idea. You should have
said."

"I don't mean their temperature, that's warm enough.
I mean the way they move. I mean where their feeling
stems from is a cold place."

"If erotic massage is what you're after then I'm the wrong one."

"Aw, come on girl. I can make my observations while you're making yours about me. It's only fair."

"What's all this stuff in here? Where does it come from? Are you a collector?"

"What stuff?"

"All this?"

"Stuff? Is that what you say when you walk in on a person's life, see it arranged before you? Would you pick up an arm or a leg and say, *What's this thing?* Assuming of course it's still attached to a being? I don't think so."

"Bad choice of words. Esther—my mother—she'd love it all. This is right up her street. Is Charles coming to help you dress?"

"When I call for him. So this, this Esther, likes fine things?" He reached for his tortoiseshell cigarette case and I watched the same procedure as that evening on the verandah—the laying down of the case, the picking out, the lighting. He drew once, removed a speck of tobacco from his tongue, drew again, watching me. The smoke curled faint between us and he allowed his arm to rest. "Damn," he said, "what *is* it scares you so?"

"I'm not scared."

"Liar. So what are they doing living in your place? Got no place of their own, your mother and your sister?"

"Not at the moment. Would you like me to call for Charles now? And I'll go and work out a regime. I'd like to give you a short treatment midafternoon. It won't be as tiring as the one you've just had. In a few days' time, if you feel like it, we could go outside, I mean, outside in the garden, not just the verandah. Right now, after you've bathed and changed, I'd like you to rest on your bed for at least an hour to reduce the swelling in your legs."

"Don't you want me to tell you about my *stuff* anymore?"

"It's better you rest now."

"Laura?"

"Robs? What is it?"

"What are you doing?"

"Trying to sleep. It's the middle of the night."

"Sorry."

"Don't be. I was only trying because that's the convention with night, isn't it, among proper people? They sleep. And I'm practicing being a proper person. What time's it with you?"

"Nearly nine. In the evening. I thought you might have come in late, not be in bed yet."

"Like I say."

"Can I ask you something? Do you remember, you and me sitting on a stair when Matthew died? Remember that?"

"Why?"

"I want to remember what you said to me. It ended with *Let's pretend we don't hear it.* I've been trying to think what came before."

"I don't remember."

"You do. I can hear you do."

"That smoke again, Robs? Someone's smoking Turkish, that's all it is. A Sobranie, maybe. Try one. They're nice. There's nothing to be frightened of, all right?"

"How do you know I'm frightened?"

"I do, that's all, and you mustn't be, because you're all right. You are, aren't you, Robs. What's the old bugger like?"

"A bully."

"There's one thing I'll remind you of about being on those stairs. We made the pact not to wake each other. Remember that?"

"I suppose."

"Well, we did."

"You said you weren't asleep just now."

"Trying, though. I'm trying hard. Keep working, Robs. Work hard like you always have and I'm going to turn over now and go on make-believing I'm a proper person, okay? And Rob? Can you not ring me in the night just in case the make-believe comes real?"

There was one thing I knew about Laura, about being far away from her, which frightened me: Anyone out of her frame for long, out of touch in the truest sense and out of sight, she blocked from her memory. And if they refused to fade, if, for instance, her affections remained tied, she desecrated their memory. I had witnessed her do this with friends and lovers alike, savage the times they had shared as though, simply because they were no longer there, whatever their reasons, each one must have been a deceiver, an exploiter, a betrayer. But not me. Not me?

———

Raoul refused to admit me to his room on the afternoon after the first treatment and kept out of sight for
the rest of the day. Late in the evening I passed outside
below his bedroom and heard from in there:

"Lean on me, now, lean on me, you know ol' Charles
won't let you fall."

"Old Charles, huh? Old Raoul too. Wasn't always so,
was it, my friend? Why, do you remember those trips to
Europe, Charles, when you and I"—his voice dropped
and was punctuated by their mutual laughter.

"Now don't go tellin' Theresa that one, Mr. Raoul."

The next morning I knocked on his door again. "Go to
hell," he shouted. The door was unlocked and I entered.
"Leave me alone. I don't want you screwing with my
limbs. Go on back to England."

"I haven't come to give you a treatment. Just to talk. It
gets lonely. I could leave but that would be a defeat for
me. And for you. And I certainly won't leave until your
nephew returns. So, there it is."

He shifted in his chair. With his right hand he lifted
his left into his lap, lowered his head to sharpen his view
of me. "Gets lonely, does it? I know. I know that. You
have a kind face, Miss Heath, despite your cold manner.
Men scared of you? I think, maybe, they are. That why
you're not married? Pretty thing like you. Tall, aren't
you, look too frail to do all that lifting of limbs. Big
heavy limbs like mine. Got fine hands though, fine
strong hands. Do your patients fall in love with you?
That why you're so remote? That why your eyes evade a
direct gaze? That what scares you? To be approached?
You had work on those teeth of yours? Only you English

tend to have bad teeth as a rule. Ha. I do like it when you laugh. Go on, laugh some more. That's good.

"Let me see now, get the beads, the beads there. No, there from the corner of the chiffonier. Mardi Gras beads, Miss Heath. The maskers up on the floats throw them down to the people in the streets. That's during Carnival. Now, that's a time in New Orleans. Kind of messy these days but back when I was a young man, well, my, my, we had some fun. See those cobra heads? They were attached to the float on which I sat as Comus during Mardi Gras fifteen years back. Number One of the Mystick Krewe of Comus I was. I have a picture of me in my regalia if you would care to see that too. It's a club, I guess. A New Orleans thing. There's others but mine's Comus like my daddy's. He was in it too. The Virgin Mary there, in front of the fire, she comes from a chapel they pulled down, stood right next to our establishment on Canal. I call her my patient Virgin. Patient 'cause she's still waiting after all these years for me to come good. See how she holds her hand? Sets her head away from me? She's saying, *My, my, look at him, what next.* Now the bed, well, well. What can I tell you? Brought it here with me when my nephew Pat—the instigator of your presence here—asked me to live with him, being all alone as he was with just his children. I said, *Pat, I have to bring my bed, Pat. Can't come without my bed. The bed I was born in. The bed I'll die in.* Why, Miss Heath, if that bed could talk I'd have to shoot it. Huh. Come here, come here."

He held out a sepia photograph, a formal portrait of bride and groom with her lace train brought in a full circle around their feet. On the back was scribbled in pencil, "14 April 1907." "My mother and my father," he whispered with awe as though they might hear.

"I see your pale face. I see you thinking they're old to be wed. Well, they were. Miss Heath. My mom, Virginie Janvier, was born in 1862 and not married till she was forty-five years of age. Living like an old maid in this house, *this* house, you see, with her brother married and his offspring running around. We have the Napoleonic code, you understand, so it was her house too, if she chose, and she did. She'd run errands for him sometimes if she was going downriver to New Orleans, pick up a new hat, maybe, waiting for him at Patout the hatters' on Canal. Doing so, she met my daddy, Alexandre Patout, overseeing, as he was, the running of his highly successful establishment, inherited from *his* daddy. Three years on from the wedding at a time of life commonly considered back then to be past that of childbearing—I know nowadays that ladies of ninety do it every day—she gave birth to me. My daddy died when I was twelve. Fell off a ladder reaching for a top shelf in his Parisian establishment—went bust, that did. Pity. Pat's father, he died when Pat was twelve. So I understood. A bond, don't you know. I traveled all of Europe, played the dilettante like a fool while my mother kept the business running, waiting for me to settle down. Then came the polio when I was twenty-five. And she had the misfortune to live and see what that did to me. Uh-huh. Died not long after. But I had Charles by me then and still had my Allie too. Am I boring you, Miss Heath?"

"No."

"You can come back later. I don't want a treatment now."

"I'll give you a massage with these unfeeling hands of mine. Just to help you relax, sleep awhile, reduce the swelling in your feet."

"Oh, young lady, I'll sleep." He mimed a kiss towards the empty bottle on the table.

"Was that a full bottle last night?"

"And if it was?"

"It's a great deal to drink, particularly when—"

"Stop right there. If I like to drink then that's what I'll do. Maybe you're the one to get some sleep. Your face looks like twenty miles of bad road."

After that he allowed me to treat him regularly at six every morning, and to begin a gentle exercise routine at intervals throughout the day. I attempted to curtail his drinking hours by giving him a massage late in the evening, even after midnight, until he fell asleep under my hands. Occasionally he was still there in his bed when I arrived first thing in the morning. If, during my wakeful nights, I saw his light come on at four or five, I would turn up, making out it was already six. This sometimes worked. In any case, he was sleeping longer due to the exercise and treatments. I used every opportunity to make him aware of his rejected left hand, to have him repossess it. "Watch that hand. Lift it to me, take mine now. Good, good." Only, I was doing the lifting, the uncurling of his fingers.

"Miss Nursey voice."

"Do you ever fish around here?"

"You know I do. I told you I do."

"You never have told me. But think about a rod in that hand, then. Think about fishing."

"Told you more than once: Never damn listen to a thing I say. Allie's better company than you. Fishing. Now wouldn't that be something?"

We had been working together for about ten days when Raoul descended to ground level—by way of the ramp—for the first time in the three months since his stroke. I walked backwards in front of the chair while Charles came behind, keeping slow pace with its progress. Raoul braced his body away from the land rising up to him, his right hand clutching the controls, his eyes wide, fearful. He was breathless when he reached me. While he regained himself I absorbed my attention in rubbing bright green mold from the glossy leaf of a camellia. He brought his chair around to assess his achievement.

"You did well."

"Guess I did at that." He raised a malacca cane resting across his lap, pointed to the ramp. "Beautiful, isn't it? Pure craftsmanship. Why, you could slide a naked babe right on down that thing. Lenny made it. There I was in my room on my return from Oschner, peacefully contemplating my graceful dying and hell, *hell,* the banging and sawing and God knows what all. And I'm cursing him loud enough so I know he'll hear me. *You fixing my coffin out there, Lenny,* I say to him. *You old dog,* I say, *Can't wait for me to be dead and gone. Huh? Dead and gone.* He shouts back at me above all his goings-on, *I'm fixing your slope to glory, Mr. Raoul, your slope to glory.* Where is he, old dog? Let's find him."

Lenny was crouched on a stool in the tack room, a

bridle in his lap and a mound of harness on the floor beside him. "Hey, Lenny. Here I am."

"I see you. Like your slope to glory, Mr. Raoul?"

"Indeed I do, Lenny. Only it's my understanding glory's up, not down. What was the intention anyway? Slide for my coffin?"

"Nope. Mr. Patrick say to make some way for you to come down and ride around in your chair. So I did. And there you are right now ridin' around."

"It's a fine slope, Lenny, proud to use it." Raoul's fingers grappled the edge of the rug slipping from his knees. I rearranged it. "See me, Lenny? Shameful. Namby-pambied like a girl."

"You go on and tuck Mr. Raoul up good. Keep them ol' knees humming nice. Ain't nothing namby-pamby 'bout a man bein' warm."

"Come on, Miss Heath. I'll show you something."

"Another day. You're tired."

"I say *now*. Hear me? *Now* is what I say"—smacking the cane across the arms of his chair.

We crossed an earth yard with three wooden sheds on the far side of it, over a track into a pine wood—it was hard going on the chair. "You'll wreck your chair."

"It's my chair. I'll wreck it if I like."

Not ten minutes from the house, enclosed by a wrought-iron fence, was a tomb, maybe ten feet high, ten deep. On top was an urn, draped, crossed with a wreath, a clutch of poppies, a butterfly. Stone, all of this in stone. The names carved below were all Janvier, Janvier, Janvier.

"My mother's in there. My father being buried where he died in Paris. And I'm asking myself, you see, I'm asking myself where'll I go? Me a Patout and all. Not pushed in with all those Janviers. If they were Juillets I might feel it to be a brighter prospect. Huh. Hear me say that? Juillet not Janvier? Never mind. But no, not pushed in there, I don't want that. And where's your daddy buried, Miss Heath?"

"I have no idea."

He sighed simultaneously with the peculiar cry of a bird nearby. I'd ask the name of it later. Not then. Not right then.

"Charles says you sleep out on your stoop."

"What if I do?"

"Says you cry out. Says he's heard you scream. Been over, checked up, and all you're doing is lying there, sleeping with your face all screwed up, uttering sounds."

"Please tell Charles to never come near me like that again."

"Like what? He's only looking out for you."

"I can look out for myself."

"Not all the time. Not when you're sleeping you can't. But that's when it gets you, isn't it? Whatever it is you're running from? But you're only human. You have to sleep, though you don't want to. Though you're scared to. Charles says you're out there on cold nights too, even when it's wet like it was night before last. I wonder what you're dreaming. What you dreaming, Miss Heath? What you dreaming, Roberta?"

"Robbie."

"Pity to do that to a name."

Dusk and I was searching for the puppy, which had scuttled into the shrubs at the back of the house. When I found her, grabbed her, and returned with her under my arm—talking, probably, in that daft way one does with animals—I saw Allie making her way down the back stairs, tapping the side of the ramp with a white cane. I'd been at Janvier some weeks and had never seen Allie standing before. As I watched her stately process she stopped, pointed with her chin. "Who's there. I say who's there?"

I reached for her arm to reassure her. She said, "Why, it's you, Miss Heath." The first time she had ever addressed me. She tucked the cane under her hand gripping the banister, leaving the other free to explore my cheeks, my eyes, my mouth. A firm touch, determined to know me. Then she cupped the side of my head and I found myself resting into the cradle of that cushioned palm. She said, "He thinks I don't hear, Miss Heath. And I do. I do. And I have my way of seeing too." She passed on down towards her bedroom on the ground floor of the dependency.

"La Passe! La Passe! C'est la qu'est mon étoile.

"C'est la qu'est mon trésor.

"Take a drink, Robbie."

He was changed and ready for bed but the signs were clear. He wouldn't go to bed tonight. He would refuse the massage that would make him sleep so I could bring the cover over him, turn off the light, and leave him there, like a child, like a child. Tonight he would drink and nothing was going to stop him. Any incident might have triggered his mood, mislaying a book he wanted at that moment, that very moment and no other. No hot water for his bath. Importune memories.

"See that? Get up there and take that down."

I removed my shoes to climb onto the piano stool and reach for a picture high above the door and hand it to him. He brushed dust from the glass with his sleeve, tipped it to the light of a lamp shaded in rose silk. "That's better. Long time since I've held it close. See what it is? It's a Chinese watercolor of the night-blooming cereus. Are you familiar with the night-blooming cereus?"

"No."

"It grew in the garden here once upon a time. Not anymore though. Don't know why. When I was a boy my mother would let me stay up late at night, just now and then, stay up to smell its sweetness. As a grown man I'd return and sometimes catch that sweetness again, floating to me in the darkness like that, stirring memories, you see, of summers long gone. I always came here summers as a child. Swam, made little plays on my own, fetch an audience from among the adults, force 'em to watch. My cousins, they were grown by then. Most of them dead now. I climbed the highest trees. Know that live oak, one outside the house, highest in the grove there? Top of that, I could get. No one ever reached me. They got so mad. Missed suppertime if I chose. Got a whipping but worth it.

"Come over here. Don't look that way. I'm not going to hurt you. How could I? Old man like me. Come here, I say." I approached the wing chair where he was seated. "Kneel down, so your face is level with mine. That's right. I want to watch you when I do what I'm about to do."

Slowly, slowly he lifted his left hand up towards me, unfurling the fingers, exposing the palm. I reached out, held it in mine. Flexion—the natural direction of the stroke—caused his fingers to dig into my palm again but, one, two, a hesitation—his lips rammed together with the force of concentration, me breathing—"Yes, yes,"—three, and four, then, last, the thumb, he extended his fingers once more. But no longer *the* fingers, *the* thumb, *the* hand. They were his again.

"Been practicing with this hand of mine. Wanted to see your eyes light like they do when you're proud."

And I leaned towards him and embraced him. I embraced him. "Fishing, next," I said and moved back.

We had worked on the strength of his trunk, leg, arm, and general conditioning. I had had him sitting on the edge of the chair—wearing his brace—and rising to his feet with Theresa there to steady the chair and Charles and me on either side of him. On the morning the walking bars, the kind that fold back on themselves, arrived mail-order, Raoul watched Charles and me erect them in his bedroom. "I'm not rising, you hear me? I'm not rising from this chair." They remained some days placed right in the middle of his room so that walking the puppy outside I heard him thwack them with his cane. "Damned ugly things cluttering up my place here." But he didn't ask Charles to remove them. All I had to do was wait. Finally, days later, he said, "Okay, now. Help me up. Man supposed to do this thing alone? Cripple like me. Call yourself a therapist? You're no help at all."

"Charles and Theresa aren't here yet and I can't support you alone."

Raoul hauled himself from the bed to his chair and crossed to the window where he pushed open the shutters. "Charles, I say, Charles, come on up here and bring Theresa too. What you doing you sleepyhead? Day's nearly over and Raoul's planning on walking, hear me? Walking." They arrived panting. "Well, did you hear me?"

"Yes, sir. Walking." Charles was still shoving his shirt in his trousers.

Confirmed by Theresa behind him. "Uh-huh, walking."

I explained how we raised and supported the weight—positioning Charles on Raoul's right, that being the stronger side and would require less of him, Theresa behind. Together we did it, the four of us, encouraging, concentrating, resting, we brought Raoul to his feet, upright between the bars. For half a minute he remained there gazing around, bemused. "Why, I'm up, don't you know. Charles man, Raoul's up." Then his color drained and I nodded to Charles and we eased him back into his chair. "Not worth it. Can't do it."

He subsided in depression and drank throughout the day and night. His door was locked the following morn-

ing, no key in sight. When Charles arrived with his
breakfast I was not allowed to enter. I remained outside
the door and listened to their voices while Charles laid
the fire that Raoul kept burning regardless of the
weather. When at last Charles shouldered out with a
tray, and the door was shut and locked behind him, I
showed him a bottle. "When he asks for whiskey, take
him this. Okay? I've prepared the rest of the bottles in
the case too."

He held it to the window, frowning at the color, shaking his head. "That's a shame."

"I know," I said. "I know, but it's for the best and he
might not notice."

"Won't be too sure 'bout that."

I lost count of how often I lay in my cabin holding the
telephone close on the pillow beside me, calculating the
hour back home. It never felt a safe one, certain Laura
would not be sleeping. Because she would in the afternoons, you see, if she had been out late or not been to
bed at all. And Will would creep in with her, lie down
too. She would open her arms to him without waking. I
trained myself to hardly ever give in and ring home, to
write a letter instead.

IV

TEDDY AND MARIE

"Know what I'd like?"

"Tell me. Watch your feet now. Lift your knee. Good."

"I'd like to set myself on the bank with a rod and a bucket of fresh night crawlers and wait for some old sac-á-lait to come by." As he spoke Raoul watched his legs the way I'd taught him to do. Stepping, carefully stepping, while I walked alongside with the chair. "Who'd have believed this of me three short months back?"

"Three *short* months?"

"You've enjoyed yourself, bossing me around like you do. A good lay's what you need." He sheltered his eyes with his right hand to view the flat water of the bayou. "Guess I'll take to my chair now."

"I'll fetch your rod, if you like. You can catch that sac-á-lait."

"No night crawlers."

"Catch one of the other kind. There must be other kinds in there. I have to fetch the puppy so I'll get your rod on my way."

He narrowed his eyes on the far bank, widened them, blinked. "Another day. Maybe tomorrow." His breath was labored. "Maybe."

"And maybe I'll leave the puppy for now." I rested with my back against the wheel of his chair just listening, seeing, easy like that. Something touched the top of my head, very light, hardly at all but so warm. I let it be awhile then I flicked my hand as if I believed it was a fly. I heard Raoul chuckle and sniff. We watched for an alligator on the bank. The day was cooling, they would be on the move. A car door slammed somewhere. Theresa off to the shopping mall this side of Baton Rouge. Or Lenny taking the pickup to fill it with diesel, fetch that harness from the saddler's. Errands. Just errands. How days pass. Children's voices somewhere. Such life in them, I was thinking. And they came closer, those children's voices, louder. Raoul craned around behind him, sheltering his eyes again, this time from the blast of sunset.

That's how it all was the first time I ever saw Teddy and Marie. He was eight, she was six. They raced up the stairs to the verandah, slid open the screen doors, out came the puppy, and all their speed ceased. Teddy gathered it up to him while Marie tiptoed around reaching for parts of it to touch.

"Why, look who's here," Raoul spoke so softly, and yet as though they had heard him—I barely had—the children raised their heads, scanning the grass, the levee, around the pigeonniers then, over to the left, they saw us all that way down there by the water. Teddy deposited the puppy and ran towards us. Marie, her interest torn, ran, returned to fetch the puppy, carried it a while, then lowered it again to run on free. Teddy didn't stop at all. "Uncle Raoul, Uncle Raoul."

"Get me to my feet. Quick." I helped him rise with my arm close by while he walked away from his chair. "Don't aid me," he snapped and raised a triumphant right hand. "I'm up and running, Teddy boy, up and running."

Teddy careered right on into Raoul, throwing his arms around his hips, nearly toppling him. Raoul embraced the boy with his right hand, reached behind with his left—*with his left*—to find mine where they were supporting him. Head thrown back, Raoul was laughing louder, freer than I'd ever heard him.

Still clinging, Teddy leaned back to see Raoul's face. I was reminded of Will, how he held me that way. "Daddy said you might never walk again. He told us to be prepared 'cause you might die."

"The hell he did."

Marie stood rocking the puppy. "Well, Allie hasn't died yet and it's her turn first 'cause she's the oldest."

"Why hello, Marie. Now where's that daddy of yours?"

"He's at the office. He had the taxi bring us on out. He said to say he's coming on the weekend but Mama's coming tomorrow and we're going to visit Disneyland with her. We rode out all on our own. I weren't scared. What's its name?"

"That's Robbie's puppy. You better ask her."

"She's not mine really, so I haven't named her."

"Did you pick her?"

"Yes, Marie, I *picked* her."

"Then she's yours and you've got to name her."

"Very well, if you help me."

" 'Bout time too. I say that she's a holy puppy, Marie, and that she's come among us to do good. Didn't I say that, Robbie? Yes, I did."

The children scrutinized the puppy and Marie found a line of brown marks on its stomach, pressed her mouth against them. "You shouldn't kiss the dog, Marie," I said.

"Why not? She wants kissing, don't you, Puppy. She likes me kissing her moles, don't you? Shall we call her Holy Moley? Shall we?" And off they ran, shouting her name.

"Do believe I lost my novelty. That didn't last, did it? Maybe I should try dying again, get some attention around here."

Raoul sat in his chair to return. When we reached the oak grove Marie was scudding in the leaf mold on the red trike, Teddy was way up the big tree, only his feet in view tucked around a knot in the rope, and Moley was underneath trying to run with her front paws while gravity held her backside. "See there? Mark it, Robbie. That's joy." Something knocked the back of my hand. Raoul was seeking to take mine in his right one without letting go sight of the children, of the puppy, of the undiluted vitality. His palm against mine was hot and damp and he gripped tight and we watched the scene in the jiving shadows. The children calling to each other, the puppy yelping, the day cooling around us. "What's that you say? Robbie? Did I hear you say *There, then* like that, the way you do when you're done?"

Yes, I was trying to acknowledge that. Insofar as one is ever "done" with any patient. He had the use of his left hand again. He was walking, no longer required the chair—we retained it from that pure laziness, his and mine, that breeds so seductively in those regions. He'd lost weight, his body was toned, he slept five hours most nights. But Miss Nursey voice, Miss MCQPD Tiddly-tiddly whose kindness came in bits, was still treating this man several times a day. She was seeking him out to spend time with him and dawdling below his window at night. A good physiotherapist remains with her patient as much as possible to reeducate the body. But there are limits. Who was I fooling by turning up at four and five in the morning to cut his drinking hours? A boozer boozes. End of story. I knew that much. I was "done."

Marie was roosted on my stoop along with Moley and a large hairbrush in her lap. "Are you going to groom Moley? She needs it."

"No." Marie pushed off the puppy. "Will you fix my hair?"

"I'm not good at little girl's hair. What about Theresa?"

"She tugs. And Allie's blind and I don't want any of those *men* messing with my hair."

"How do you want it?"

"I just want it nice for when Mama comes. I don't want that." She lifted the nest of rubbed hair on the back of her head, the same as Will had in the mornings until

Laura, chatting and singing, smoothed it, groomed it smooth. Marie positioned herself conveniently between my knees and rubbed her own while I was brushing. I noticed the state of her fingers. "Would you like me to cut your nails?"

She buckled her hands in her armpits. "Guess so."

So I did, and even before I'd finished she had kicked off her sandals. "Toes too? They've got kind of twisty. Mama's a lawyer in Washington, *D.C.* My daddy's one too but my mama speaks-for-those-who-can't-speak-for-themselves. Daddy said that's the finest thing anyone can do so I said why didn't he do it too if it was such a good thing and he said that someone's got to make a buck around here."

She was playing with the implements from a manicure set, turning them in the sunlight, when I noticed the buildup of wax in her ear. Every Sunday night Will patiently offered this side, that side of his head, allowing himself to be attended by Laura, collecting her care, her love, storing it in his stature, reflecting it in every move he made, every word he spoke. Marie permitted me to clean her ears. "Do I look pretty now?"

A pallid little face, deep-set eyes, close together, an anxious triangle of green, muddy like the bayou. Had the answer certainly been yes would she have asked? Laura would have known how to answer without lying, taken her onto her knee—I could picture that—and talked to Marie about all manner of things important to women of six and thirty-six and ninety.

"You look charming."

She picked her nose to deliberate, rolled the findings between finger and thumb. "Okay."

So easy? Just like that? Okay, because I was the one who knew such things and the lesson for today was Acceptance: Pretty was what she had wanted. What she received was a word she didn't understand. This is how it was and always would be. Okay.

Teddy arrived, squatted beside her to pull off a sneaker, shake out a pebble. "Will you come on in the boat with me and Marie?"

"I have to take care of your Uncle Raoul. That's why I'm here, you see."

"But he's walking. Why can't you play with us now?"

"Because I'm not employed to do that. It would be wrong not to be with your uncle. Your father wouldn't expect that."

"But Uncle Raoul's *better.*"

"Yes. So when your father comes home I'll make arrangements to be on my way."

"Where'll you go?"

"Home. I suppose."

Home I suppose to a place too small for the four of us, for Esther and Laura and Will and me. Home I suppose although I could hardly bear the climate of my mind there—or here, or anywhere.

"See, we're not allowed to go alone."

"Where?"

Speculative eyes guessing I'd forgotten our exchange of moments before and deciding something about me. Possibly that after all I was not a suitable person to go alone in a boat with.

"It's okay, Mama's coming today to take us on visiting places we haven't been like Disneyland."

"Disney—Disney—I don't want to go more places I

haven't been." Teddy was red-faced with the effort of tying his sneaker. "I want to stay home."

"Washington, *D.C.,* 'll, be home too, Ted."

"Hush up, Marie. You never even been to Washington, *D.C.*"

The pair of them spent the afternoon on the verandah stairs, spruced up and waiting for their mother to arrive. At six she telephoned to say she was delayed on a case, couldn't make it this time. While Raoul was resting I sought them out, found them in the oak grove transported into make-believe, requiring no one. Laura and I had done that when we were little girls, we entered make-believe requiring no one. During the evening Teddy breezed into my cabin while I was washing my uniform. "Uncle Raoul says would you come on up."

"Is he all right?"

"I guess he wants you to play with him. He sure doesn't want to play with us."

The verandah was littered with toys and unfinished board games. Teddy, who'd run ahead of me, was letting out death cries as he twitched the controls of a noisy computer game. When I tripped over a circle of stuffed animals and dolls Marie shouted, "Hey, careful, they're doing group therapy." Allie was murmuring about crooks and pop stars, untroubled by Marie having possession of her hand, painting the nails various colors in felt-tip pen.

Raoul was slumped on a chaise longue, face in refuge behind his hands—no table, no cards, no book, no bottle. "Where the hell have you been all day?"

"With you, most of it. When do you children go to bed?"

"You ignoring me? That it, *Miss Robbie?*"

"When someone puts us."

Their bedroom was at ground level, directly below the verandah, a dark place even in daytime. I hadn't yet learned the value of cool rooms. Precise in their routine, Teddy and Marie undressed, folded their clothes, brushed their teeth, knelt to say their prayers. Someone had instructed them and they had not forgotten, hung on to it in the absence of that someone. All they required was that I should be present.

I stood by the door with my hand on the light switch. They sat bolt upright in their beds, quilts drawn to their necks, expectant faces balanced on patchwork heaps. Yet I could think of nothing that had been missed. "All right, children?" They subsided an inch or two. "Goodnight, then." I snapped off the light.

Allie had gone when I returned to the verandah. I cleared a table and placed it beside Raoul. "Where are your cards?"

"Get me a drink. And I mean the bottle, for God's sake." I brought one to him with ice and a glass. "Now sit by me awhile." Something had gone out of him, something of light or hope. Sonething I'd seen grow was gone again. "What's on your mind, young lady?" I was messing with Teddy's computer game, trying to turn the thing off. "You thinking of leaving?" The green robot was firing at the red robot that vanished. "I asked if you were leaving?"

"When their father comes. It's only right I wait to see him."

"What you going back to?"

"Work. My family."

"They draw you, your sister and your mama. It's not how it should be. You're thirty years old. You should think about a life of your own." He pulled out the tortoiseshell cigarette case, withdrew an oval cigarette.

"I'll come back later when you're settled."

He retained my wrist. "Don't be silly. I won't light it"—trailing the cigarette down my cheek, under my nostrils. "Not if you tell me why it is you hate them so."

"They bring things to mind. Things I don't want to remember and *don't* remember clearly. But something's driving my thoughts back, pulls them in every idle moment, and when I sleep, to a place I was when I was little. I don't want to go back, but whatever it is makes me go there in my head. There? Satisfied? You shouldn't smoke so much. It's not good for you to smoke. Laura smokes too much."

"Know what happens to your face when I light up? It comes apart. Comes apart like a jigsaw and the pieces mix up. Then you reassemble them, Robbie—and you always do—you remake your expression but one is left reminded that that is what it is, a construction, an artifice, a pretense."

"I don't like talking this way."

"Maybe you don't. It's like the night-blooming cereus is for me, the way the scent of my cigarette stirs your memory."

"Yes."

"But not fine ones."

"No."

"What kind, Robbie?"

"I can't say."

Tasting the blood of my fingertips, I am led by the stranger. The door closes. The stranger's hand lets go. My face is covered. The scent of those cigarettes, sounds, glass on glass—why glass on glass—someone moving near, touching me. I'm seen without seeing. Voices, voices, *Mummy doesn't want you anymore—where's Laura—where's Laura—sent Robbie all alone—you can't go home again.* I turn in my darkness to where he will be, where he always is at the source of the smoke, and I know the cloth of his trousers, wrap my arms around his legs, lay my head against them, feel the warmth of his hand through my hair, his hand pushing me away while my arms are unwound. There is no other world now and no words. In that room, during those times, how many I don't know, my identity took its leave. Mirrors would always be empty.

"Hush now, Robbie. Didn't mean to upset you so. Come, easy now. Hoped maybe you'd tell me something, free yourself from whatever it is. Your mama and your sister, if it's them. It would be the natural thing to do. I'm not saying desert them but think of your future. Hereabouts perhaps. Old man's dream."

"It's a good dream."

"Not so hard to make true. Who knows? Don't rush away from life. Slow down and take it to you."

Patrick Janvier did not arrive at the weekend. He telephoned to say there was too much on at the office. Every morning the children collected Moley from my stoop and I wished they would keep her, relieve me of her during the nights as they did during the days. But they insisted she was mine because I'd darned well picked her so she slept where I slept. My evenings were spent with them on the verandah until their bedtime. Allie maintained her impassive presence, content to be attended by the children as though she were a giant doll, so long as neither of them touched her earphones, or the transistor they were attached to. When they made that mistake she swatted them until they rushed shrieking to the rail where they ducked, giggling until she resumed her dialogue with the airwaves. "Uh-huh, ain't that the truth, man—"

Late at night, before attending Raoul for his massage, I would walk to the levee, back around the house, and that's when I'd linger under his window, kneeling in the grass where the light, spilling from his window and across the verandah, paled and faded over where the magnolia grew. That's when I was comforted by the sounds drifting from up there: the chiming of the mantle clock behind the patient Virgin, the delving of tongs in ice, and Raoul's voice now more, now less coherent, sometimes addressing Charles, *Ah well, my old friend, times long gone, don't you know,* and, *You don't say,* and, *Remember when . . .* And Charles's responses, always the same, his cackle and his *Don't go tellin' Theresa that one*. And Charles cajoling Raoul towards his bed with the unspecific, almost sung, *Uh-huh, uh-huh*. A Southern sound, a conversational litany that ribboned along bayous, across swamps, around steeples, through pews and superstores and gas stations and out of the mouths of not only Charles and Theresa and Raoul and Teddy and Marie and the pipe-smoking black women hired to pick the snap beans and the man Allie called a vote-begging no-good who came banging on the screen door, but across tables in the diner at Dawson Switch too, and in the darkness of bedrooms, *Uh-huh, I hear you, uh-huh, I wait, you know I always wait, uh-huh, uh-huh, uh-huh.*

And I was sitting below Raoul's window, listening to such things, when a figure in a pale suit wandered into the far side of the light. The dark head was bent in study of something he held and that he returned to his inside pocket on becoming aware of me.

"Hi. Are you Miss Heath? I'm sorry. I scared you. You startled me too."

"Yes, I saw. I'm sorry."

"I'm Patrick. Patrick Janvier. I arrived only a minute ago. I guess the kids are sleeping by now. I didn't call to say I was coming in case I'd have to cancel again." He paused so I could respond, only I wasn't quick enough because he continued. "I haven't even been inside yet, not even said hello to Raoul. But he's told me when we've talked on the telephone everything you've done for him. Miss Heath, I thank you, I really do. He says he's up. Is that so?"

"He is."

"I'll be. He's all I have, after the kids, that is. See, his father was married to my great-aunt Virginie. The Patouts came from Paris about the same time as the Janviers and I'm talking about a time not long after New Orleans was little more than mud. Course his people were merchants and mine were, well, back then they were more." He ran dry.

What a compulsion these people had to set off an historical infantry before them, possibly to prepare the way for any shortcomings in the existing individual. I felt expected to deliver a few foot soldiers of my own, so, "Well, I'm called Robbie. Roberta, really, but no one ever calls me that."

His eyes were on my mouth waiting for more words to come out. I had none, and understanding this he returned his concentration from far away. "I never believed he'd walk again."

"That's why you had the ramp built."

"That's right. Only, to be honest, I didn't think he'd even live."

"Then why did you leave for so long?" I had been cross-legged and sometime during our exchange he had come to sit the same way beside me. Now he drew back as though surprised by my being there at all.

"I can't answer, not clearly. It's been a bad time all 'round. You see, my wife, my ex-wife"—he was feeling in his inside pocket for whatever it was he'd returned there earlier—"didn't come for the children when she said she would."

It happens. You find you've said something that restakes the boundary of acquaintance, creating greater license, and don't know what enabled you to do it. Perhaps it was that way he had settled next to me, leaning

forearms on knees like it was time to ask, time to tell. Or
perhaps it was a resemblance to Laura that vanished as
soon as he spoke. But before he did—it could even have
been her there concentrating on something in her hand.
There was nothing effeminate in his bearing. Feminine,
yes. Just as there was something unaffectedly masculine
about Laura.

"No. She didn't, did she? She's joined this firm in
Washington. Big-time firm. It's a great chance for her.
And Washington's her hometown. I guess she didn't root
here too well. We met as law students at Tulane. She
gave it up to settle here after Teddy was born, then
Marie. And well, well—I don't know. It's not as easy as
people make out. Getting divorced, I mean. Or do I mean
staying married? Either way."

Did I know that? Did I know it was not as easy as
people made out? His eyes were the color of whiskey,
malt whiskey. I had never seen such pale eyes. His
mouth had a current of humor running through it, as if
still amused by something his other features had forgotten.

"She left me, you see"—fist in palm to enforce the
statement. "That's how to put it, I guess. It's important to
me these days to have this understood—and it's been a
year since the divorce. I wouldn't have broken up or
risked my family for anything in the world. Nothing. It's
embarrassing to find myself saying this, but it's like a
truth that pushes itself right out of me. All the time with
the three of us alone in Europe, it would arise, where's
their mother? And I found some of them were assuming
she was dead. So I had to have people know she was alive
and that I'm not a widower, which would be nobler, in a

way, wouldn't it? Although I'd have done nothing to earn the nobility. I've tried explaining Louise not being around in more evasive ways like *We're separated* or *We decided that* or *It didn't work out.* Ways that made it sound like we'd made a joint decision or that the situation was something beyond the two of us. Neither of which is true. What is true is that she left. I didn't want her to, but she did."

His eyes were asking me to please not leave him suspended in silence.

"It's all right. Be patient, it will mend. It really will." What was I saying? What did I know?

"Thank you. Thank you for that." So then it was too late to warn him that I knew nothing.

The atmosphere coming from Raoul's room was heavy with the weight of suspended movement. I placed a finger against my lips to indicate the eavesdropper and formed a vision of Raoul in his wing chair with one hand raised aloft for absolute silence from Charles, from Charles who would be waiting with the sheet raised for Raoul to cross the room and maneuver himself into bed, from where he could listen all he liked and let Charles go back on down to his cabin where Theresa would have a po'boy waiting for him brought back from that diner in Dawson Switch and a cold beer, too, set on the table, because that's what they liked to do on a Saturday evening and this was one, only Raoul wouldn't let him do that because he didn't want to miss any of our words or have us think he was listening. That is, until he wasn't interested anymore, when he wouldn't care anyway if we did know he was listening.

Patrick frowned, half-guessed what I was trying to tell

him, raised his voice, "Anyway, it's good to know Raoul's more mobile. Like I said: It couldn't have been easy."

"No it wasn't." I raised my voice too, although we didn't have to because our voices would have been clear, peculiarly close, the way the voice of someone many yards away can carry around stone and whisper right out of it. "It's been a great strain and I don't know how I've stood it. He's spoiled and capricious and, given half a chance, downright lazy. Why, the things I could tell you. Do you know what he said to me once—"

Sure enough, the tension above altered. That tangible stillness was broken. The private life of Patrick's mouth took over from all the weariness and joined with his malt eyes in laughing as he mimed the question *Was he listening?* and I mimed *Think so,* and he laughed silently again with his hand covering his face until he hissed in a stage whisper, "Course, you know Patout is a Cajun name—"

And Raoul bellowed from above, "Cajun, my eye. I'm a New Orleans boy and my daddy was, and his daddy before him."

"I better go and give him his treatment."

"Treatment? At this hour? That's why you're dressed that way?"

"Yup. Stops him hitting the bottle. The treatment, not the uniform."

An ice bucket was rattled and we heard, "Huh."

Raoul wasn't waiting in bed but fully dressed in his wing chair. "Come in, come on in. Heard him telling you about himself. Leave me alone, I don't want messing with. Settle down now. How do you like him? Fine boy, no? Good-looking?"

"I suppose so."

"You so frigid you can't even see a good-looking man and know it? I said settle down, Robbie. I can make my jokes, can't I? That's right, you take a drink. Nice to see you're cultivating some healthy habits." He sniffed and smiled, watched me carefully as I filled my glass. "Soda's right there by your hand. Maybe I do have an exaggerated idea of his worth. He is, I admit, the son of my imagination. Has been since he was born. You think it was you made me live? For him I lived. The thought of my boy alone again, like he has been before. Keeps happening. First his daddy when he was no more than a child, then his mama when he was still a young man, then his wife through no fault of either of them. She's ambitious. I guess he's not. 'Less you count the hardest ambition, which is to create a life for his children that's secure and filled with joy the way he'd have liked his own solitary childhood to have been. So if he talks a little too much, right off, forgive him, Robbie. He's had a hard run and sometimes people respond that way. So. That's enough from me. You leaving now, leaving us here at Janvier?"

"I should."

"Give it more time, why don't you? See this left hand? Well, we're only freshly acquainted, a chaperone is called for. Who knows what it'll get up to with you not around? Huh. I'd miss your laugh."

"I'd miss laughing."

———

A weekend followed and I was invited to join Patrick and the children in everything they did—the walks, the games, the swimming. And Raoul told me, "You go, you go," and left me no choice. Then it rained on Sunday night and all through Monday, plain-dressing Janvier, making it sad. Patrick had left at daybreak for his office in the city. There was no sign of the children. They didn't fetch Moley. Come the evening, Patrick banged on the door of my cabin and entered without waiting. I was lying on the bed listening to the ringing tone back home—surely one of them had to be there, didn't they? He made a gesture of apology, backing out into the rain again, and I called for him to stay. The short run from the house had soaked his through, slicked his hair to his forehead. He rubbed it back, pulled his hands down his face. "Finish your call, really. Would you care to come up for a drink after?"

"I was ringing home. They're not there. Come in and have one with me. I've only just got dry myself."

"What's that song you're humming?" he asked while I was opening a bottle, and I had to think for a minute. Then all the scenes filled my head. "Something my sister sings to her little boy."

"I know it. 'Skip to My Lou,' right?"

"That's right, that's the one." We sang together, more saying the words really, tacking them onto the tune, the words here, the tune there. Not the way Laura would have sung it.

"It's a Southern song, Robbie. What's your sister doing singing a Southern song?"

"She knows lots of them, and blues too. She loves the music from this part of the world."

"Was it your sister you were calling just now?"

"Yes. She's never in if I call and doesn't want to talk if she is. She doesn't answer my letters. I need to know if she's all right."

"Why wouldn't she be?"

"What?"

"Why wouldn't she be all right?" Hesitating long enough for an answer if one was coming, then, "Hey, you know who I learned that song from? From Allie. Did I have fun with her when I was a kid. Jesus, she was a thousand even then. So your sister sings?"

"She's a singer. That's what she does."

"Is that so? Would I know her? Has she made recordings?"

"No. Nearly, but nothing ever quite comes off."

"Yeah. I know about that." He watched my mouth again while his concentration drifted as it had that first evening. "So: Has Raoul been very difficult?"

"Not impossible."

"Has he talked about himself? How he used to be? I guess not. Bet he gave you all the history though, *that* he does. He's looking good, Robbie. Better than even before the stroke. You've done so much for him. But you like him, I can see. You been happy here?"

"Yes."

" 'Cause, we were wondering, all of us, we'd like you to stay on, if you would. There's plenty else to do. By the way, I'm embarrassed on thinking how I opened up the other night, talked on how I did. Hope you didn't mind too much."

I let him understand that I hadn't and we sat quiet. It

was pleasant. It was pleasant until he covered my hand with his and began talking and talking away out of the window to where the rain was still rattling down. Then I forced myself to look at him as he was finishing whatever he had been saying. And now it was, "What? What is it?" The weight of his hand on mine. Mine cold. He pulled his own away, withdrew both his arms from the table, banished them beneath it, untrustworthy things, disowned them, don't want these arms anymore. "Jesus, I'm sorry. I didn't mean anything. Don't look that way. Hey, please, Robbie. Did you think? Oh my God. I meant nothing. *Nothing.*"

"It's all right but just—" Why did I always struggle to speak at these times? Why didn't I just let him, and all the rest of those who made such gestures, *be* sorry, the way they said they were, and *be* embarrassed and *be* aware that I did not want that. I had never wanted that.

"It wasn't intended as anything. But I see what you must be thinking. Oh boy."

"What were you saying before? You were telling me something?"

"Oh, oh right. Well, let me see, okay, thing is, the children's mama's coming in a few weeks to take them on and settle them in Washington. They've missed half a school year what with one thing and another, mostly my wish to have them with me while I traveled. Having taken them out of the local school once, I don't think it's fair just to pop 'em back in like that, only to move on a few weeks after. We'd all be glad if you'd stay till then, Robbie. I'd be around all I could but . . . anyway, I guess you won't now." He was backing to the door again.

"All I can say is I'm really sorry. Sorry. Sorry. Why you smiling?"

"You remind me of someone."

"Esther?"

"Robbie, Dear? Is that you?"

"Yes. How are you?"

"Are you all right, Dear?"

"Where's Laura? You still there? Where's Laura?"

"I don't know, Robbie. She's not been back, you see. Often out now. I don't know."

"Do you cope all right, with Will?"

"He's very well, Dear."

"I'm coming home, Esther."

"You've got the sack."

"Don't be ridiculous."

"Are the family back?"

"Yes."

"They don't want you anymore?"

"I just want to come home."

"Why? Why, if they want you?"

"I want to see you. I want to see Laura and Will."

"I've told you they're very well. And the job, you might never get—just a minute, I can hear Laura. *Laura, Laura, Robbie on the phone. She says she's coming home.*"

"Robs?"

"I want to talk to you. You haven't written once."

"Sorry."

"Esther says you're always out. Where were you this time?"

"Nowhere much."

"I'm coming home."

"What for? To check on me? For Christ's sake what for, unless you have to? You made the break and you were right. I'd give the world to do what you've done. And I can't. I'm trapped. There's nothing here, Robs. Stay out there. You're in the light at last even if you can't see it."

I waited on the bayou for the fishermen to pass. And when they did they waved to me as they had on my first morning and mornings since. Then I heard his car start up, Patrick away to his office. I dashed over the grass, around the side of the house. He had almost reached the gate, which stood open, always open, so there would be no need to slow down and he would not see me running along the drive now. But he did slow and stop and let the window down.

"I'll stay until their mother comes. Okay?" He gave a great whoop that rang in the air even after he had gone. The same sound Laura had made that night in the sad club. Had she been in a similar place last night? Would she be again tonight?

The heat of the summer commenced. I insisted on maintaining the routine with Raoul as well as joining Patrick and the children in boat rides, in cart rides with the mules hitched up, and camping by Lake Fausse Riviere, a cutoff arm of the Mississippi without outlet, which turned out to be where the fishermen headed.

"Hey lady, what you doin' down this way?" And they gave us fish that we fried in a pan.

I passed my evenings with them even after the children had gone to bed, and alone with Raoul again, when Patrick stayed back in New Orleans for the night. We'd work out the crossword, competing for who guessed the most clues, joint efforts not counted.

"Gettysburg. I win."

"The hell you do"—slamming down his pencil, raising himself exactly as we had practiced, using all the right muscles.

"That's so good, Raoul. See how you're using your latissimus dorsi less and less, and your quads and gluts more. Your triceps are stronger too. I'm very pleased with you."

"Stop that claptrap talk. *Pat? You back? That your car I heard?*"

"Uh-huh." Unseen but close.

And from the top of the stairs, the screen still shut across them and his hands spread on it as though caged, Raoul yells into the night, *"Well, hey, Pat, it's my belief this young lady's a virgin. Now don't that seem a pity to you? I mean isn't that a shame? A condemnation on the young men of her generation?"*

"Your uncle's a bad loser. *Bad loser. Junior crossword too.*"

"Liar."

Marie's talk was all of her mother arriving in six weeks, in five, in three. She had a chart and crossed off the days. "Mama'll be here soon, Teddy. You ready? You packed?"

"Don't want to live in any city."

In one of the wooden sheds, on the far side of the earthen yard, Marie found a leather cabin trunk with brass locks and corners. She dragged it back to their bedroom and filled it with her possessions, with T-shirts and dungarees—dirty, clean, made no difference—her Beatrix Potter storybooks, illustrated prayer book, and the pillow from her bed. Acorns from the grove filled the silk pockets on the inside, along with half-finished packets of biscuits, a dog lead, a rubber hooter fallen off the trike. "You think you can take Moley and the trike, and I know you can't. No dogs and trikes in Washington, *D.C.*"

"You been looking in my trunk, Teddy?"

"Everyone knows what's in your trunk and no one cares. It's just stupid. It's too big anyways. They won't let you bring it on. They'll take it away."

She kept the trunk in the corner of their bedroom. Every evening she traded items in and out of it—her only seclusion being the depth of her concentration—whispering all the time, remonstrating with herself for including this and forgetting that, explaining to one doll or stuffed animal why it had to come, and to another why it had to remain behind. She was usually finished when Patrick arrived from the city, ready to play awhile and read to them before bed.

The first time he saw her struggling to reach into the trunk, muttering to herself, was the night before my birthday. He sat on the bed with his hands clasped between his knees, smiling, smiling. Then less so. I bid goodnight from the door. They did not hear me. I waited.

Patrick said, "Marie? Hey Darling, maybe it's time for you to stop that and get into bed and have me read you a story?"

She ignored him. He came close behind her, picked her up, and right away she was kicking and screaming. "Don't look, don't look, that's mine own stuff, let me go, set me down."

Patrick reached for the lid of the trunk, slammed it. "See Darling, I'm not looking. It's your secret, Baby. That's okay." He walked the room with Marie, hysterical, in his arms. Gradually she calmed. "You ready for a story now, Honey, would you like that?"

Teddy approached, subdued by his sister's violence. "Can I listen, Daddy, too. I like Beatrix Potter just like Marie does?"

Patrick knelt down to encircle Teddy. "Course you can, man, but maybe I've got a better idea. How about us three watching a video? I've got nothing else to do and who wants to sleep anyway?"

Much later on the same night—the stairs damp underfoot, the screen doors stiff to part, lamps on the verandah extinguished—I returned to the house. The door to Patrick's bedroom was half-open. A television was chattering in there. By its cold, animated light I saw him, still dressed, asleep on his bed, the children cradled in his arms.

———

"*Raoul?* You didn't have Charles call me." A spark shot from the fire. He swept it from his lap, reached for his cigarettes. "Why not?" I sat down with the Virgin between us.

He poured a drink, held it to the lamp with the rose silk shade. "You water it down, Charles beefs it up. Everyone's doing their thing. Ha."

"Ha."

"Booray with the boys. Long time since I played a hand of booray."

"What's the matter? Why didn't you have Charles call me when he left you?"

"Pass Pat's room, did you?"

"Yes."

"Saw him in there, no doubt, asleep with his babes. Did the sight not stir you, Miss QP-little-c? I guess not. Any more than the hoo-ha I heard coming from Marie earlier this evening. I saw you crossing to your cabin and Patrick arriving with the two of them perched on his arms and a plan to amuse them. Who killed your heart? Can you not see how that young man is suffering at the prospect of his children going? Don't you have any more to give than this, this efficiency? If you reassure yourself that manipulation of human bodies is involvement with your fellow beings, you're wrong. Can't you see he likes you?"

"What are you getting at?"

"Come on. You know very well. All it would take is a little warmth, some spirit, to have something going between you. What's the matter with you anyway? What did you stay for?" His freshly dyed hair—it would be unruly and stiff for a day or two until it settled—covered half his face, leaving one glaring eye. "Well? Go on. I see you have something to say. Spit it out."

Was he really going to insist on the base coin of language when his body knew my hands as they did—had done for nearly five months? And my hands knew him; he'd responded to the change in that cold place he once claimed my feeling stemmed from. All right. Very well. If words were what he wanted—

"Wait." he pulled slowly forward in his chair, color rising in his cheeks, cleared the hair from his eyes, and plucked an elastic band from the breast pocket on his caftan to hitch it back. He sat erect now, arranged his shoulders, pulled his sleeves, allowed himself a coughing fit. Done with that, he was composed. "I want to tell you something about myself. I was fourteen when I had my first intimate relations with a woman. And it was good. So good I couldn't leave them alone for a minute. Lost count of how many other women passed under my fingers between that first one until the polio. That slowed me up. Slowed me up enough to fall in love. Forty-one years ago and I could still tell you about a certain amber in her hair when the sun shone. The tiny marks on her neck, how they darkened in times of emotion. One on the inside of her ankle"—he traced a finger against the air where his gaze was fixed—"another at the base of her spine. Freckles, I guess you'd call them—peculiar word." He dismissed his vision. "Turned out what she felt for me was pity, no more. Pity for the cripple. Fine, I told myself, if pity's the bill of fare then I'll make do with it. And I worked on all the other women's pity. There was plenty of it. And I made them all pay for the hurt that she, Rose—Rose, she was called—dealt me. Wasted my money traveling around the world in style with Charles. I can tell stories. The kind of stories men tell to make other men jealous. The kind they tell to good husbands and fathers to offset their own emptiness. But time sneaks by. Charles was smart. When he turned fifty— same year I did—he married young Theresa. I never got the knack of commitment, and lost any I had for true feeling. Then I was old. Just like that"—raising his left hand to snap his fingers, which didn't respond, and he scoffed at them—"*old.* Old enough to look back, find nothing of value. And too old to change.

"Hope you don't mind me talking about myself. Felt like it, that's all. Now what were we saying? Ah, yes. Young Patrick. And you."

I got up, lifted his left hand, examined the fingers, flexion, extension. "We're not puppets."

"Oh, *please.* Go to bed now, Robbie."

He was right. It was best just to leave him with his patient Virgin. First I brushed sparks from the back of her robe. The door was almost shut behind me. "Robbie? I say, Robbie?"

"Not so loud. You'll wake Patrick and the children. What is it?"

His right arm was draped over the Virgin's shoulder. "Six A.M., remember. Now don't be late."

"I'm never late."

V

'SPECTING COMPANY

And I wasn't late, Raoul was up and bathed and back on the bed when I arrived. He'd slept well and looked years younger than I'd seen him yet. When I was through with the treatment he said, "Happy birthday, by the way. How old have you got to now?"

"Thirty-one."

"Jeesum. That's old. Why don't you take the station wagon. Go visit Baton Rouge. Drive around the country-side. Any rate, I don't want walking or messing with today 'cause I got company, see? I want to rest up for my company tonight."

Back in my cabin Teddy and Marie arrived with a clutch of birthday cards signed from Moley and the mules as well as themselves. There were cards from

Laura and Esther too. Will, like Teddy and Marie, had drawn his own. It was a picture of a house with a chimney and a door and four windows, three of them filled in yellow, one in black. Teddy and Marie compared the cards then Marie told me, "We got to go now 'cause we're helping Lenny build a bonfire. A huge one for the barbecue tonight, and Daddy's off in town picking up company."

During the four months I had lived at Janvier there had been no visitors. Raoul had no social life and if Patrick pursued any it was in New Orleans. The Bizets were cleaning the cabin next to mine and the other empty one opposite. Rugs thrown over the rails, the knocking of a broom from within, Charles and Theresa calling to each other, and she confirmed to me, "Uh-huh, we're 'specting company."

The noise of Lenny's chainsaw riddled the air while I wrote letters and rang home—rang home only to have my own voice informing me I was not there. I knelt among my photographs spread about the floor, the framed ones from the shelf: Laura holding Will at his last birthday party with my face out of focus behind her shoulder; Esther cradling newborn Will; another of Laura and me in school uniform—pre–nail scissors. Yet I couldn't find my favorite. I'd pulled the books off the shelf, pushed aside the pitcher, glasses, and bottles, tossed the cushions out of the armchair before I remembered, and yanked the covers from the bed. There it was, black-and-white, yellowing, pinched from Esther's own box of photographs stored among her other possessions behind my sofa. The image was of the three of us at night in

Trafalgar Square, Laura and me as tiny girls holding tight to Esther's hands, our eyes rendered vacant by the flashbulb. We had been to see the Christmas lights in Regent Street, Esther told us. She had paid a street photographer to take our picture. I have no memory of the lights or being there at all but retain a commonplace nostalgia for the scent of nighttime London after rain. And something else—harder to express, harder to erase—an awareness of Esther's diligent pursuit of familiar pleasure that she must have known by then, would never be as she had dreamed.

Moley was barking somewhere and the children were shouting as they ran around helping Lenny. A car drew up and I heard Patrick's voice calling for Charles to come, and Charles, disturbed from his afternoon sleep, stumbled through the door of his cabin, yanking on his cloth jacket.

Despite the arrival of the visitors, Marie came to stand in my doorway as she sometimes did in the afternoons, waiting in silence to be noticed and invited in. She would clonk around in my high heels or pretend to cook at the kitchen bay or, best of all, she liked to collect the photographs from the shelf and hold them close to her face.

"You got your pictures out. You homesick again? Being your birthday and all?" The hard-skinned pads of her fingers stroked my forehead as she cleared my hair to see me better. "Don't be. Everything's going to be all right, you see. Mama's coming in thirteen days' time and we'll go live in Washington, *D.C.*, and you can go home. Know what? Theresa's baked a cake for you and we're giving it to you tonight. That's a surprise and I'm not supposed to tell you but I think you want something nice right this minute." She shook her head. "Can I say something? Only don't be mad now?"

Marie was examining her favorite photograph, taken when Esther was still young, glamorous as a forties film star. She and a friend had visited a studio in Oxford Street and paid extra for a makeup artist and the hire of jewels and furs—*What fun we had, Robbie, such fun*—but there's no fun reflected in her eyes.

"See, I don't think this lady is your mama like you say she is."

"No?"

"No."

"And the other one, is she my sister?"

"Oh yeah. Anyone can see that. I have to go now but Uncle Raoul says you're to be sure to join us for supper tonight." Superbly solemn, one warning finger raised, she departed, backwards.

Nearly time now. Time to leave and allow to pass all that goes with leaving, the series of small releases, each one stabbing until the job is done.

It was dark when I raised the telephone receiver one more time. The bonfire was alight and the glow it threw way down the lawn seeped into my unlit cabin. The creaking, cracking, and bursting of the logs filled one side of my head while the other was filled with the ringing of my own number in England, the click as the machine picked up. It would have been nice to hear Esther's voice, Laura's, *Hello* and *Hello* and *Happy birth-*

day, Robbie. Try again before you go to sleep. The best time to talk to someone you love.

I dressed in my white dress and carried my shoes because I would take a walk before turning to the house where the verandah rose tall in candlelight. The silhouettes of the guests were added to those of Patrick and Raoul. I would be visible in the dark if they looked this way, my white dress shining. And they did because I half-saw them draw up to the rail, voices hushed to point me out, no doubt. The English girl, the physiotherapist who had stayed on awhile to help with the children.

Moley barked as I approached the steps, greeted me at the top. Now the verandah was deserted and the voices were coming from inside. If their guests had not visited Janvier before, and did not know the family, Raoul would be telling telling telling of his mother Virginie and his father the hatter from New Orleans and of mirrors backed with diamond dust and seventeen-year-old brides. I sat on the swing with Moley in my arms, turned her over, unable to see her moles in this light, pressed my mouth to the place where they would be. I had never kissed a dog before and learned the consolation. They would be in when I rang later, Esther and Will, maybe Laura too. I might wake them. I would certainly wake them and hear their contained impatience urging me towards goodbye.

Patrick stepped from the house wearing the pale suit I had not seen him in since the night he arrived back at Janvier. I caught the tone of it, you understand, and of the one wearing it, but hadn't looked up because, right then, I needed a moment to sharply adjust my mood, hide what my face would have revealed. I gave Moley more attention, pretended not to know he was there. Nearly ready. A moment more would do.

He approached, crouched down, wrapped his arms all around me. So thin. His head deep in my neck. My hands were raised, poised above him. Touch him? Hold him in return? All right. So thin. Never this before. "Happy birthday, Robbie." Not his voice. Her voice. "I've missed you so much." Laura in my arms.

Then bang bang bang on the boards. Will there too. And Esther. There was Patrick. Teddy and Marie crashed onto the seat on either side of me. "Happy birthday. Surprise. Surprise. Say you're pleased, say you're pleased."

Laura withdrew to allow Esther near, Esther so short and round and stiff, bewildered and trying not to have it show. Marie's confusion that afternoon blinked in my memory. Even I had retained the image of a different Esther, younger, more vigorous, but was glad of this one, the one I really knew and always had. "Hellooo Robbie, Dear." All new clothes, she was wearing, and her favorite scent, the special one she had made last for five years, Estée Lauder's Youth Dew.

"When did you arrive?" I managed as she helped Will scramble onto me.

"This afternoon. Patrick had the three of us hide in his room and we kept very quiet and even had a bit of a sleep. Happy birthday, Robbie."

How long was I paralyzed, sort of laughing, sort of crying? I still believe it is not right to shock people even in the name of love. When I landed, as it were, pegged down my responses, I saw Raoul keeping apart from the melee, wearing a cream tussah suit and white shirt. He was observing me. Me and the rest of it. I'd never seen him in a suit before. It displayed the work we'd done.

Laura danced up, held my hands. "Poor Robbie. We *are* real, honestly."

"I tried to ring you. You were out."

"When?"

"Just now."

"Well, we would have been out. Just now. Wouldn't we?" She held me again, whispering, "Sorry about the shock but it's so wonderful to see you. I'll give you a minute, okay? See you below." She swung away, hoisted Will to her hip and grabbed Teddy's hand. "Let's check the barbecue. Come on, everyone. Esther too, come on."

They toiled lightheartedly around the bonfire. Charles and Theresa fetched tinfoil parcels from the kitchen to tuck in the embers. Patrick set up a spit for the meat. Will was already in possession of the red trike with Marie following close, insisting noisily on her seniority. Teddy and Moley chased each other's shadows. Someone started the music loud.

The murmur of the cloth of his suit, the scent of patchouli oil.

"You're looking good, Raoul."

"Thank you, Robbie. You look fine yourself."

We watched as Laura bent down before Teddy, her arms extended, and he reached to touch one of them. She was nodding, emphatically explaining, only we couldn't hear her voice. She straightened and, arms still stretched, began to run, dip left and right, Teddy, in imitation, behind. Will saw them and clambered from the trike, knocking it over in his haste to join, followed by Marie. All of them ran in the wake of Laura, arms akimbo like hers, planing all the way down into the night and back into the bright of the fire, where she flopped to the ground and all the children climbed on top of her. Esther waved and Patrick was pointing with a long fork. Theresa and Charles, who had been arranging chairs in a circle, had also stopped to watch, she with her hands on her hips, head to one side—*My, my. Kids. Good Lord never gave us no kids*—and Charles slapping his thighs, rolling his shoulders—*I ain't never seen the like*—and all their laughter, all their laughter. The only thing you could hear above the music.

I turned to Raoul and saw there was a great alteration in his expression. Something had been understood by him, told out of the air, seen in the play below. But when he spoke it wasn't to tell me what that understanding was. "What happened to her face, do you suppose?"

Her poor face. Not now. Not now.

Raoul raised his right hand for me to lay my left upon it and together we descended. The party was good. Patrick made cocktails and we all drank those. And Charles and Theresa stayed. And Alice Wine came and Lenny too with his wife, who looked no more than fifteen years old, and who did not speak a word all evening but danced. We all danced because when Patrick turned on the Cajun two-step music Laura got up all on her own and danced until Will toddled up to her. So Patrick invited Marie, Charles drew Theresa to her feet. Esther was eager and leaning forward, clapping her hands, all but dancing herself with Raoul next to her clapping too. A dance of their own. Alice Wine rose up, earphones off for the first time that I had ever seen, hands high with her head back like the music was straight from above to herself alone and she moving like a goddess. Who would have believed it? Esther touched my hand. "Ask Teddy, go on, go on." So I did and he said, "Dancing's sissy." Esther insisted. "Don't listen to him, take his hand." So I clasped his hand, little hand, and we danced too. He was glad not to be apart. You could see.

Will was the first of the children to fall asleep. Esther slipped him from her lap into Laura's arms and Laura raised him this side, that side, so her lips could reach the cheeks of Raoul and Patrick and kiss them and thank them so much, so much, and Raoul most of all for it being his idea, *Thank you,* and never for one second waking Will, *Thank you, goodnight.* Her poor face.

Patrick accompanied us to the cabins, Esther's opposite mine, Laura and Will's next door. He offered Esther his arm, which she accepted with studied grace, as though long ago she had been primed for this manner of respect and accident had denied it until now. When he opened the door and stood aside she gasped. "Oh, oh this is—Laura, Robbie, come and see, this is *so* pretty. What an enchanting color the walls are and look at the bed. That quilt." Using the study of that quilt as an excuse, she sank deep on the side of the bed, suddenly and completely exhausted while Patrick demonstrated all the features of the cabin, the telephone by the bed, the stocked fridge and corner kitchen, how the air conditioning worked, and, calling from inside the bathroom, "See here, you have jets in the tub, neat hey?"

Laura pressed behind me in the doorway, her chin resting on my shoulder to peer into the warm-lit room, Will still fast asleep in her arms. I could hear her amused staccato breath and she dug me in the ribs to have me pay attention to what was going on: Esther leaning this way, that way in the direction of Patrick's progress. Finally he stopped in front of her, hands in pockets, head sunk like a son who considers he has done his best and knows that would always be good enough. Esther reached up to him with her wrists pressed together. He brought out a hand to place within hers. "Thank you, Patrick. It's going to be a very happy visit, I know it."

We left her to sleep and crossed to Laura's cabin with Patrick ahead of us again to switch on the light, draw back the covers from one of the two single beds. Laura lay Will down, kneeling beside him, sorting his hair, gazing into his face as though to determine the depth of his sleep, the quality of his dreams. She whispered inaudibly and we were held by the sight of her, Patrick and I, although it was in some sense a private act—we were unable to stop watching. Then she jumped to her feet, beaming, and in a normal voice, not hushed on account of Will sleeping. "This is so, so lovely, Patrick," speaking through clenched teeth, fingers kneading the air, eyes wide. A bridled, tense enthusiasm, having him understand that the loveliness was almost too hard for her to bear. "Shaker, isn't it? I mean this blue and the beds? All of it? Esther's cabin too? Done in the Shaker style, am I right?"

"Hey, absolutely right."

"Robbie, you never said. Did you choose it all yourself, Patrick?"

"No. Louise. My ex-wife."

"I'm so happy to be here. We just don't know what to do to say thank you enough, Esther and I."

"Well, you mustn't because it's our thank-you to Robbie. I guess I'll leave you to rest."

He ushered himself from the room with his arms raised as though to embrace something not there. Then it was there: lightly, briefly, Laura kissed him once more on the cheek, her hand resting fraternally on his shoulder. "Goodnight."

The door shut and she rummaged in her bag for a bottle of vodka, pointed it at the wall. "Your place or mine?"

"Okay, I admit I was wrong about you coming over here. You did good, girl. Landed square on your size sevens." She was hunched on my table, singeing the edge of it with her cigarette, swinging her legs. "Doesn't it seem to you, Robs—oh sorry, didn't see that—that this is one of the places we invented when we were little? Remember our worlds? You had Backland and I had the Land of Ice and Fire?"

"Your ice palace."

"Right, but we never imagined mirrors backed with diamond dust, did we? Never anything as fantastic as that. Blimey, what's that doing there?"

"Drying."

"You wear your *uniform?*"

"Of course. When I'm treating Raoul."

She sat down at last, the table between us. Her poor face. "They're the ones Matthew smoked, by the way. Raoul's cigarettes. In case you were still wondering."

"I know. I've been remembering things, Laura."

"Shh, shh. Diamond dust, *yeah.*" She reached for my hands, pressed her lips against them.

"I don't have a face in my dreams. They've taken it away."

"Who?"

"I don't know."

She released my hands to cradle herself. "You do, though. I knew you would one day. So what do you remember?"

"Stairs. Harsh light. A black place again. Confined. No air."

"Am I there?"

"No."

"I'm sorry."

"What for?"

"Not being there." Her chair scraped the floor. I watched her cross the cabin—pigeon-toed, very slightly pigeon-toed. Strange, the things it hurts to remember. She let herself out. The shadowed pigeonniers, a ragged black line of pines behind, the Bizets' cabin and Esther's, the house with all detail lost, these things I was seeing while Laura was turned into the night itself as though she and it had business. Until she let it go, dismissed it, and clasped my shoulders. "Let's go back in. That bottle's too full for its own good."

She tipped her chair. "You can't look back. The past

doesn't count. Tell yourself there's only the present and future tenses. And here you are in this beautiful place."

"How come *you're* here?"

"Raoul wrote to Esther saying how grand you were, then he invited by letter, rang to invite again because she was too timid to respond. I think he hopes us being over for a couple of weeks might make you decide to remain."

"I can't."

"Why not, for God's sake? Aren't you well, Robs? You look a bit tired."

"I've got too close."

"Gone on, say it"—nudging the air—"you've fallen for the heavenly Patrick. Cool."

"No."

"*Not* Patrick?"

"No. And not that sort of close."

"Then what's the matter? You're in clover, girl."

"The whole place has got to me. And the people, all of them. It shouldn't be that way."

"Why not? Let it be that way."

"I've done my job."

"You and your *job*. Lighten up and look around, Robs. They're great people and they want you here. There's no more to it."

"There is for me and it feels—"

"Well? *Well?*"

"Unsafe. I want to come home now, Laura. I'm ready."

Laura rolled her glass between her knees. "Pity. So what's ruined your sleep, what are these things you re-member—if you want to go into this, if you really must?"

"I've woken up and the woman Jane is lifting you out of bed. She takes you away. I follow but you've gone and I don't know where. I wait on a stair then she's at the top coming down with you in her arms. Your head bangs the wall and—"

"Not me, Robs."

"No. It is. This isn't a dream."

"You're wrong. Stop it. Okay? You're just wrong."

"Don't. Please. There's only you."

She lit a cigarette. I pointed to one still burning in the ashtray and she frowned as if uncertain of what it was. "It's yourself you're seeing. It's yourself you followed, Robs. I saw her come and take you and I knew. And I didn't go after but waited like a coward. Didn't protect you like I should have. You think I like remembering that? You think it's easy for me? You were four. Sometime after, next day maybe, I don't know, I found the woman Jane in the Healing Room with Matthew and told her I wouldn't fight anymore or be difficult or threaten to tell—although I'd never tell because you can't, can you? I mean you wouldn't? Would you? *Would you?*—no, it's okay, I'm fine. You asked, right? Okay. They knew I'd never tell. I said anything was all right so long as they left you alone. She laughed at me for that. Then she sort of turned it off, her laughing, and said to Matthew, *She hasn't learned yet, has she? She doesn't understand we're healing her.* I saw his face. He looked driven and wretched and I said, *Poor Daddy,* which made her look at him. She snapped her head 'round as if she suspected him of making gestures behind her back. Then she got up and reached for me. Remember the noise of her bangles clacking, remember? But Matthew said, *No, Jane, leave her alone.* That was the only time I ever heard him assert himself with her."

"Was she insane?"

"Don't know."

"Was he?"

She shrugged. "Have you had enough of this yet, Robs? 'Cause I have. I don't want to go on."

"But there was a time, wasn't there, when we were little and we still called Esther *Mummy* and everything was all right? Then there's time after when everything's different. Only I didn't know the reason. What came between?"

"You find paradise and your head treks back to hell. I'm not blaming you, only I wish I could find a paradise for me. My head wouldn't trek back. I wouldn't let it. See if I wouldn't. Strikes me they could do with a hand gardening in paradise, Patrick and co. Not the happiest faces in the world. You could stop around, help them out, share it. That's what they want."

"What happened between?"

Laura could hold her gaze into another's eyes for so long that the other was forced to turn away. I never asked her where she learned the trick or why—because that's what it was: a trick, a power play. There, that night, at that moment in my cabin, was the only time I ever stared her out. Her wrist was cocked to support the mounting ash on her cigarette and I watched how her body filled and minutely diminished as she breathed, a twist in the corner of her mouth, the unrelenting flicker of a nerve in her lower left eyelid.

"All right, Robs. Do you remember how one weekend I wasn't well so you went to Matthew and the woman Jane alone? After you'd gone, the doctor came and confirmed I had mumps. I lay in bed listening to Esther ringing Matthew, insisting you stayed there until I was better. They had a row about it, she said she couldn't, wouldn't cope with the two of us and risk you getting the mumps after me and all that time off work for her. She told him it wasn't fair. And I tried and tried to be better. Hung my head under the cold tap to make the swelling go down. You were away eleven days. I counted every hour, and my eleventh birthday was the last day. That's why I remember the number of days. A sort of omen. When you came home you didn't speak for weeks. They sent you home from school because of that and because all you did was sit around scratching the backs of your hands raw. Every time scabs formed—great whole scabs like maps of India—you picked them off and scratched till they bled again. Until then you'd been an ordinary, noisy, messy little girl. Even after you began speaking again you were quiet and whispery, always washing yourself, tidying your things. Enter Robbie neat-freak. God knows I wanted to keep you safe. You were so little. When you were born I pretended you were my little girl. You wouldn't remember. But I failed you."

"You were a child yourself. What could you do? Why did he have it happen? *Any* of it? You knew him better than I did. You must have understood something. You say you remember his face that time. Tell me things. Tell me things to make me understand."

"I can't. Listen, do what I've done: Take all the things you knew and forget them. Rub them right off the board.

That's the only way. Forget questions. Because that's what drives you mad in the end, when there's no one left to answer."

"But there is someone."

"Not me, Robs. Not me, right? I can't answer any of your whys or mine. I did anything I had to get through—me, us—through, safe. Played safe and—don't ask any more. I'm never looking back again. This was the last time. There's only going to be good things now."

"Esther knows."

"I said don't. Okay?"

"She must know."

"Just stop. There's no more to be said. 'Cause sometimes the cost of an answer's too high. Not worth the risk."

She unbuckled her body from her own grip, stretched with her arms above her as though slipping free of a skin. The tips of her fingers touched the rafters, then she bent double to rap a fast rhythm on her thighs. "Hey listen, let's be happy now, right? Think of it, Robs: us. Here. Louisiana. *Diamond dust.* I can't get over it. And those trees with the moss like you see in books? And the ol' Mississippi slopping right by the foot of our beds. And, blimey bummers, what about that Allie person? And don't you love their voices? That accent? And the words like *bayou.*" She'd whispered the word and sang, soft, soft:

> *Goodbye Joe, me gotta go, me oh my oh*
> *Me gotta go pole the pirouge down the bayou.*
> *My Y-vonne, sweetest one, me oh my oh*
> *Son of a gun we'll have big fun on the bayou.*

Jambalaya and crawfish pie and fillet gumbo
'Cause tonight I'm gonna see ma cher amie-o.
Pick guitar, fill fruit jar and be gay-o
Son of a gun we'll have big fun on the bayoooooo.

"Take happiness, Robs. It's not so hard if you practice. What are you looking at?"

Her poor face. Her poor face. And I'd been thinking, What's happened to you? You've never been so thin, your eyes so hollow. Except onstage I had never seen you so masked in makeup. Masked to hide cuts and bruises. Unspeakable. Your hair was struggling back from a recent attack with your nail scissors, that zigzag look. And I told myself I was seeing the face of the bravest one I was ever likely to meet.

"Darling little Robs," she said and pulled me against her so as not to have me look at her that way.

With vision halved by the line of her shoulder, I saw across the room, through the window, another face with a hand beside it, finger crooked to tap the glass. "Hellooo Babies. I couldn't sleep and saw the light on here. I thought you'd be together. Shall we have a cup of tea?"

So we drank tea and more vodka and talked on until Laura burst out, "Robbie says she's not staying on here," right in the middle of Esther's description of the woman next to her on the flight over who asked if she, Esther, would hold her hand during the turbulence. "And I'm trying to tell her she should stay. That this is paradise. You tell her, Esther."

"Well, I don't know. They do seem very fond of you. Raoul's better, is he?"

"That's not the point. They want her to stay anyway."

"I've done all I can for him."

"Well, you've done a wonderful job, Dear, and you don't want to overstay your welcome. There'll be other positions. I've always been lucky. Until now, that is, but something'll come along."

Laura slammed her hand on the table. "But she mustn't be like you."

Esther withdrew as far as the chair allowed, then on into herself, leaving her features faltering in an effort to show she understood, and that Laura was right, and that she knew Laura had not meant to hurt but that it hurt just the same.

Laura gathered Esther's hand, wagged it by one finger. "I only meant Janvier is too lovely to leave and that they're nice people and they all want her to stay. So why not?"

"Because," I said, "I want to come home and have my own life again, my old life. I want everything to be like it was before."

They stared at me until Laura said, "Is it you two who's mad or me?" And Esther and I chimed, "It's you, Laura," together, like that. "It's you." And we all laughed. We laughed.

There was light in the sky when they left my cabin. I slept for an hour or so before waking with a terrible need to be unconfined. Laura was out on her own stoop, slid deep in a chair, feet up on the rail, so still. A stranger could have believed she was sleeping, but just as I had seen her a few hours earlier involved with the night itself, now she was welcoming Janvier into her being with calm intensity. Certainly she had not been to bed. She had drunk more than any of us, her makeup mask had worn off and the pale linen suit—the one I had mistaken for Patrick's—looked chewed and spat out. All this, yet Laura appeared renewed, a different Laura from the night before. Gently she interrupted her communion with the place, the day, to wink at me—I could almost feel all that wonder holding back just long enough for her to do it—and I passed on, too late today for fishermen.

When I returned Laura was way down the grass hand in hand with Will, crossing towards the house. She glanced back over her shoulder, inclined to Will, and he too glanced back at me. Then they both turned around, relinking their hands, walking backwards to wave at me, me up there on the levee. They waved hard, swaying with the movement and beckoning, *Come on, come join us,* although something prevented their voices reaching me. A breeze, maybe, or an aircraft overhead.

The continuity of that visit escapes me now. I remember no more than a collection of incidents. But, for me, they sum it up:

Lunch on the verandah, the nine of us together with the spirit of vitality. Patrick seated at one end of the table and Raoul at the other, informing Esther at his side, "The house of Patout, you see, was opened on Canal back in 1803." Esther bowing her head as near as convention allowed to catch every word. "Jean Patout, there's him, isn't there? A dress designer?" And Marie holding forth with her, "When we live in Washington,

D.C., we'll see the president every day," and Teddy, "You're so dumb, Marie, that's not how," and Laura settling the matter with, "Well, you tell the president that Laura and Will say hello. Gosh, imagine it, Will, the *President.*" While Will is transfixed by Allie's masticating jaw above him, until she—forward-staring, crowned with her headphones—imperiously rises to her feet, her slow-clapping hands powered by the bellows of her elbows. What begins as a moan becomes song:

> *Fix me, Jesus, fix me right,*
> *Fix me so I can stand,*
> *Fix my feet on solid rock,*
> *Fix me so I can stand.*

Laura hums along. Will claps his hands in time with Allie. Everyone has joined in when Teddy reaches over and pulls the jack out of the transistor. Allie swoops around with her great palm raised right by his ear but he has slipped under the table, just in time, and Patrick grabs the wire and rams the jack back in, guides her back in place while she challenges Raoul, "You got no sway anymore, letting 'em push your old nurse around?" And Raoul lifts her wrist as if gauging her pulse. "S'okay Allie, sing your song. I remember it." Then Allie catches Teddy's hand periscoping from under the table, in search of the unfinished hamburger on his plate—"Gotcha, varmint," *"Daddy, Daddy"*—and Will withdraws to the safety of Laura's lap. "Sing your song, Allie." Raoul's hand is loaded on top of hers. "Ain't no more song. Song's over. New show now so hush up." "You're as deaf as you choose, old lady, aren't you?" Esther has tilted back for a view under the table—"Come out this side, Dear, that's right"—while Marie whines in her ear, "Don't help him out, let him stay on down there. He's just a show-off anyways."

Hot, hot afternoon. "Psst, hey, Robs, come up here," Laura rasps from the verandah, childishly skitting from foot to foot. Signaling for me to keep quiet as I approach. She links her arm in mine to draw me past the east-facing windows. Just short of the corner where the verandah broadens, she tiptoes ahead, barring me with her outstretched arm to spy around the side of the house, circling her hand for me to come closer. To gain the same view, without being seen, I kneel with my head between her legs: I see Esther reclining, feet up, on the swing with Will spread on top of her, thumb in mouth, his sleepy eyes lowered on Teddy and Marie, who are cross-legged on the floor, their upturned faces concentrated on Esther, who's telling them, "—on Saturday nights I'd go to bed with my hair in rags to make ringlets. On Sunday morning Mother made me wear a white smock over my dress that reached all the way to my button boots. They stopped at just about there on my legs and had tiny little buttons all the way up, so small you needed a hook to fasten them. My brothers would wear their hats and sailor suits. Only they weren't sailors, they were only little boys, not a lot older than you are now, Teddy. As soon as we were all ready we'd set off in good time for our grandmother's house and wait for Mr. Dickens to arrive. After lunch he'd read to us."

"And was he there *every* Sunday, at your grandma's house?"

"Oh yes."

"And did he read the *Christmas Carol?* Mom read that to us."

"He used to read that at Christmastime. Usually he read the latest installment of whatever story of his was coming out that month."

"And was there fog all the time and little window-panes with globby glass and snow in the corners?"

"Certainly. And those were the days when they pushed little children no bigger than Teddy up chimneys to clean them. What's that noise? Will, go and see if that's your mother being silly." He trotted down the verandah and found us. "Is it Mummy there, Will? Laura? Is that you making that silly noise? What's so funny?" We present ourselves, straightening our faces, hiding our mouths.

"Will's grandma's telling us all about how——"

"About my childhood, that's all. Nothing you haven't heard. Just a bit of fun." Esther points towards the boathouse. "Patrick's been looking for you, he wants to know if you'd like to go in the boat. He went that way."

"Boats. Cool, c'mon everyone." Laura departs at a run with her tagalong trinity, while Esther droops a hand above her eyes to watch them out of sight.

Raoul dozing where the bayou curls, propped against a canvas backrest, a panama covering his face, fishing rod on the ground nearby. I settle so as not to wake him. A cricket climbs a blade of grass, swaying in the momentum of its own weight before dropping precisely on the edge of the tartan rug and proceeding into the luminous shade of Raoul's white sleeve. On reaching bare flesh, the cricket pauses and rears as though contemplating the mountain of hand before him, and I wonder how overwhelming is the heat, the scent emanating from that hand in the scale of the cricket's universe. And when, as it reaches with one threadlike leg to begin his ascent—and his world darkens under the shadow of my own hand blocking his path— how prolonged for him is this change in the light? Raoul's hand turns over, palm up, and the cricket jumps from sight. Raoul has been watching me, his eyes unclouded by any recent sleep. Voices carry from the water, followed by the boat party rounding the bend. Patrick is poling from the rear with Laura in the middle, clutching Will by his collar. Teddy and Marie are in the bow, shouting at the tops of their voices. They don't see us.

They are late. Raoul has been on the bank shining a torch for over half an hour while Esther has remained with Allie asking, "Should they be gone this long?" "Is it far up that way?" "What sort of a boat are they in?" And Allie keeps silent. Well past suppertime we see lights far up the bayou, hear the plashing of the water, and last of all, drifting close, fading, then nearer, always nearer, a loud-whispered unison:

> *Jambalaya and crawfish pie and fillet gumbo,*
> *'Cause tonight I'm gonna see my cher amie-o.*
> *Pick guitar—*

Bursting out, when they stamp up the steps, *"Son of a gun we'll have big fun on the bayoooooooo—"*

Raoul has gathered his cards, making out no one's worried on their account. That is until Allie barks, "That you, Baby Pat? That you who worked my Raoul in such a state? Thoughtless boy is what you are." And Laura pulls Patrick's sleeve to have him notice Will, always fascinated by Allie, drawn up close to her with his mouth hanging wide. Patrick sweeps him up. "Hey little fella. She's a cross lady. What'll we do about that?" Will hisses, "Say sorry." "Okay, Will. Sorry Allie, sorry Allie." They all hold hands to dance in a circle chanting, "Sorryalliesorryalliesorryallie."

On passing the dependency I hear an unfamiliar sound coming from the kitchen. Further on I find Raoul and bring him back to stand with me and we listen together. I suppose I know we're listening to laughter and couldn't have explained why I should want Raoul to identify it with me. But he's there and together we concentrate, then he holds my chin to inform me, "That's the sound of your mom laughing, Robbie. That's what that is." I skulk along the bridge to gain—between a tumble of cashmere bouquet and a corner of mesh come unnailed from the door frame—a sliver of the kitchen's interior. Esther and Theresa face-to-face shucking peas into a bucket on the floor between them. Esther's leaning forward to beat on Theresa's knee with one fat pod, saying, "Picture it, my dear, there's me, rigid there in the dark, thinking it was a—what did you call it?"

"A hont."

"That's right, a ghost, more of a spirit, really, from the other side. And I lay there in bed hoping it will communicate with me, a message from my mother, dead for thirty-five years. I'd have liked to hear from her. Well, I waited for as long as I could bear it, then turned on the light. What do you think it was? The little green light on the iron, that's what." Theresa rocks on her stool, using an empty pod to hide her teeth all uncovered from their sheltering lips. "Why then," she gasps, could barely bring her words out. "Why then we's all fools, ain't that so?" They are laughing so much they lean with their foreheads pressed together for support.

Esther and Theresa leaving to go shopping in Baton Rouge while Laura and I straddle the gate waving at the two of them set up in the back of the station wagon with Charles in front like he's their chauffeur. And Laura shouts to the children, who have left the gate by then and are harnessing Moley to a miniature cart, "You've lost your granny, kiddies. She and Theresa are off to have a hot time." Will pipes up, right on key, *"We gonna have a hot time in the old town tonight."*

You've lost your granny. She had said it to all three of them, embracing Teddy and Marie into the relationship. Then from the house Patrick calls through cupped hands, "Hey? You want to hitch the *real* mules, instead of poor Moley there, to the *real* cart and we all go riding?" "You bet." Laura cups her hands the same way he does, although there is no need, he could have heard quite well without.

We're trailing lines from the flat-bottomed boat. Will falls in. Laura screams, *"The alligators, the alligators,"* but Patrick hocks him out with no fuss. "What gator'd want to eat a fish like you? Yuk." "I'm tasty, they'd like me." The two boys are naked but Marie's kept her vest on. Teddy teases her for that and she yells, "Girls don't show their bosoms anyways." "They do too. I seen Allie's. She ain't showed me but I seen 'em." *"Hasn't* shown me," Patrick corrects automatically, dreaming, hardly present, leaning away on the pole. "See, Teddy, Daddy ain't seen 'em." *"Hasn't,"* Patrick repeats, abstracted as ever. "So you couldn't've seen 'em, Teddy, so there." "Did too. Through the bathroom door while Theresa's swabbin' her down." Laura slides low in the boat, pretending to cough. Patrick pays attention. Marie insists, "Any rate she ain't got no bosoms." "Jeesum, kids, *hasn't, hasn't* got any." "See, see. Daddy says." Laura cuts in, "Excuse me, Marie, but if Allie doesn't have breasts then what does she have there, because I mean, well she's not exactly flat, is she?" I say, *"Please, Laura."* "Actually this is really interesting, Robs." Patrick is smiling, shaking his head while Marie stands with her legs braced and fists jabbed into her waist. "Why, she's got cloth there, that's what, mounds and mounds of cloth, you know? Like the stuffing that's coming out of that split teddy bear of mine." And Patrick sits down to laugh and laugh, hanging on to Laura while the boat tilts and sways and Laura's shouting, "Stop it, Patrick, we'll drown, we'll all drown," not believing it for a minute.

One day was different from the rest. For one thing it rained. Patrick had to go into his office in New Orleans. The children were restless and bored and even Laura was more still, withdrawn, less resourceful. He hadn't returned by the children's bedtime so I accompanied Teddy and Marie down to their room. Once she had settled Will, Laura lunged around the door, singing, "Hi, kiddies. Will's asleep, why aren't you? What are you doing that way up, Teddy?" He was practicing yoga. She flung herself on Marie's bed, covered her face with a pillow. Teddy launched himself onto her and they wrestled until Laura noticed Marie at her trunk down at the far end of the room. She held Teddy at bay for a moment, before gently pushing him aside. She swung her feet to the floor, engrossed in Marie's ritual. Her expression lost all light and became drawn, haggard as it had been on her first night at Janvier, when we had talked and she had told me what she told me and not referred to it since.

Teddy and I hunted for his roller skate. I emptied the bath, tidied away the boats and water toys while he brushed his teeth, and when I came out of there Laura was still gripped by Marie's feverish sorting, her incoherent monologue. I said, "Hey, Laura?"

Without removing her attention from Marie she rearranged herself to respond halfheartedly, "Right, then—so—what do you want me to read, Teddy—only not that crappy comic."

Teddy had his computer game pressed up to his face.

Laura didn't ask again. She moved closer to Marie. I said, "Give me a hand over here, Laura."

"Righto." She helped me tip toys into the bright red chest, but even before we had finished she veered back to Marie and moved up close, as though she couldn't help herself. Marie instantly slammed the trunk shut, sat on it, hunched up, her face set firmly ahead. Laura remained still, without speaking, her hands linked loosely between her knees. Suddenly Marie threw herself into Laura so hard she had to use all her strength to maintain balance and hold Marie fast in her arms while Marie wailed, "She won't ever come, will she? I know she won't, she won't."

"Shh, Baby, hush, everything'll be fine, you see, you see . . ."

Then Esther had her accident. She slipped on the steps of her cabin. She had left us after supper on the verandah, Patrick and Raoul with their heads close over a chessboard, while Laura and I lounged in steamer chairs wrong-guessing the stars. The children had been asleep some time. She had departed as she preferred to do—without bidding goodnight, not to have a fuss, have anyone disturb themselves to accompany her down—so that later we were unable to say how long she must have been lying there, unconscious, bleeding from a gash in her leg. Charles and Theresa found her on the way to their own cabin, and when Charles's call—"Mr. Patrick, say Mr. Patrick"—cut through the crickets and nightjars and our own chatter, Laura immediately snatched my hand, wrenching it against her. "It's Esther. It's Esther, isn't it?"

I sank down where Esther lay. "Esther? Mummy, what happened?" I shouted back to the verandah for Laura to come—could see her standing up there in the light, shaking her head, her mouth moving but no words coming out. Charles brought quilts to cover Esther, Theresa hovered with towels and water. Patrick was inside on the telephone. We could only wait with me calling to her, calling to her, not to have her drift too far—to have her know there was me there—me to be there for—*Mummy please don't go*—and I turned back to Laura again and again. Why wouldn't she come? Why just stand there that way gripping the rail, staring down? Won't she help me to call her back—

The medical helicopter landed in the middle of the grass between our four cabins. If I had been capable of expectation then it would have been for a regular ambulance and a longer wait. As it was, the power of its lights as it circled above blinded me and the force of its blades tore up the night, shook the cabins and drove the trees wild and everyone was shouting to be heard above the din. The lights grew more brilliant, too brilliant now, and the night too dark to see. Men came rushing between Esther and me. They unrolled a stretcher beneath her, swaddled her in blankets, strapped her up, and lifted her away from me, from where I was still kneeling in her blood as paralyzed as Laura was. Then I looked for Laura up there but could see nothing beyond the floodlit pool of our drama. As they raised Esther up to the cabin

Patrick swung himself in too. And then, at the very last minute, before the door slid shut and the machine rose to sashay two feet from the ground—further tormenting the trees—Laura came running out of that killed world beyond the lights and leapt in too, before it tipped to the east and was gone.

Charles, Theresa, and I remained on the stoop, staring into the traumatized night long after the lights and the noise had died away. And then I remained long after they had departed hand in hand.

"Robbie?" I heard. Raoul was halfway down the steps, ready to descend farther if I didn't respond. We sat together on the swing, the rattan swing, without speaking. I heard the clock chime in the drawing room, heard it again, and yet again after that, and understood hours were passing. Only I'd lost the power of counting, lost the feel of time. The telephone rang. Raoul arranged himself without haste and entered the house. "Janvier," I heard through the window behind where I sat, his voice steady, prepared. "Uh-huh, uh-huh. Okay, Pat. Whenever. Yeah, I'll see to that. I'll see she does." The receiver was replaced. No sound of his footsteps. Raoul did not return. He would be waiting, deciding how to say it.

A slip on a step and Esther no longer there for Laura, for me. I wanted her. I wanted her. I wasn't ready yet.

The weight of Raoul's hand on my arm. He dried my face with his fingers, rubbed his palm as though my tears were ointment. "She's going to be all right, Robbie. Hear me now? They're keeping her overnight. Home day after tomorrow, they reckon. Patrick and Laura are staying nearby."

All the time in the world now to go on not asking.

When Esther returned she was confused and frail but mending. She was settled in bed, raised on pillows, a cage lifting the sheet clear of her leg. The children shuffled around her until Laura asked Teddy and Marie to take Will off and play. Except Will couldn't stay away. He kept slipping back to stand quiet and as close as he could to Esther, while outside Teddy and Marie pressed their faces against the window, gesturing apology when they caught Laura's eye. Esther was only vaguely aware of Will. Her attention was way off, through the window, beyond the two little faces there. Once or twice she patted the air next to her bed until her hand rested on Will's head for a moment before she withdrew it, wanting all of herself collected up to concentrate, concentrate hard.

"Esther?" Laura leaned towards those preoccupied eyes. "Mummy?" and stole back a hand. Patrick knocked and pushed on the open door. Laura carried Will across to him. "Could you take him, please? We kind of want to be alone with her, Robs and me."

"Sure. We'll all go visit the alligator farm, they'll like that."

"Thank you, Patrick."

You could never tell what lit Laura. Circumstances that shriveled others, made them gray, could do it. That day I was shriveled, gray. She was lit and indefinably different. Patrick too. Funny how the sharing of a shock, a trauma, or a really good joke can alter the way people move around each other, change the tone they use.

Laura and I sat at the back of the cabin so Esther was relieved of the weight of our presence. Yet we craned to

register every movement—the fingers of her left hand
searching to scratch the back of her right, her lips forming an absent word, her eyes opening to respond to scenes
of which we were no part. We took turns holding the
water glass to her mouth, wiping her face with a cloth.
To every ministration she murmured "Thank you, thank
you" and "How kind" with a formality reserved for unknown attendants. There was a long, still period when
she might have been sleeping except that her eyes remained open. Suddenly she spoke and her voice was the
one we knew, not vague or feeble. "What are you doing
in those? You look ridiculous. They're *his* trousers, not
yours."

I knelt by the bed. "Mummy?"

"It's you, Baby. How did you get up here?"

"We're at Janvier. Remember? Louisiana?" For all that
it sounded unlikely.

"You'll be better in no time, Esther, you really will,"
Laura spoke past my shoulder.

"Better? Better? Yes, Dear. All right. Leave us alone to
talk now"—turning away from us. "Do you think I iron
them for you to wear? Ladies' maid? Is that what I am?"
Her head shaking in anger for a long time before she
slept.

Laura drew me outside into the formless day. We
heard the car, the children's voices and Patrick's, "No,
Will. You come on this way, Darling, and let your
grandma rest some more. We need a hand unpacking the
Chinese, don't we Marie, don't we Teddy? You ever eaten
Chinese take-out? Come on, kids. That's right." And all
their voices faded.

"He's such a kind man," Laura said. We were lolling

on either side of the screen door, unwilling to go farther than that. A soft light glowed through from the bathroom at the back of the cabin. "It's the painkillers making her mind wander. The doctor said they might. They couldn't stitch her, you know. The steroids for the Crohn's has weakened her flesh so much that stitches won't hold." A long while passed before she added, "She won't die. That's not in the cards at all."

"What do you mean?"

"I'm just telling you she won't die, that's all. You don't want her to die, do you? Is that what you want? You want her to die?"

"Stop it, for God's sake. But she's not young and she's not fit. You know that. We've both known for years. I really thought she had died the other night when you left me here alone. When you went off with Patrick and her in the helicopter. I had to think about it then. Face it. Not for long, but I faced it. The day'll come, that's all. It's natural, in the way of things."

"What do you know about the way of things, anyway? Don't. Okay? Just don't. She won't die. She *won't*"—kneading her forearms until her hands remembered and journeyed to her back pocket where she kept the cigarettes. She lit one and was pacified. "So who do you think she's talking to, Robs?"

"The woman Jane wore his clothes, didn't she?"

There was movement inside the cabin. "Laura? Is that you out there, Dear?"

Laura charged inside, clasped Esther's hand. "Mummy, you're awake. How do you feel? Are you hungry? You must be hungry. I'm so glad you're all right.

We were so frightened, weren't we Robs? You must be careful from now on, you really must."

"Laura, Dear, there, there. And Robbie too. What's the matter, Robbie?"

Although her recovery was rapid, Esther wasn't going to be able to travel for a few weeks longer. This wasn't discussed because the greater event now was Louise arriving to take the children away. This was the milestone dreaded by Patrick and anticipated by Marie with such confusion. Teddy wasn't confused and hid away for hours. We understood what he was up to, but there was always the fear of the water, so we couldn't leave him be, and we called him and called him. Searching for Teddy occupied a lot of time. Raoul would stand underneath the largest of the trees in the oak grove, scanning its branches, in search of, not Teddy, I don't believe, but his child-self still hidden there. It was usually Lenny who arrived and whispered behind his hand to Patrick, not to have the world know Teddy's hiding place.

Marie's trunk ritual had become mania, interspersed with fits of tearful frustration. The only one able to subdue and distract her was Laura. But now Laura was constantly with Esther. Forgetting Patrick and the children, even Will, sleeping on the second bed in Esther's cabin, she wouldn't leave Esther's side. On the night before Louise was due to arrive I heard Marie's screams from where I was, all the way down on the levee counting the flickering bats. I ran to the children's room, certain there'd been an accident.

Patrick was pressed up against the trunk with Marie in his arms kicking and punching. He staggered to fend off her fists, avoid her feet, and yet embrace her too, to not let her go, or have her fall. Teddy was cringing in the corner, biting his wrist. When he saw me—gaping, useless in the doorway—he rushed to press his face against me and cover his ears.

"Robbie, Christ, Robbie," Patrick's voice was breaking up, "couldn't she come for a minute? Only a minute? Couldn't Laura come?"

Teddy wouldn't let go of me, so we ran together to Esther's cabin.

The three of them, Esther and Laura and Will, were laughing at a show on the television at the foot of the bed.

"Laura," I called and she did not hear, had not noticed us. *"Laura."* My shout startled them and Teddy's grip tightened. "Marie's bad tonight. The trunk thing. Patrick says please will you come."

She disentangled her arms from Will's. "Oh my God, of course. Oh I'm so sorry, Robs. I'm so sorry," as if only now she realized how absent she had been.

Patrick's face when Laura entered the children's room. His face. When Marie felt the touch of her hand she ceased her attack on Patrick and threw herself into Laura's arms with terrible convulsions.

"Come on, little one." Laura rocked and reassured in a firm voice. "Come on, shhh. It's late." She caressed the wet hair from Marie's hot face, ran her mouth over her forehead. "Come on my baby, my little one. Everything's all right, you'll see, you'll see," she spoke the words like a song, like a song. Teddy loosened his hold of me. Patrick sighed and sank down on the bed. "Shh, shh, Baby, listen, listen. Shall we have a story? Shall we have 'Mr. McGregor's Garden?' Or maybe 'The Story of a Fierce Bad Rabbit.' Mmm?" Laura reached behind without looking for who might take her hand, and Patrick sat forward as if he might, but Teddy was first. Laura continued her unbroken rhythm. "Shh, 'cause Teddy likes that one too, don't you Ted? Shhh. Teddy likes it 'cause the tail gets shot off though, bloodthirsty little git, shhh, shhh." Teddy began to giggle, she reached to ruffle his hair and he giggled more. Still shuddering and retching, Marie tried to giggle as well. "I-like-it-too."

This effort of Marie's, to conform, to forget despair, defeated Laura. Now she was the one fighting for control, rocking Marie faster, harder, whispering, "No. You don't have to, Baby. You don't have to do anything you don't want. You can choose, no one's making you."

At first Marie was her shield to hide behind, so that no one should see her face, what was happening to her. A second after she slipped Marie into Patrick's arms and turned away, hiding her head in the crook of her elbow. Then she swung back again, meeting the misery in Patrick's face with a glorious smile. She curled her hand into her shirtsleeve and used the cuff to wipe Marie's cheeks. "You choose the story, Darling."

"Mr.-Mr.-McGregor's-Garden-'cause-Teddy-likes-it-too."

Laura held her by the shoulders, stared hard into her eyes and let go. "Cool. So that's what we'll have."

Patrick dragged his hands from the top of his head to

his chest. Then he rolled onto the bed with Marie and Teddy bound in his arms and Laura leaned against him to read aloud.

Esther was asleep. Will was craning towards the television watching slapstick in deadly earnest. "Psst, hey Will?" He had no intention of acknowledging me so I lifted him from the bed, which he allowed me to do without breaking his concentration.

Esther half-woke. "Robbie, Dear?" intoning more, wanting me to understand the rest of the question without her having to ask it—the question being, *What was the matter?* Why was my behavior a little bit, just a little bit different, only she could not have said precisely how? "Robbie," she repeated without the inflection this time, to have me know the question didn't matter. It was enough to see me.

I settled Will to sleep as I had done every night since the accident. He had accepted this change in routine without question, and now he circled my neck, drew me close to kiss my cheek exactly once. "That's for you, Auntie Robbie." And again. "And that's for Mummy. Look at me." He lay down stiff, reached to smooth the quilt over his breast and reslot his arms on either side. His feet formed a tiny alp halfway down the bed. "What am I?"

"Tired, I hope."

"I'm a knight lying on my tomb."

Couldn't Laura come? I rinsed my uniform, hung it to dry. Turned on the television. Turned it off. *Couldn't she come for a minute?* His face when she entered the room.

"Hi." Laura loomed around the door in her music-hall mode. "What a storm, eh? Poor little Marie."

"You were wonderful. Any sign of Louise?"

"Well no, not yet. It'll be all right, I expect, once she gets here." She lit a cigarette. "They're both asleep now. Patrick didn't wait. Left while I was still reading."

"He left?"

"He was crying." She reached for the vodka, was about to pour. "Hey, let's not stay here. Let's go and sit with him and Raoul."

"You go."

"Not without you."

"Why not?"

"They'll be sad, Robs. Raoul worships the children as much as Patrick. He's going to miss them too. We could cheer them up a bit, you and me. Come on." She wouldn't look me in the eye. Or be alone with me any longer. We approached the house together.

"Hey, there you are, I was wondering where you'd got to," Patrick called down.

"Yup, right here. Hey, make us one of your fancy cocktails, Patrick, won't you? And I'll make believe I've got an umbrella and a cherry in mine."

"Sure thing, Laura. Love to." But it was an effort to sustain the light tone. And before he reached the door to the house, he flopped into a chair with his eyes shut. Laura seated herself on a footstool, close enough that he would feel her there. "Will doesn't get that way, ever, does he?" he said with eyes still shut.

"Well, no, he's——"

"He's secure. That's why he doesn't get that way. You made him secure. He believes in himself and you and the world. And Louise and I, between us, we've screwed up our kids——"

"They'll settle down in Washington. They'll come here for holidays and such. It'll be fine and——"

"*No it won't.*" Patrick lunged from his chair, knocked over a card table. "*No it fucking won't.*"

"Pat, come along now, Pat," Raoul called from over by the chessboard. "Hold on, boy."

"They won't settle in Washington, Laura, because they're not going to Washington. Louise rang this morning. I couldn't find the right time to tell the kids and I did it then, before you came in. And you saw. Jesus, you saw. Louise has a case, but told me it's not just that. She told me she'd faced the fact that she couldn't cope with them, was scared. Scared of her own kids. How many times have I had to explain to them that their mom's not coming for this reason, that reason, but that next time. Well now there's no next time. I'd set up the school there. Went with Louise to check it out. Make it okay for Teddy 'cause he didn't want to go anyways, explained why it was best he did. Now I'll have to think why it's best he doesn't. But Marie wants her mom, we all know that. We've all seen the trunk routine. Sure it hurt me to watch it, you know. But I understood. And I do, how a little girl wants her mom." He punched a cushion over the rail. "I've got to think. Really got to think."

"Think what?"

"Huh?"

"What have you got to think?"

"What to do tomorrow, make it all right for Marie, leastways not too terrible. Have to come up with something. Done the boats. I have to think of something new." He retreated inside the house talking on. "Done the cart with the mules"—we heard his voice away down the passage—"Done picnics"—and his bedroom door shut.

Raoul stood up, brushed his lap, and bowed. "Goodnight, ladies."

I returned to my cabin, pulled out my case. Laura watched me, keeping pantomime paces with every step of mine. "I don't believe this," she said. "You're not really packing, are you?"

"Yes."

"But you know very well Esther can't travel yet. She can't move yet, and the children—well, the least we can do is stick around till they're settled again."

"You can."

"You're mad."

"Don't start that."

"I'm being serious. You're either mad or you're heartless. I'd prefer mad." She pinched my chin. "You can't leave Patrick and the children now, not right now."

"I think I can."

She released me, sort of threw my head aside, and sat at the table, blew on it and rubbed moisture of her breath into the grain, blew a second time. "What's the matter with you? Why can't you let go and for Christ's sake *live.* They need you, Robs. What in the world have you got to go back to anyway? Or me, for that matter, or Esther?"

"My work."

"This is work. This is real life. Being paid by the hour to sort someone out is different. You're distanced that way."

"They still pay me here. Should I stay and get paid or should I say, *That's all right, I consider myself a member of the family now.*"

"So petty. Who cares anyway? Grief, Robs, I'm only talking about staying on awhile, just until—anyway there's Esther. I can't leave her—bugger, I don't have to say it again. You've made up your mind." She wiped her last breath from the table with her sleeve. From the door she said, "So I'm not leaving. Okay? Sorry. Sorry, Robs, but I'm not."

Hers was the first voice I heard in the morning, calling from her cabin, "Hey, Patrick? Hi. Morning. Listen, I've had an idea," followed distantly by his response, whatever it was. Then a thud when she jumped from the step, the pounding of her feet on the parched ground.

Esther was up, dressed, and preparing to sit outside, expose her leg to the fresh air. "It's ever so much better, Robbie. Look, I can walk quite well." She winced as she shuffled. "So I would have been able to travel, we're not to stay on on account of me. Such a shame about the children's mother, but it doesn't do to judge in these matters. One never knows."

"I'm leaving tomorrow just the same."

She maneuvered to reseat herself on the edge of the bed. "Laura said Patrick wanted us to stay?"

"I'm sure he does. But I'm going anyway. Laura's in control. And it must be better for you to wait awhile."

"What is it, Robbie? Tell me. You've been so, so—" Whatever I had been she couldn't find the word for it. "Please tell me what it is?"

"I can't. I can't, I—"

"*Stop it.* Stop it, do you hear me?" She was shaking. Her rare, petulant anger still checked me, silenced me as it always had. "It's bad enough when Laura does that, that silly *I can't* nonsense. Now if you're starting too, well, for goodness sake take a pull. I asked a simple question. If you don't want to answer then don't. You're an adult now, behave like one. All this silliness." Sweat stood on her upper lip as she talked herself back down to gentleness, twitched her woven wicker fan—a present from Theresa the day they'd shopped in Baton Rouge. "Look, Dear, if you feel you want to go, and you've got your ticket, then do so. Laura knows what's what. If she didn't know she was welcome then she wouldn't think of staying. It'll only be a day or two, I expect, then we'll all be home together."

The only soul present on the verandah was Allie, humming to herself on the swing. "That you Robbie child?" She gathered my hand between both of hers, brought it to her lap. "Things in the air. I feel 'em. Uh-huh. I feel 'em. My Raoul's gone fishing. Bring on home some ol' thing not fit to eat. Always the same."

"I'm going home, Allie."

"Uh-huh."

I passed the barn, heard the children's voices inside, not their usual squealing banter, but considered and low, strangely studious. I turned a bucket over and stood on that to reach a knothole, peered in. They were at the far end, lit in that obscure sunlight that was diffused by ambient particles of hay and oats and cobweb. A platform of hay bales formed a stage where Marie—a feather in her hair and clothed in a cutoff sack tied at the waist—was strutting and proclaiming. Laura and Patrick were behind her, hitching blankets onto a line, pegging them together. Teddy and Will were working on upturned crates, one writing, the other striking a xylophone. Patrick and Laura came to the foot of the stage. Their silhouettes made one shape that divided to display their astonishment and admiration to each other for Marie's performance, then combining as one again to concentrate.

I found Raoul as I had often before, resting against a half–deck chair affair, the line running between his feet to the water. "Good to see you, Robbie. Where's Pat?"

"Laura in the barn."

"Children?"

"They're all there, making plays."

"I see, right. So that was her big idea. I heard her say she had this *brilliant*"—his English accent—"idea. Poor Pat. He needed one. He was right about something dif-

ferent being called for today. Clever girl, your sister." He
reeled in his line, flipped open the basket next to him,
picked a crawler from a jar, hitched it on the hook.

"You do like her, don't you?"

"Couldn't not. I believe no one could dislike Laura.
She has a way with her." Tossed the line in the water.

"Has she mentioned about staying on awhile for the
children's sake?"

"Uh-huh."

"Anything else?"

"No. I merely heard her inquiring gently of Patrick if
he might prefer you to remain, postpone your leaving
until the children are settled once more."

"Was he glad?"

The reel whizzed. "My, my, could that be Mr. Sac-á-
Lait? That you ol' Mr. Sac-á-Lait?"

It was not Mr. Sac-á-Lait. Just weed. "Raoul, I'm leaving tomorrow as I planned."

"Is that so."

"Did Laura tell you?"

"She didn't have to."

"Esther's not strong enough to travel yet, so Laura will
stay to look after her and come back when she does."

"Will she indeed?" He felt across the grass for my
hand. "You know, Robbie, don't you, that it wasn't my
intention to have it this way? That my aim was to have
you remain—"

"And *you* know why I can't, that I have no business
here anymore." No more words between us. But then I
wanted to be sure he had understood, to have him understand and see that—

"Shh," he said, "say no more, Darling."

VI

BACK AGAIN

Say no more, Darling—a snap of fingers and back again, back again in autumn London, shopping at an all-night store in Notting Hill Gate, feeling cold. I had arrived home late, no food at home, of course, and so I was shopping, hardly knowing what to choose or where I was. Back again.

The play had been charming with Marie as Pocahontas, Will a confused Captain Smith, Teddy confining himself to the slaughter of soft toys, Patrick and Laura earnest in their tasks as stagehands, prompters, and providers of incidental music. The rest of us were audience—Raoul, Charles and Theresa, Allie, Lenny, Esther, and me.

I found the studio painted yellow as Esther had announced when she was here and I was there. I had forgotten. It was a shock. Esther and Laura had imprinted their lives more forcefully on my home than I ever had: Will's pedal car parked in the postage-stamp hall, a dried-out tangle of his laundry in the bottom of the washing machine, a dirty load nearby on the kitchen floor. Esther's belongings were now liberally distributed—raised from refugee status to full residency—and Laura's stacks of dog-eared albums and racks of discs and sheet music were strewn over the floor in the bedroom and the studio. I was glad of it all.

The last time I glanced back through the departure gate, Patrick was carrying Marie on his shoulders with Teddy's hand firmly grasped, and Laura was bent towards Will, indicating which in the crowd was my retreating figure. I rang them to say I was home—"Hi, I'm home, I'm safe," and their excited voices around the receiver as it was handed from one to another. Laura promised to ring when she knew their plans—"A week or two, no more," she had whispered in that moment after Goodbye when I always waited and she knew I always did, and her voice had echoed inside her cupped hand.

Days passed before the city came easy to me again, with its rucked pavements, wind-bullied litter and roadwork and traffic and crowds, the emptied-out streets at night, the clatter of the underground trains, the hunting-howl of police cars flooding and receding, leaving the atmosphere retracted and alert. They were six hours behind in Louisiana. Were they fishing from the boat? Riding in the cart? Or asleep as my day began? The time lapse made their continued existence feel unlikely, and any pause during my full days instantly exposed my longing to reach them, to reach Esther and Laura, to hear their voices and be reassured. I tried not to call them. Instead I would lie in bed and picture them, irrationally idealized, no unspoken past, no unasked questions, only the gestures and attitudes that confirmed the root-deep security we drew from being together, from one another's continuing life. Sometimes I failed in my picturing, could not bring them up at all. So then I conjured the others at Janvier instead, or the place itself. When I failed in that too—as I frequently did—it would seem then that they, and all that was Janvier, had gone and I had missed my chance forever. Whatever that chance might have been. It would be the same now if Esther and Laura were far away in some other sunlight; I would need to confirm they breathed. I would need to reach them and hear their voices, however unsettling. But it can't be the same now because they are gone. They no longer have any existence to doubt. Their nonexistence is the only certainty.

I was quickly reestablished in my work. Former patients returned, new ones came recommended by contacts from training years, people who were now GPs or specialists. I was welcomed, appreciated, had even been missed. I attended the Royal West London Hospital on Fridays, the practice off Kensington Church Street on Monday afternoons and Tuesday evenings. The rest of my time was taken with private patients, chronic and terminal cases, usually chests. My spare-time preoccupation was house hunting. The bank confirmed I could take on a higher mortgage, so I searched for a house large enough for the four of us, with a garden, either in Wandsworth or Stockwell or Kensal Rise. Because Esther, when she came home, wouldn't be able to work anymore, whatever Laura wanted to believe. Laura and Will would be returning to homelessness again, when Will should really be settled in primary school. Life as it had been in my flat would be intolerable. We would be so happy in a house, the four of us. How Will would love a garden. Esther too, she liked gardens, birds and seeing things grow. Should I find the house first and let it be a surprise? Of course if I found the right place, something really special, I would be too excited not to tell.

"Laura, how are you? Can you talk? I'm longing to talk. How's Esther?"

"She's good, Robbie, toddling all over the place. She's right beside me. We're all here on the verandah. Indian summer, don't you know"—laughing the laugh she made for others. "Here, Will wants to talk, go on Will, go on."

"Hello Aunt Robbie," he was distracted, challenging Marie over some present interest.

"Hi, Will, how are you?"

"Sorry, Robs, his mind's on other things. We got your letters, we all did. Great that work's going so well."

"How's Esther?"

"I told you, she's good. *Aren't you, Esther? Robs wants to know how you are.* I'll let you speak to her, Robs."

"Don't go, Laura. When can we talk? I mean when's a

good time when you're not—only it's been three weeks now and I was wondering."

"Hang on, hang on, listen, here's Esther. I'll get back to you in a second." A child was screaming nearby.

"Hello Dear, is it you?" Despite the racket Esther's voice came vague and removed, as it always did on the telephone. The house could be burning around her and she would still inquire cautiously of the telephone receiver, "Hello Dear, is it you?"

"Yes, it's me. What's going on there?" I had heard Patrick guffaw and there was a roar that could only have come from one person. "What's Raoul laughing at?"

"They're all being very silly. Well, we all are, really."

"No point in asking to speak to him?"

She held the receiver away, still sounded like a speaking clock. *"She says, she says—Raoul? Listen, she says, 'No point in asking to speak to you?'* Hello, Dear? Are you there? He's sort of waving his hand, you know how he does. Oh, he says he's written you." She used *written you* as though trying on American to feel how it suited.

"When are you coming home?"

"Better talk to Laura. Only she's run off down the stairs now."

It was always that way or similar. Laura was never alone when we spoke. If I asked how it went with the children—were they more settled now, steadier? Could she think about leaving?—she would be someplace from where she could not talk—the verandah or inside the house with everyone around—and I wanted to say, *So go somewhere you can talk.* Only I never did and nor did she. All Esther ever said of herself was her usual, "Very well, Dear, nothing to worry about here." And her hand would have been on her breast to indicate there, in her delicate body. Every time she said that on the telephone, me in England, she back there in Louisiana, a memory formed. And I can form it now, this very instant: Esther is in a kitchen of a long, long time ago—I don't know which of all the kitchens it is—with her feet in a bowl of water. She is sighing. Laura and I are nearby, we are still only girls, the age when giggling is the wild intoxicant. We are teasing her and she tells us quite seriously, "You see I look after my feet because they've done me well, they've stood by me." And there we are pointing, covering our mouths, spluttering. "They've what, no say it again Esther, what have your feet done?" "Well, it's true, they have stood by me, my feet," only now she self-consciously smiles. "It's still true."

Sometimes I had breakfast in my usual café. It was good to be among familiar, nameless faces. One morning Sam's friend, the Rastafarian, tapped my elbow. "Hey, Sam said you'd gone to the States."

"I'm back. Laura's still there."

"Hey, man, I thought you were Laura. Right, you've got that hair, she got the other. Right."

A couple of days later Sam's polished head gleamed through the window of the café. It took a minute to find him again among the chattering crowd inside. There was a line three deep for service at the counter, people hunched at marble tables barely wider than a hand span, others in search of a vacant seat, or an inch of clear wall to lean against. Some simply stood with elbows drawn tight, sipping and nibbling as best they could. Funny how the café three doors down was always nearly empty. I knew by his face Sam had been waiting for me. "Dan told me you were back. Came here yesterday and the day before." I mentioned Laura's name first to save him from asking. He did not pretend he was there for anything other than to hear about her. And he wouldn't have known how to disguise the hope and regret flowing in his eyes, working at the corners of his mouth as he listened to my measured descriptions of Janvier. I listed everyone there by name and described them, dwelling on those I thought would interest him, like Raoul and Allie. I invited him over for supper. "Not if Laura's back."

"Not yet. But quite soon, I expect. Come tomorrow."

"Can't till next week. Got a gig in Leeds, then Torquay."

"Next Wednesday, then. I promise I'll ring you if they're back by then."

"Righto, 'ta, Rob. Very nice."

But I couldn't wait another week to tell someone about my idea. "Only, Sam, we'll be moving soon. The four of us. I'm looking for a house. There's no room in the flat. We'd all go mad."

"You are all mad."

"Thanks." And they were with us all of a sudden, Esther and Laura, evoked by that "all mad" routine. He had heard us do it. He knew it too. "Anyway, I've been talking to estate agents. Even seen a couple of places and—"

"Is it such a good idea, Rob?"

I did not want that question, or to see his eyes when he asked it. "Well, Esther won't be able to get another job. I'm not sure she even wants one, but that's all right because with what I make—well anyway. And, you see, Will can start school properly and Laura can—"

"Listen, I got to go. I'll see you next week."

I finished my coffee with a stranger in Sam's place at the table. Could it have hurt, what I'd been telling him? Hurt more than he was already. Still hurting.

"—and there's a garden for Will to play in, with trees in it and shrubs, and a bedroom each and a kitchen, of course, and a really nice one where we'll talk and talk and talk. Because we do that when we're all together, you see. It's a place for all of us to be at last. And Esther won't have to go out to work anymore and"—and I was doing it again a week later, hurting Sam because that afternoon I had seen a house I liked and was unable to contain myself, not even to spare him or me from that left-behind look in his eyes and that other expression too, the one I did not want to see.

"Have you told them?"

"Not yet, but I'm going to later on tonight. If I ring about midnight our time they're bound to be around. It'll be suppertime there."

He talked about some new songs he had written and wished there was a piano in my place. We recalled how he and Dan brought the piano in for the party and joked about that until we remembered further and stopped. There was no path that did not lead to more anguish for Sam, and he said, "I can't seem to get over it, Rob. I mean Laura. I can't get over her." He kneaded his eyes with the mounds of his thumbs, stubby fingers splayed on his forehead. It's a myth about musicians' hands being so beautiful. They aren't. Not all of them. Or maybe it is the composers and arrangers who have those thick, urgent, clever hands, enduring hands. "I like your hands."

"What? What?" He lifted his head out of them, eyes all red, and observed his fingers as though they had confided in me something they should not. "Little fellas. They're all right. Do the job. Thanks, Rob."

We ate fish and drank a lot of wine. Softly and carefully he sang the latest of his new batch of songs, humming the piano where there were no words. I had been waiting for the husband of a patient to ring. A high diver I had treated for four years just because she once agreed to perform at a water festival in Sydney. She had hastily prepared a comedy act in top hat and tails and told me that two thirds of the way down she realized what would happen if she did not take off the hat. But the thought came too late, only not too late to know beforehand how things could be for her when—if—she came up. The impact of the water meeting the brim broke her neck and shattered her spine. She was paralyzed from the shoulders down. She had had yet another operation that day. I told Sam about it and he was waiting for the call as keenly as I was. When at last it came we both gasped, "That's it," "That'll be it."

"Robs? Robs, it's me. Did I wake you?"

"No. I was expecting someone else. What's the matter? Are you all right? Is Esther all right?"

"Everyone's fine. Expecting someone, eh? Now that's good news."

"Not like you think. There's a friend here."

Sam knew. He knew and would have liked to leave his place in the armchair but could not make himself, not for courtesy, not even for his own sake, he just couldn't trust his legs to hold him right then, that all written on his face with embarrassment and longing.

"Who's that, Robs?"

"Well it's"—Sam crisscrossed his palms at me—"a friend of mine. Hey, I've been dying to talk to you. When are you coming home, 'cause I've had a brilliant idea."

"Cool. We've had an idea too. They gave me five minutes, then they're coming in."

"Who?"

"The family." The family? *"Hey, no fair. That wasn't five minutes. All right, come in then, I don't mind.* Robs? Sorry. You still there? What's your idea?"

"You first. It could be the same. Is *we* you and Esther?"

"No. Guess what?"

"I can't."

"No, do."

"I don't want to."

"Okay. Ready? We're getting married, Robs. He asked me this afternoon and I said yes, yes, yes, like that. Didn't I? Didn't I, my love?" For a moment her voice was lost among others and when she spoke next it was as though she were struggling to reach the receiver. "And all these smelly little kiddies are driving us potty." Noises off, disgust mostly. *"You are, you are, hey stop it, let go."* Her voice was submerged in squawking children.

"Hi there, Robbie. It's me, Patrick. How about us, hey?

Aren't I the luckiest man in the world? Are you there? Robbie? Listen, here's your mother."

"Robbie, Dear? Robbie?"

Hadn't I known since she danced down the steps at Janvier and planed over the grass with the children all behind her? Since, with his altered face, Raoul took my arm before we descended and he said—what? Anything? Did he speak at all? Hadn't I known from the look in Sam's eyes in the café and didn't want to see? Wasn't knowing, after all, why I left? Because of the proximity of her—of Laura's—glorious vitality to my etiolated soul.

"Rob? Come on girl. Guessed as much, didn't we?" Sam sniffed. "Here, anything left to drink? You didn't mention him enough, see, the other morning in the café. This invisible fellow, this Patrick-with-the-kids."

The telephone rang. The call I'd been waiting for. *"She's come through. She's going to be all right."*

"She's going to be all right," I told Sam.

"Will she walk?"

"She could, Sam. That's the point, you see. That's why she had to risk it."

"Good luck to her. Here, let's fill this up. Drink a toast to all and sundry, eh? How long they known each other, then, Rob? Can't be, what—"

"Seven weeks."

"Seven weeks." He stored this to make sense of later, meanwhile came and sat next to me. "Come on, Love. I'm the cast-off, not you. What is it?"

"I don't know. Laura gets on, doesn't she? When she arrived at Janvier, well, she just *was*. Like that. And mesmerized everyone. She's so powerful. I never realized. Except once perhaps, just before I left England, when I saw how she managed an audience. You were there in that club, remember? When you played the bongos from the back of the room?"

"Right. I followed her everywhere for a bit, she didn't know, except that time of course."

"I'm all right when she's near, part of my life, coming and going like she did. Me the stable one with an income and a place of my own. Somewhere for her to be on and off, Esther too, and I can moan about them being there. When Esther comes back I could still get the house for us, couldn't I? Sam, couldn't I do that, and Laura and Will would want to visit, wouldn't they?" I stopped long enough to register that expression in his eyes, telling things I wouldn't admit. "You don't think she will, do you?"

He pulled my hand to his lap, played with my fingers. "I don't think so, Rob. It always looked to me like Esther tipped up wherever Laura did. And now, if Laura's over there, well—" He gave it back, my hand, laid it on the sofa between us, scooped my shoulders into his arm.

"Raoul and Patrick wanted me to become part of their family. I didn't understand exactly how though, it was vague and I suppose I couldn't handle it. I might have learned. Something hinders me from being close to people, the same thing that drives Laura right up to them I suppose, that drove her wandering the way she did."

"I know where we are now." Sam withdrew his arm as

though at this point he needed all his consolation for himself. "We're back with those bastards, whoever they were. Got to Laura when she was just little. And not just her, right? I always wondered. Laura never said much. She didn't seem to be able to. Even if I asked ever so gently she couldn't say, like she was physically incapable. But I watched her closely, knew all her responses, listened to her talking in her sleep. All the things you do when you love someone and want to learn more about them, everything about them. 'Cause you can never know enough about someone you're in love with, can you? What I gathered about her young life was so horrible. It's a bloody silly term, *abuse—child abuse*. It's abomination. It's violation. The casual destruction of a child's faith and security, the invading of its body—it's all evil. Those vile wretches put out the light in her life and left her in darkness. That's the worst of it. It can't be undone. And where are they now, I'd like to know? Old people, are they, with kiddies of their own, grandchildren? *Bastards, bastards, I'd kill them—*"

"Hey, Sam."

"I mean it, Rob, I'd kill them if I saw them. Only he's dead, isn't he? Your dad, and he's the one who—"

"Stop it."

"See? See?" He jumped up and shouted in my face. "It's bloody *stop it* isn't it? You too, *I can't, I can't, stop it.* Bet you said that then when there was no one for you and I bet—"

I forced my head between my knees and felt his hand come softly on the back of my neck, his other supporting my forehead. The sickness passed.

"Sorry," he said. "Sorry-sorry-sorry, like Laura says. Sweet the way she does that, isn't it? Can I just say—try to say—what it's like to be on the outside of someone like Laura, maybe even you? I fell in love with her before I guessed about any of that—what?—darkness, okay? Only that darkness must have been a factor. Once or twice she got hysterical when we were making love, attacked me, like I was trying to kill her or something. It happened a couple of times before I understood it wasn't me she was fighting. She didn't know what she was doing and could never explain after. I'd follow her those nights she went walking. And Dan would go if I wasn't around. She never knew. Till that last time. You see, I made myself part of her past. I let myself in to try to be the one there for her, the one who wasn't there when she was little, to protect her and get her away. I thought that if she lived how she had to live—even if that meant screaming at me sometimes when I was only trying to love her, beating on me, or her getting involved with vile sods in the back rooms of clubs or whatever—then okay. I was up for all of it, Rob. She could turn around and find I was still there and we'd work it out together."

"Why? With it all so grim, what was there for you to stay for?"

"Go on. You're not really asking me that, are you?"

And I wasn't. I wasn't because I knew the answer and still, "Yes. Why stay with all that—that *darkness?* Who'd want it?"

"But, like I said, that darkness is what she's been given. Where she was put and left. But she has a way of recycling all that so that what she *gives* is light. I never laughed so much with anyone else, never felt so alive, or so useful, or clever. Everything was all right when we were together. She made everything all right for me and I wanted to do that for her. Now I can't try anymore to take her out of her nightmare. 'Cause nothing's changed, Rob. Nothing's changed."

"It has. She's all right now. She'll have security."

"You think so? This—this Patrick person. What's he like?"

"He described himself to me once as a simple man."

"Lovely."

"No, he's a good man, Sam."

"And does he know about the nightmare? Has he guessed yet, do you think?"

I gathered our glasses and mugs. Would I tell him I had seen a different Laura, a different sister? Someone set on walking in joy, determined on nothing but fulfillment, refusing that there had ever been, could ever be anything other than that for her. So much so that she would no longer look me in the eye, no longer allow herself to speak to me alone for fear that just for a second she might remember who she was and lose her footing.

"Thought not." Sam pulled on his jacket.

We were down in the hall. "Will you come and see me again, Sam?"

"Sure." He was through the door, I was closing it when he pushed it back against my hand, without returning or showing his face. "One thing?"

"Yes?"

"Good-looking sort of a cove, is he?"

"They look alike."

"It's often the way. Lots of dark hair?"

"Well, sort of."

"Tall, lean, not the chunky type like me?" He knew I wouldn't have answered that, did so for himself. "Well, he wouldn't be, would he? I mean if they look alike."

He sustained his pressure against the door. The light clicked off and he fell back inside, against the wall, bathed in a cadmium wash from the street lamp. With his face still averted he rubbed his neck. "So it's a beautiful spot this Janvier?"

"Yes. Vaguely unreal."

"Well. Couldn't have given her that. Couldn't give her *unreal.* What'll happen when he does find out?"

"Maybe he won't have to. Maybe you're wrong and I'm right and she's changed."

He faced me then so I too fell back against the wall so he couldn't. Together we stared out at the side of the steps, a bag of rubbish, a cluster of empty milk bottles. He walked out after a bit and I shut the door, listened for his footsteps. Listened. Twenty minutes passed before I saw him from the studio where I had watched for him with the light off, saw him crossing the road, going away.

Silly, my idea about the house.

A few days later I was heading for the main road— nearly midnight but no matches to light the cooker meant no tea before bed and I had to have tea before bed—when I heard Esther's voice, *That woman, the woman Jane, took a place down that way—there would be*

the crescent—the church—five roads down, I guess—a
ground-floor flat in a corner house. I went there once, just
to see, to see her face after he'd turned her out—there she
was with her arms crossed, still wearing those blessed ban-
gles—

I craned down that narrowing perspective of streets
where Esther had once stood reliving days before I was
born. On that lonely corner in the middle of the night I
peered and shifted for a view like a race-goer in a crowd,
as though at any moment, just before vanishing point,
something might pass, someone, left to right, right to
left, pass, stop, even, and look back at me. A man or a
woman? A child? Who would I see? Would they see me?
It became an obsession. I could not pass that corner, day
or night, without stopping, my hand involuntarily lifted
to shelter my eyes. Sometimes there was no perspective,
no possibility at the end of all those crossroads, between
all those houses and shedding trees. But I stopped just
the same, every time I walked that way.

Sam was right about Esther. Her letters revealed in
stages the diminishing possibility of her return. She
would not come before the marriage since it was already
November. She was still weakened from her fall and
might stay on until the better weather arrived in England. Laura needed help with the children. She was
unhappy about leaving Will and so on. Laura came to
the telephone once—"You will come for Christmas,
Robs, won't you? We won't have a big wedding but we
want to make a fuss of Christmas. Patrick says to book
your flight early. It gets insanely busy at holiday time."

Sam did come to see me again. He came often and we

had pleasant times. We did not always talk of Laura but she was always there.

We were finishing a take-away one Sunday evening when he announced, "I'm off to la belle France tomorrow, Robbie, and I'm stopping. A friend of mine's opened a little place in Arles. Know Arles, do you? I don't. He wants a piano player for the flavor." He was rooting through the boxes spread between us on the studio floor, picking out with chopsticks whatever he could find. "Now, see, if I was like you and had studied, trained for something, things might be different. As it is they're tough over here."

"And you're going tomorrow?"

"Yup. First thing. He rang me the other day, made the offer. I thought about it, didn't take long, said yes. Like that."

A kind of singing in my ears. Life passing me by.

"—my mum's a bit sorry of course. Down in Plymouth, she is, and I don't see her much as it is. Told her she could come out. So can you, Robbie. Would you?" He wiped his mouth, wrapped the chopsticks, rubbed his hands, settled them on his knees, lifted his face all bright and optimistic and flying free. "What's the matter, Love?"

"Nothing."

"Come on. What've I said. Me off, is it? I'm serious about you having a career, caring for people. You don't know how much I admire that. You're a *valuable member of society*, Rob, and don't forget it. Well, you're reminded of that every day, I expect. Grateful patients and all. Here, how's that diver?"

"The operation helped. She's in less pain. I treat her most days."

"Bloody hell, girl, there you go. Fantastic."

A silence. He could have asked, *Well then, so what's the problem?* But a man's instinct for self-preservation is very strong, even in one as tender as Sam. "I'd like to ask you something, Sam. It would mean a lot to me if you didn't say no."

"Then I shan't. What is it? No, go on, don't be shy." He mimed a nudge with his elbow as Laura used to do.

"Shall we clear this stuff away?"

"Righto."

And we did and we talked some more after that. Then he left. I did not ask him. It would not have been right, I thought, not of the lover—ex-lover—of my sister.

VII

ALL THE JOY

". . . then you were gone." Patrick smoothed the cloth, realigned the cutlery. "Just your back view disappearing through the departure gate. And I'd given you not a word of thanks, Robbie, for so much. For changing our lives, Raoul's and mine. Although I didn't know even how much. Were it not for you, well, there'd have been no Laura. That's why I brought you here, so we could be alone and I could do that, say thank you. I composed a lot of letters to you, wanted to describe my feelings, but, well, with so much going on—you know how it is."

Patrick had met my plane, brought me into the Quarter for lunch before driving on out to Janvier. "How is Laura?"

"She's good." He raised his eyes to me, lowered them. "Really, she's looking good. Hair's grown. Face is all"—molding another face in front of his own—"healed."

Why now? She had arrived in July and it was already December. Why refer now to that which had been so immediately obvious? Did he want to find out about the one he had married, already married, quietly in a civic office a month before with only Esther and Raoul present? *Robs, are you there? Don't be cross, will you, but we've done it, we wanted it quiet, you do understand, don't you? Robs?*

"This establishment's been here for years, you know," Patrick informed my silence to save us both. "Why, that waiter who's taking care of us, he took care of my daddy, so he tells me, and I know it's true. That's how they do it here: A waiter has his clients, you see. That's a bit of tourist information. Thought you'd like to know." He sighed. "Were you very shocked? Speed of the wedding an' all?"

"Yes."

"I'm sorry. It's going to be all right, Robbie. We're only looking ahead now. It doesn't matter what went before in my life or hers, I've said that to Laura."

"She's told you about *before?*"

"Nope. And I respect her silence. She understands that by not asking her a lot of questions—questions my friends don't refrain from asking about her—I'm demonstrating my trust. That it's only from now on that counts. We want to create a happy, stable base for the children. Can that be so hard? I don't think so. To be honest, my work doesn't intrigue me the way it does some of those I work with. And the way it intrigues my ex-wife Louise.

The law I practice takes me into a corporate, purely business world. Earns me good money. My name is first on the firm's letterhead, sure, and I have meaningful clients. But, you know, it's not time-intensive. Doesn't have to be, at any rate. It's my fig leaf, you could say. I want to be with my kids and with Laura as much as I can. Too many years have been wasted. That's right, isn't it, Robbie? Isn't that the way to play it?"

"*Play* it?"

"Uh-huh. Play it."

Is it possible to live with another and leave a history unspoken, unknown—possible to even want to? Wouldn't it devalue every effort made towards peace and commitment, not knowing the price that other pays to handle what went before? And did she still wake up screaming, and if she did, didn't he hold her and ask, *Hey Darling, what did you dream?* He'd find it was always the same. Could every signal of Laura's suffering have vanished so fast, so completely—her drinking, her chain-smoking, her pacing and pacing and going without sleep for days and the crazed look in her eye that came with all that— *play it?* Is that what you do?

"Hey, Darling." A dark-haired woman leaned around Patrick and cupped his face to kiss it. "I guessed it was you. Why hi, Laura," she added, and then, "Oh. Excuse *me.*"

"Daithel, this is Robbie, Laura's sister."

"Well, I'll be." And the rest of the group who'd entered the restaurant with her—three more women, two men—crowded around to marvel with her on my likeness to Laura.

"And Patrick, thank you for that great evening. If you

give parties as good as your sister does, Robbie, then you're okay. That girl's a pistol. We love her, don't we?" Yes they did. " 'Bye now, Patrick, happy holidays. 'Bye, Robbie, great to meet you. Hey, gimme another kiss before I go." She lifted his face again, released it. "Mmmm, that's *right.* 'Bye."

They weren't the only ones to stop by the table to thank for recent good times.

"See? All my friends love her. Where were we?"

Nowhere. I wasn't going to enter where he and Laura wouldn't tread together. "I can't wait to see her."

He glanced at the brass-bladed fans above us, around the mirror-lined walls, and retrieved his composure. "No. I know where we were. You didn't like my *play it.* Well, I'm not a stupid man. We don't speak of Will's father. I've no idea who he may be. She's offered no information. I know she's never been married before. Nor do we speak about that—that face thing. Was she mugged? I don't think so because if you have been it's a tale you tell. God knows it's happened to friends of mine. And you get instincts about things. I've never asked her, or you, or Esther, just to show you all—and above all Laura—how that's okay with me. Why, I believed in Laura from the moment she, she—"

"Ran down to the levee in the dark. And all the children—"

"That's right. That's right. Wasn't that the most beautiful sight? She has a capacity for joy like I've never met. And kindness too. Sure, there's things about Laura's past the nature of which I can only guess at. She tells me what she wants me to know and it's not much. No picture. Sometimes I get nervous, see something in her manner. She's private, goes off for the day to the city and—"

"And what?"

"Oh—and nothing. Good Lord. See? I always did talk to you, say things. Remember that first evening, me yakking on that way? God, I felt a fool when I woke."

"No need."

He unclenched his fists on the table. "I know that. And thank you because"—he closed his eyes, shifted his knees aside from under the table, lit a cigarette, laughed away the smoke, and beamed—"because life at Janvier these days, it's something else, it's *great*, I tell you."

There was a Christmas tree with real candles inside the house, beyond the verandah, and the scent of cinnamon and cedar and oranges and a gabble of voices coming from the salon—a room I remembered as cold and austere. More candlelight, delivered from mirror to mirror, finessed the scene in there: Allie, beside the fire in a fan-backed chair, knitting and nodding into her earphones. Laura, Teddy, Marie, and Will crouched in concentration over crepe paper and scissors and no end of glittering things—"No, Will, that's the snapper. It goes inside the cracker and makes the bang, don't pull it." *"He pulled it."* "Did you see that, Marie? He pulled it. Will, you silly billy." "Silly billy, silly billy." "Look-it, Will, the bang scared Moley."

Moley was not scared. She had seen me and was gathering herself for a greeting. Laura looked up, saw me, and dashed the contents from her lap to the floor, crossed the room with her arms wide. "Robs, oh Robs. I've *missed* you."

The children tumbled around and we somehow ended in a muddle on the floor. Before I knew it, still in my overcoat, I was making crackers with them while taking in the changes. Will a little taller, less baby fat, whereas Laura had gained. Her skin was radiant, her hair fuller, longer than it had been for years, and indefinably formal. I couldn't keep from staring at her lowered head as she cut at bits and pieces for the crackers. She didn't look up, or cease her fluent recount of events at Janvier. But she knew, she knew I was seeing the difference in her. Several times she shook her fingers free of the scissors to touch her hair where my eyes rested. And when I faced away, that was when I felt her eyes on me. But all the time the two of us were talking, talking until from behind me, "Hellooo Baby—"

"Granny, look," Will called before I could turn, "look, Aunt Robbie's here."

Infected with this business of welcome, Teddy and Marie rushed to Esther, who was leaning on a walking stick. Keen to demonstrate their possession, they brought her forward. "See, Granny Esther," "Come on, GrandEst."

"Robbie. How are you, Dear?"

She was wearing a new suit, light-colored with gold about it—the buttons, I suppose, I cannot remember. But I do remember she appeared different, groomed, no more crazy ragbag look. No more bun slipping off the top of her head. Her hair was short now and back-combed and lacquered. I had never seen her so lithe, so rested and composed, tanned yet from summer. Only her hands in mine were the ones I knew, active and fragile, seashells in paper, and always that extraordinary warmth. One time, when I was very little, I had watched as she cupped a maimed bird between those hands and seen it revive and fly away. Magic.

We led her to a straight-backed chair and Patrick joined us and somehow we were all, except for Esther and Allie, sitting on the floor again. Allie was near enough for me to reach up and stroke her shoulder, whereupon she claimed my forearm and rested with it, apparently content until she raised her choral voice, "Raoul. She come. The child come home."

Raoul stood in the doorway taking in the scene as I had done, a scene of which I was now a part.

"Look, Raoul, here's your favorite person," Laura said, which struck me and I didn't know why.

He was wearing his suit again, his tussah suit, and I knew it was for me. His hair was blacker than black and he held his left hand aloft, nodded at it to have me notice it—as if I wouldn't have. "Embrace me, Robbie, I insist." And when I was as close as that he said through my hair, "Welcome back." What I didn't feel coming from him was the power that had always been apparent. A quality I had marked in my original notes—the ones I made before he had addressed so much as a word to me—a quality that cannot be clinically quantified but you know when it's there. And when it's not.

Esther pointed to a chair with her stick. "Get him a

chair, Teddy Dear. No, not that one, a nice straight one like mine. It's more comfortable for us elderly people."

"No thank you, Esther, I don't feel the need."

Esther smiled her boys-will-be-boys smile. "Leave it there, Teddy, he'll want it in a minute."

"I will *not* want it in a minute. Thank you." He didn't move well, towards the tray of drinks where he poured himself a whiskey then frowned at the empty bottle. "Hey, where'd all that go?"

Esther made that noise with her tongue, that click of disapproval that I had thought was reserved for me alone and irritated me so much. My anger swelled, overwhelming my jet lag and exhaustion and elation. The force of it took me by surprise. How dare she make that silly noise at him, at Raoul of all people? "I'll fetch another bottle," I said.

"No need. There's one right here." He pulled one from a stash in a cupboard behind a panel in the wall.

"Well, I'm going to help Theresa in the kitchen. Poor soul has plenty enough on her hands." On her way out Esther returned the straight-backed chair to its place in the corner.

I was ready to sleep long before the rest of them. Laura was studying plans for alterations to the house. Patrick was standing behind her, binding her close to him. "You're not looking, Patrick. Do look. See, those are all new windows." She traced a finger across the paper. To my goodnight she answered, "Sorry, Robs, but I must make Patrick pay attention. I promised the architect the go-ahead tomorrow."

"As if she'd listen to me anyway." He wrapped her up more and kissed her while she struggled and laughed. "No, seriously. Concentrate."

Esther organised herself at the top of the verandah stairs, removing her stick to her left hand, grasping the rail with her right, and descending heavily a step at a time. Her frailty was even more apparent during our process towards my cabin. "No, I want to come. I want to settle you in, Dear." And she groaned as she sat down at the table. Everything in there was as it had been when I'd first arrived.

"You look thin, Robbie." Her hair had been blown about and something of the real Esther was back.

"Been working hard, that's all. I want to save enough for a good down payment on a house."

"I wouldn't be sorry if you moved from where you are. That area is so," she poked her stick at a knothole in the floorboards.

"It's so what?"

"What?"

"You've never liked my flat, have you?"

She agitated her stick. "You've made it nice. It's that part of London I don't like. The types, I suppose, and the—the "

Memories? And types like the woman Jane? I thought, and waited for more, but her concentration had drifted, anchored only by that beleaguered knothole. "So, anyway, I'm working hard for the down payment."

The ticking of my traveling clock. A tap dripping in the bathroom. I went through, turned it tight. I returned and she was saying, "—right on the corner opposite his house. Close enough to spy on him, see him with the other women he had after her. *She* discovered what it's like to be turfed out."

"It's never stopped hurting, has it?"

"What are you talking about?"

"That memory. When Daddy and the woman Jane—"

"You know nothing about it."

"You've said things over the years. I know enough."

"You weren't born. Just Laura. Laura was born. You always do it, don't you? You're not here five minutes and you're digging things up, things we don't want to think about. You never change. Why can't you love life like Laura does? Make an effort like her? Here we are in this beautiful place and Laura happy for the first time in her life then you come with—with—with the way you are. Don't you think she'd like to have been clever at school like you? How do you think she felt with you being successful and earning good money when she was struggling so hard? And now she has this nice young man and a lovely home here for Will and, and I don't know *what all* and here you are *remembering* things. Going back over old ground."

Dizzy. That singing again in my ears. Her furious eyes won't let me go. Say something light to her, something to make it all right so we can talk in a friendly way before she leaves me alone, so she'll call me dear again when she says goodnight. "You're sounding Southern," I said and kind of laughed. *"What all,* that's Southern, isn't it?"

Someone outside was whistling "Some Enchanted Evening." The door banged open. *"You will see a strang-*

ahhhh, naughty-naughty-naughty, chatting after lights out."

"Hello, Dear. Come in, shut the door, there's a breeze."

Laura attacked the remainder of my unpacking. "Leave it to me," I said. "Did you bring the Marmite?"

"Loads, in that bag."

"Cool."

"Does Patrick like the plans, Laura? You must show Robbie tomorrow. It's very clever, Robbie, because they're going to make the attic into a whole floor for the children, bring them up from below. Isn't that right, Laura?"

"Certainly is. He loves all the ideas and he said *yes-yes-yes,* like that. It's a huge unused space, Robs. Fabulous."

"Do you know what I'd like, girls?"

"A cuppa tea," we answered, Laura and I, together. While I was making it, Esther asked me, "And how are your chests, Robbie, tell us all about them?"

We shrieked so loud that Patrick, taking a breath of night air, called, "Hey, you all okay in there?"

"Just saying goodnight to my loonies here," Laura shouted back and sat herself on the arm of Esther's chair to hug her. "Isn't she sweet, our little Esther? Do you think she does it purposely?"

"Don't be silly. Robbie knows I mean her patients."

"Oh. Right. Only I was going to say *Still as flat as Laura's chests* but I can't. Because look at you."

Laura stroked her left breast. "I know," and waved away the tea. "Hate that stuff at the moment, just the thought of it makes me—" She did not finish.

I set the cup back on the table. Finished for her.

"Throw up. Right? Just the thought of tea makes you want to throw up. You're pregnant."

She beamed long enough for me to jump in with her, jump into the beam and congratulate and say all the things people do at such news when all is right for it. Only I did not jump in, and there was a silence. Not a long one but something of our show had gone when next we spoke. I was first.

"Does he know?"

"What do you mean *does he know* like that? Of course he knows, Robs. He knows, Esther, doesn't he?"

"You told me you told him, Dear." Feeling around for her stick.

"No, don't go yet," I said but could not think of anything to add.

"Say you're glad, Robs?"

"He didn't mention it to me."

"It's a secret. We're not telling the children or Raoul or anyone for a month or two yet. I'm only just."

"Is that why?"

"Why he asked me to marry him? No, he asked ages ago. You know that. I've only just found out and I wish just once, *just once* you could accept things for what they are. Can't you see we're happy? Can't you? Are you blind?" More anger in her face than I'd ever seen before.

"I'm going to bed, girls. I think we all should."

They left. I sat on the bed—don't know what I thought—sat on the bed vaguely surveying the turmoil of contents from my case. How was it possible Laura could have spread so few things so far in so short a time?

I nearly laughed but—never so angry, Laura. I arranged my things and remembered how meticulously I'd done that the last time, the first time, I'd been here in this cabin, itching to ring them back home. *I've arrived, I'm safe.*

A knock at the door, it was Laura. She'd been crying. "Sorry, Robs, sorry-sorry-sorry. I didn't mean it. You know that, don't you?"

"Course, silly, course I do." We held each other until she ruffled my hair. I would have ruffled hers back only its new tidiness discouraged me. She washed her face. "Do I look okay? Would he know? That I've been crying, I mean?"

"You look good. But can I just ask something, so I'm clear, that's all, okay? Who does know and who doesn't?"

"Right." She slumped against the wall to count off on her fingers. "Patrick does." Twisting her fingertip into the corner of her mouth, nudging the air with her elbow. "Well course he does. And Esther knows but *absolutely* no one else. And, listen, Patrick doesn't know that Esther knows because she wants him to know she knows only after we've been married for a bit longer. Don't ask me why."

"Wouldn't dream of it."

"Robs?"

"What?"

"Please say you're glad?"

"I am. And everything's going to be okay. Right?" It was all she wanted.

"It is, Robs. It really *is* this time. I know all the things you're thinking. But nothing's ever been like this before and I have the strength to make it good, keep it good. Believe in me, okay?"

Raoul's room was unaltered: the sconces sprouting their sago palm, the draped bed, the watercolor of the night-blooming cereus high on the wall above the piano from where I'd once lifted it, a fire burning behind the patient Virgin. I sat to one side of her. Raoul had pushed his own chair up close, in front of me, and was reaching forward to take my hands in his and read my eyes for longer than I usually allowed anyone to do. "Taken no man to your bed yet, I see."

"So sure?"

"Uh-huh. Time you did so. It's not healthy, you know, leaving such things."

"I'll bear it in mind."

"Your mind's not the place, *huh.* 'Scuse me. So." He pulled a leather case from his inside pocket, withdrew from it one of two cigars. "Mind if I do? It's not Sobranie. No more Sobranie. I've taken to these boys now since Laura's given up. Mutual support, I don't tell her about these." He rolled it, clipped it, wet it, held it in a match until his fingers scorched, and lit another until his fingers scorched again. Finally, suffused in smoke, he settled back, lids half-closed. "So. My guess would be summertime."

"For what?"

"The baby, what else?" He grinned back at my expression.

"Are you glad?"

"Patrick is *happy*. The only word. Laura the same. There's a fervor to it all I don't understand. Maybe because I'm old, forgotten such feeling. But I watch. Lord made me a passenger, not a driver. Can I ask if you're taking your mama home with you when you go?"

"I'd like her to come."

"Uh-huh."

"You don't get along, you two, do you?"

"The grain of sand in the oyster. Your mama disapproves of all men, I guess. A disappointed woman is usually critical. To her, we're all heroes or scum."

"Does she disapprove of Patrick?"

"He's still a hero."

"Are you exercising, like I showed you?"

"That's my business. No excuse to mess with my limbs anymore, Miss Tiddly."

"Would you like a treatment?"

He sighed and rubbed his right thigh. "I guess I would."

All the rush of Christmas followed. Patrick and Laura in their firmament of children and plans and secrets and hopes—no, wrong, not hopes. There was nothing so vague, so dependent on faith as hope. There was absolute, unfailing certainty in their process. Laura was always observing too, judging what might be at play between the children, ready to diffuse jealousy, insecurity, squabbles. Whether she was dealing cards, grooming Moley, brushing Marie's hair, whatever the activity, she never missed a beat of what was going on between them and adjusting the mood. It was Laura who established teatime at Janvier. Teddy and Marie told me they couldn't believe, at first, that four-thirty in the afternoon, every day of the week, was a good enough excuse in itself for a feast of sandwiches, biscuits, and cake. I longed to ask Laura, *Where did you learn all this, these subtle skills of family life?* But didn't in case I should do it again, spoil things by reminding her of our history—of the good times, I say, the good times—that she, and Esther, had chosen to forget. And, by forgetting them, so removing them from me as well. Undiscussed, unshared, these things die. Don't they?

I remained for ten days. Long enough with a family so involved in their own present and future plans. Esther spent much of her time in the kitchen with Theresa. I overheard her once, "—so just tell him you don't *want* him sitting up all night drinking with Raoul." Charles would have been in the tack-room with Lenny.

I wanted to warn her against stirring long-founded understandings between Theresa and Charles and Raoul, knocked on her door one afternoon while she was resting. When I pushed, it gave two inches and no more. "Esther?"

"Robbie? Wait, wait. I'm coming."

She was over three minutes removing a piece of furniture before the door was cleared, and then it was to tell me, "I'll come over to you, Dear. Go on. Don't wait for me."

"No, it's all right." I pressed in to see the interior of the cabin that had so delighted her once. It was completely rearranged. No, *arranged* is not the word. All the furniture had been shoved to one end: the bed lengthwise along the window, with the chest of drawers at its foot— this is what partially blocked the cabin door and had to be lifted aside for access. The wardrobe was beside the bed, too close, again, for its doors to fully open. The bedside table and chair were at either side of the wardrobe. The rest of the room had been cleared of its rugs and lamps and pretty things. She had achieved the look of a makeshift living space in a storeroom, such as a night-watchman, or undiscovered vagrant, might set up.

"What have you *done* in here, for goodness sake?"

"Don't sound like that. I just didn't want to mess up their nice things. So I've put them safely away. You know how things get messy so easily and I'd hate to be responsible for, for—and I like seeing out of the window first thing. I can reach the drawers, and the wardrobe, from my bed you see, like this"—she demonstrated. "It's very convenient."

I pointed to her suitcase gaping on the other single bed shoved into the far corner. "You're packing. Does that mean you're coming with me? Because you could help me choose the house and—"

"Of course I'll help you choose the house. When I come back. But not this time, Dear, because I can't leave Laura. Not with her having the baby and needing help."

"So why are you packing?"

"I'm not. I just like to keep my things handy and I don't want Patrick to think I'm too settled in. Overstaying my welcome."

It was disturbing. Not funny or sweet, which Laura thought it was when I tried to talk to her about it. "Of course I've been over there. That's how she likes it. It doesn't matter, Robs. She can have her room how she chooses, can't she?"

My next visit was in June. I have a vision of Laura, calm, confident, gloriously pregnant. Her hair is already past shoulder-length and she's holding it up off her eyes to call to the builders on the roof some instruction about the pastel-stained windows being set into the frames on the new nursery floor. "I must have the children sleeping upstairs, Robs. It's not right they should be below-ground." Patrick had been there when she said that, vigorously agreeing, shocked that he could ever have been so insensitive to allow it. I didn't point out that they'd been level with the ground, and not below it, and free to run on the grass first thing. Esther had been there, too, listening, saying nothing, smiling, observing things made right, which, in her discarded past, had stayed wrong. "And it's going to be beautiful, Robs, our nursery floor. A room for each of the children, set around a huge play-room, and the colored-glass windows too. Imagine how the sun will shine through on us, pink, yellow, green. I don't want any blue. Blue's sad. Can't risk sad."

Will, Teddy, and Marie appeared always to surround her, follow her everywhere. They were fascinated by and protective of her condition, fetching her cushions and tisanes and requiring her to be still awhile to play an-other game with them. When Laura was resting they focused on Esther instead. Lying on the swing, she held their attention with her stories.

"—so I crept upstairs and into the twins' bedroom.

There was the dressing table all covered in lace. I climbed on the stool and found the lipstick, just like before. I was smearing it all over my face when mother came in and shook me and boxed my ears."

"She did what?"

Esther mimed her fists banging over Teddy's ears. "Only much harder than that. I couldn't hear for I don't know how long. But I certainly didn't forget I'd been a naughty girl."

"Your mama *hit* you?"

"It served me right. I never disobeyed her again. She could have lost her job and then where would we have been?"

"You were only little, GrandEst, you didn't know."

"Oh but I did. Or I should have. I had no business there, especially with Mother no more than a tweeny. That's a maid who's not allowed in the drawing rooms or the family bedrooms at all, except to lay the fires. She cleans the stairways and halls and senior servants' bedrooms, that's all."

The children shivered for her, and hugged Esther, and moaned, "Gaaaaad," patting her and smoothing her, reassuring that she was far away from this kind of treatment. None of that would happen while *they* were around to see. And Esther was amused and detached and content.

Should Raoul have come upon them like this he'd turn right around the way he'd come. More than once I'd seen him below where we were on the verandah, raising his head, as if sniffing the wind, and deciding on another route into the house. If he arrived inside the house behind the French windows, and paused to listen with his hand resting on the inside handle, he would still go away again. Not bother with company.

One time he did open the door and crossed the verandah to stand at the rail, scratching his behind through his caftan while he considered the folding day. Esther tried to pretend not to have been disturbed by his presence. But she was and concluded briefly, "So that's enough of my nonsense."

"No, go on, GrandEst."

"Go on, Granny Esther. Did Mr. Dickens tell you about Pip and Miss Havisham? Did you help him with the stories?"

Raoul stretched his hands on the rail, spoke over his shoulder, "I can only say, Esther, that I congratulate you."

"On what?"

"On your constitution, that's what. It's my understanding Mr. Charles Dickens, the author under discussion I take it, died in 1870. Which would make you—five, you say you were?—one hundred and thirty years of age at this point. Or am I wrong?"

The children clamored in her defense. "So what? So what?" And Laura dismissed him, laughing. "You *are* a naughty man, Raoul."

I don't know why I minded so much. Only I saw the look on her face.

Laura had composed her idyll there at Janvier, with Patrick and the children. And she never failed to remind me that I had a place there among them whenever I chose—which was every Christmas for a week, every summer for a month. Life continued this way for three years. I would walk the same places at the same times of day—the levee at dawn, to wait for the fishermen, sometimes they'd pass, sometimes not, and down past where the magnolia towered, to the barn, lively now with ponies for the children along with the mules. Sometimes in the early hours, if I wandered outside, below Raoul's room, I heard him in conversation with Charles—the way I used to in my own early days at Janvier. Then on returning to my cabin I might see Theresa out on her stoop. "Hi Theresa, not sleepy?"

"Guess not."

Sarah was born three weeks after I left, in that first summer. The changes to the house had been completed. The world was ready to receive her. We wouldn't meet until Christmas, Sarah and I. And when we did I found it good to hold a baby again, already six months old. By then Will's accent had a Southern lilt—Laura's too, more the fall of the words than pronunciation.

I bought my house the following spring. A Victorian terrace house in Wandsworth with three bedrooms and a garden. It was already May when I received one of Laura's rare telephone calls.

"Robs?"

"What? What is it? Is Esther all right?"

"Yes. How are you? Tell me what's new."

"Is it Raoul? How's Raoul?"

"Honestly, Robs. He's the same as ever."

"Can I speak to him?"

"He's not here, is he?"

"Don't get cross. Nothing much this end. Busy. Going on a seminar in Eastbourne this weekend."

"Cool," whispering aside with the receiver covered, *"Going to a seminar in Eastbourne. A seminar on what, Robs?* No, go on. What? Stop laughing, Silly. Tell me."

"Chests." And I heard her laughter through my own.

"Why are you calling?"

"Tell me more about you? Come on. There must be something."

"Well there is something. I've bought a house."

"Brilliant. Why didn't you say? *Guess what? She's bought a house.* So whereabouts, Robs?"

"Wandsworth. You'll have to come over and stay when I'm ready. Tell me something about you."

"Well—well"—so there had been a reason for the call—"it's just that, just that I'm pregnant again"—a background cry of *"Whooeee,"* as well as the children's voices, then I knew she had been speaking in a roomful of people all waiting for her to make the announcement to me. The receiver was passed around the family so that I spoke to each in turn.

Charlie was the baby she was carrying then, to be born in October. And for a second Christmas running I held a new baby. I tried to warn Laura, "Why the hurry? So many babies so fast. You'll get ill." Only why listen to me? What did I know? Honestly, what did I know?

I had been settled back in my London routine for some weeks when I received a letter from Raoul:

My dear Robbie,
I write with sad news. My Allie has died. She died
last night in her sleep, as gracefully as she lived. She
always knew the things I didn't say, thereby made me
lazy, I guess. One tiny thing to blame her for and so
ease my pain of missing her. I wish it could be so. She
was a rampart of my life. Now the walls are coming
down. If you were here we'd take a drink together and
speak of her, wouldn't we? We'll do that in the sum-
mer when you come? You will come, won't you?
Raoul

Why wouldn't I come? I always did. But a doubt was
there. Just as if he knew, the way Allie used to know, all
manner of things.

They say one does nothing by accident, yet it is difficult to believe that the day before my fourth summer
visit to Janvier I purposely stepped off the curb into the
path of a courier cyclist, causing a taxi to crash into us,
crushing my skull. The cyclist's face was horribly cut—I
saw his scars months later at the hearing. The taxi
driver, who was carrying no passenger, was relatively
unharmed.

The operation to my head was very soon after the
accident, although I have no recollection of any event up
to or emerging from the anesthetic. I'd find myself lying
awake listening, seeing the life of the ward around me
before falling, softly, back into fabulous dream. I collected voices and visions that became distorted as I journeyed with them back and forth between unconsciousness and something just this side of waking. Among the
voices was Esther's, warm and broken, and it filled me

with longing. Esther's voice—*I don't understand, I don't understand.* And one of the visions was a young Esther in the doorway filling our nursery with the scent of outdoors and night and the world of adult enterprise, incomprehensible, thrilling. Rain glistens on her round black velvet hat with the tiny silk balls dancing around the crown and rain glistens too on her skin. She will turn and leave—*Too late—asleep—fast asleep*—my bed giving to her weight as she reaches for my hand. I want to speak to prevent her from leaving—she leans to kiss me, her cheek smells of the elements she brought with her, the outdoors, the mystery, the night and face powder—and she pulls back, her face stiff with horror. *Seventh grade—to tell you he caught a sac-á-lait at last—we call her 'Miss' Moley now because she's had puppies so she's referred to with respect—Nurse, nurse, I saw her smile. She smiled.*"

I opened my eyes to find Esther beside me, lined and tanned and luminous. Foreign, somehow, and not as I knew her. "It's all right, Dear, I'm here. I came right away."

She told me she had been allowed to sleep nearby in a cubicle off the intensive care unit. When I was moved to the general ward she settled in my house, although I hardly knew how because she appeared to be constantly by my side, speaking softly of familiar things, my house and Will and Laura.

On the day they removed the bandages from my head, Esther approached my bed with her hands pressed against her mouth.

"What? What's the matter? Do I look horrible?"

"No, Robbie, of course you don't. You couldn't. But,

my goodness me"—coming to terms with her amazement before sharing it—"you could be Laura there. As she was when she liked her hair so short."

After she left, I picked up a mirror the nurse had laid on the bedside cupboard—"Take your time to have a peep. Just so's you know you don't look like something out of *Star Trek*, Love. Only look if you want to"—and I saw a face cut and bruised, head shaved. Laura.

Esther collected me on the morning I was discharged. In the taxi home she reached shyly for my hand—shier than she had been in the hospital. "Robbie, I'm in the little bedroom at the back where I found you'd put all my belongings. You don't know how happy I was to find them. The stools and so on. Thank you for not throwing it all out. I've had such a lovely time sorting through." Her hair had something of its old disarray. At that moment, she was cruising a strand around the top of her head in search of a pin.

More weeks passed. I remained mostly in bed, sleeping for long periods during the day. Whenever I woke Esther was always there, not too close, but close enough to reassure. She prepared lunch for us both and served it in the garden during those hot days, with delighted attention to detail. A baked potato became a feast in its starched napkin with the tray arranged just so. Afterward I would lie down again in the cool sheets—which Esther changed every day—and there I would sleep, drifting now and then towards wakefulness without breaking through, vaguely aware of Esther beside me. Vaguely aware of gladness.

Once, as I lay there, my sleep a river running around

sounds—lawn mower, dustcart, the squeak of a neighbor's gate—I was drawn to a surf of urgently whispered words. The troubled unwinding of my own mind, is what I believed it was, until I realized Esther was seated nearby muttering to herself. I half-opened my eyes to see her on her upright chair, inclined forward as if communicating with someone in authority. *"Let her be all right, please let her be all right."* She secured the hem of her skirt across her knees. *"Don't take her."*

"Mummy?"

"Hello, Dear." She smiled instantly. I pressed down the pillow to see the part of the room she had been addressing: the rug with sunlight on it coming through the window, shadows of the blowing curtains.

"Was that a lovely sleep, Robbie? Sleep's the best thing. You look so much better. I've made some lemonade, here. Get up slowly now. Nothing to hurry for, it's only us." She was the old Esther again, the real Esther in a muddle of unmatched clothing retrieved from those boxes, and her hair was precariously pinned.

"Look how well my lavender did. I bought that when you were in hospital, and the rosemary there. They've done well for their first season. They'll be double that size next year. The man next door gave me a rose he's grown from that lovely one on his front. The one we've admired, you know. He asked after you and told me how you'd helped the lady over the road with her arm. I told him you preferred chests. Lungs, I said. Not chests. Told him they were your specialty."

"Like in a restaurant?"

"What?"

"Nothing," only I couldn't wait to tell Laura about the man growing things *on his front* and my *spécialité de la maison.*

"I'll start feeding the birds next month if it gets much colder. Mustn't start too soon though or they become dependent."

Autumn and Esther had stayed. We never spoke of her leaving. "I'll start work again in January," was my only reference to the future, and I watched her concerned face, how she scanned my eyes, my eyes, then the air around my head as though that might reveal something.

Laura telephoned every day and I would observe Esther in the exact posture I had pictured on all those occasions when I was the one far away: She sat well forward on the sofa, poised for flight before lifting the receiver with her fingertips, straining her head to the angle imposed by her own right hand, while her left hand beckoned distractedly for me to come and take over. "No-no-Dear-I-said-Robbie's-much-better-quite-her-old-self. What? Oh-oh, Laura you are naughty"—covering the mouthpiece delicately to reassure me, "She's only joking, you know what she's like"—then back to the receiver, "I'll-put-her-on-Laura-Dear-no-yes wait a min ute."

The first time I was well enough to grasp the receiver from Esther, Laura was still talking, ". . . no but, Esther wait, don't go, just answer will you, when are you coming back?"

"Who me?"

"Oh, Robs. I thought you were still Esther."

"No I'm still me."

"God, Robs, it's been awful. We've been so worried about you. Is there any left?"

"Brain? They scooped some off the road."

"Do come for Christmas. Esther won't commit. I miss you both so much."

"Is Will there?"

"No. All out." This was followed by a familiar ejection of breath.

"You're not smoking again, Laura?"

"Just one. Now and again. You are okay, aren't you? Joking apart?"

"Really. I just get tired and that'll stop too. Complete recovery, the man tells me."

"Could Esther come before Christmas, then. Do you think?"

"Ask her yourself, she's just in the kitchen. Guess what she's been doing?"

What she had been doing was sticking another layer of plastic on one of Bud Flanagan's stools. "Mummy?" I shouted and heard for the first time what I had been calling her, concluded self-consciously, "Laura wants to say something."

"Send my love to Will for me, Dear, will you?" she called from the kitchen, and the garden door banged shut.

"She says love to Will."

"But can I speak to her?"

"She's gone outside." How well I understood the silence that followed.

"I want us to be all together again, Robs. It's been
ages. You don't know how long it's felt because you've
been ill. It's been ages."

"How are the children?"

"Oh fine, fine." There was impatience there and she
must have heard it herself and added, "No they're sweet,
really. Will's always going on about you and Esther."

"Got to go, Laura, sorry. It's that tired thing, headache
and stuff."

"Christmas? Say yes?"

Of course we said yes. A week or two before our
departure, Esther began to inquire, "You will be all
right, won't you Dear?"

"What do you mean? I'm coming too, remember?"

"Yes but," she would stop whatever she was doing, and
as though there were a point I hadn't grasped, one too
subtle to explain, she would finish. "Yes, of course you
are. Silly of me. Course you'll be all right."

She packed and repacked her possessions—the ones I
had arranged when she was still at Janvier, and she had
rearranged, as I knew she would. She returned everything to the old suitcases, the same cardboard boxes, se-
curing them with the same lengths of string, each cob
bled from several pieces knotted together to make one.

"Why don't you leave your things as they are? I promise I won't throw them out."

"I don't think so, Robbie, not this time."

Long before we all met up in the holiday crush at New Orleans airport, we heard Laura shouting above the clamor, "There she is, there she is, Patrick. I see her. Look at Robs's hair. Over here, Robs. This way."

Esther gave my arm a squeeze. Such a light touch. Yet I recalled it when I had returned alone to England.

We made for the shore of faces beyond the barrier, where Laura's was now bobbing intermittently beside Patrick's. The first thing she did was ruffle my hair the way we used to ruffle hers, before frowning into each of my eyes. "You are really all right, aren't you?" Before I could answer she was asking, "Where's Esther? Where is she?"

"Right here"—tucked behind me in the throng.

Laura hung over Esther in the back of the car while I sat beside Patrick, who was driving. "You look pale, Esther," she was saying. "You must rest as soon as we get back. Robs too."

The ashtray beside me was overflowing and Laura lit up as soon as the doors were slammed shut.

"So much for giving up then?" I half-turned in my seat.

She was holding Esther's hand. "Well it's okay now, see? We've had all our babies haven't we, Patrick? He's still not smoking, though. He's made of stronger stuff. Aren't you, Darling?"

He winked into the rearview mirror. His eyes slipped across to me. He knew I was trying, even at that stage, to assess the nature of the change. Because there was a change. So slight. So slight. Imagination, probably. Long trip. Tired.

Esther was gazing off to her right at, I suppose, the lights of the oncoming traffic. That is all there was to see. Laura reached to touch me.

Patrick said, "So, anyway, welcome back to both of you, eh? Have I said that yet?" His enthusiasm was different too.

Our headlights shone up Will, who was balanced on the gate to meet us. He was seven years old and taller yet. His limbs were temporarily outgrowing his body, so the others called him Spiderman. He slipped down to run beside the car, holding my hand through the window. Patrick stopped for me to climb out. As we neared the house he stopped and I looked around to see what had caught his attention. It was me he was staring at. I knelt down for him to close his arms around my neck and he gripped me hard until we heard voices. "Will? Robbie? You out there still?" And the sound of Teddy and Marie's running feet, Miss Moley barking.

We climbed the stairs to the verandah towards the tree within, resplendent as ever. Raoul had selected his station beside it, his hair—was he using henna now?—caught into the thinnest red ribbon on the nape of his neck. I came home to his embrace. He released me and inclined his head, confirming that later, yes later, we would talk as we always did once the hurly-burly of arrival was done. Sarah was two years old and Charlie one. They contributed as much as anyone to that hurly-burly, without any clear memory of who I was. Not then. Not in those early days. They were Laura's satellites and twinkled with fury if their fingers were uncurled from the folds of her long skirts, refused to be dealt with by anyone else unless she first covered their tiny faces with kisses and muttered promises.

The ceremonies of Christmas—carols around the tree, Christmas Night bonfire, roasting chestnuts—meticulously orchestrated by Laura on previous years, were conducted this year by Patrick and Raoul. And more than once I found Raoul reading to Marie, making fishing flies with Teddy. He even managed to distract from a tantrum with his hunter watch, spinning it at the end of its chain, because Laura wasn't there, wouldn't come to bath her. Wouldn't come because she was with Esther, who could no longer quite keep up with Laura and all her tasks. "You go, Laura Dear. Robbie'll help you. I'll be along in a minute."

"No, I'll stay with you. Robs? Robs? Could you manage the babies without me?"

Other times Laura found it as hard to leave me. If Theresa called her for help in the kitchen, "Come too, Robs. Please be with me. Esther's resting again. I'll teach you the secrets of Theresa's chicken stew. Promise."

When Laura and Patrick were invited to dine with friends in the city, she said, "Not if Robs can't come."

I could have gone but did not want to. As if strung between Esther and me, Laura was anxious for whichever one of us was out of her sight. Then there was the supper when Sarah picked up the glass spoon Patrick had used to mix his cocktails. She was chiming it on the rim of her drinking glass. Laura had removed it from her fingers once, twice, in that absentminded way mothers monitor their little ones' behavior while speaking to another. Sarah retrieved the spoon each time and continued—continued until Laura suddenly snatched the glass from the table, smashed it to the ground, yanked the spoon out of Sarah's hand—Sarah, white, white, silent, and rigid—and snapped it in two, yelling, *"Stop it damn you, Damn you and that noise,"* then shrank, curled her head under her hands. "Robs? Robs, help me . . ."

I held her and rocked her, tried to bring her back, have her how she'd been, where she'd been now for so long. Long enough to believe the past really gone, as Patrick— as she—had always said it could be.

"After your mother left to be with you, Laura got nervous. Pat and I assumed she was tired, you know, having her babes so fast an' all. Tried to make her take a trip over, see you both, only she wouldn't hear of leaving them. I watch her sometimes, Robbie, and I see confusion there. If she catches me at that she smiles like she does and, hell, I can go on believing there's not a single cloud in her sky. What about yourself now? All healed up."

"Yes. No, Raoul, don't," he was closing in for the ritual eye inspection.

"Uh-uh. Got to keep abreast of things. Come on, look me in the eye. There now. Damn it, woman, still taken no man to your bed. It's a crying shame and if—"

"May I come in?" Patrick leaned through the door. "Laura's fallen asleep on the bed between Sarah and Charlie." He pulled a hassock near the fire, accepted the brandy Raoul poured him. "Robbie? It's just that she's weary, right? I don't have to be afraid, do I?"

Laura slammed into my cabin, lit a cigarette, cupped her elbow, and paced. "Sit down, Laura. You're making me nervous."

"I'm fine. Fine. She's asleep already. Esther is."

"Of course."

"I know but—but other times she would be happy to sit up and talk about the old days. We always do that. And we haven't once yet, this time, have we? She's different."

"Just older. That's all. I think that's all. We have to be patient. My accident shocked her quite a lot."

Laura collapsed on the side of the bed, covered her eyes. "Jesus, Robs, it was horrible. The thought that you might not be there anymore. Not *be*. Just not *be*. I couldn't go on, you know. If that did happen, if it did"— she uncovered her eyes to prove the truth of what she was saying. But the truth I saw in them was a different one.

"What's going on, Laura? What's happening to you?"

"You see it? Oh God, do the others? They mustn't. You must help me hide it, Robs. Make everyone happy. This must be the best. The best of all."

"What must be?"

"Everything. This life. This life. I must make it the best. When Esther went away for so long, to be with you, I began to think things. Things. You know. Those things that happened to us. Damn. Damn. And I was alone again. Without her and you."

"You could have come for a visit. Why didn't you?"

"And leave the children? All my babies?"

"Why ever not? Just for a few days?"

"*Anything* could happen to them. *Anything.* Besides—don't tell, don't tell will you?—but I'm frightened that if I go it'll all vanish. That it won't be here for me to come back to. Now you're going to laugh."

"Has nothing from the past few years given you strength to draw from? This security? Patrick's love for you? He worships you."

"That's why he must never know. You wouldn't ever tell? Things."

"No. But you're not being fair. Janvier is you, now. If you're sad so's Janvier. You've made it work that way. And something's wrong. I knew it right away."

"You did? You did? That's terrible." She lifted the blinds as if gauging the proximity of an enemy. "Well, I won't be sad anymore. I promise. I really do. I'll be happy. You see. All right? Only listen, you must be careful from now on. Very careful when you cross the road. Stop laughing. I'm serious. And Robs?"

"What?"

"I don't suppose you'd stay, would you? You know, stay here? Live, I mean?" She didn't force me to answer. Replied for me. "No. No. Course not. Sorry. Sorry. And don't worry, I won't forget. About *happy*, I mean. I'll make everything lovely again. Trust me."

She was different over Christmas. Esther and I heard her laughter coming from the house even before we reached the verandah carrying our stockings—the oversize stockings, stuffed with gifts, that she had laid on our beds sometime during the night. And not only Patrick, the children, and us, but Raoul, Charles, and Theresa, too, found brimming stockings propped outside their doors. We all gathered in the salon where Laura was kneeling among her five children while they unpacked, exclaimed, and hugged and thanked, and Laura threw back her head to be kissed by Patrick standing behind her. The rest of us circled in their aura. That was the year I gave Will his Spanish guitar. Even before the day was through he was cradling it in his long arms, producing the sweetest chords.

Rain drove us to abandon the Christmas Night bonfire, indoor games instead. Esther and Raoul presided in straight-backed armchairs—she accepted the cheroot he offered her—while the children had us make-believe we were fruits and had to describe ourselves. No one understood the game so they delivered poetry learned at school. Then Will loped into the middle of the room, nervous and determined. "Ah, okay everyone, guess this, Granny helped me learn it."

He arranged himself with the guitar while Patrick created an extravagant cocktail at the far end of the room. Will strummed some chords and, hard though I listened, longing to guess, they meant nothing to me.

Suddenly Laura leaned forward on her chair, chin on fist, and cried out, "You are *too* brilliant, go on, go on," then she jumped up, spun in three turns towards Patrick, had him set down the bottles, and brought him back to dance with her. "Hey, Darling, I can't dance. You know I can't dance."

"You can. You can 'cause Frenchmen do. You're a beautiful dancer and Will's playing our song."

"How do you do, Mr. Right,
Can it be true? Well it might.
I could search the whole world over,
It's like looking for a four-leaf clover
Out of the blue, Mr. Right—"

Esther was clapping her hands and singing too.

"Now I've found you, Mr. Right,
I'll stick by you day and night.
If you were to make advances
And imagined that your chances might be bright
You'd be right, Mr. Right."

Laura called, "Anyone know it? Join in if you know it." Nope. No one did. *"Flanagan and Allen,* that's who. Bud Flanagan and Chesney Allen. No? Still not?"

Raoul touched my arm. "Who's Bud Flanagan?"

"You may well ask. Esther's got his stools."

"That's too bad."

"Esther, come on." Laura beckoned and beamed and not a soul in the world could have said no.

Esther grasped her stick, rose to join Laura, while Patrick slid free. "What's it to be then, Dear?"

"Will, Darling, you pick up with us where you can. All right? *Music, Maestro, Please."*

"Lovely. My favorite." Esther linked arms with Laura. Too stiff to move much, she swayed while Laura stepped left to right, raising her leg music-hall style the way they had—the way they had—a long time ago in my kitchen.

Just in time I called, "You're both mad," before they broke into song and they answered, "No *you* are. We *all* are. *Hooray.*"

> *"Tonight I mustn't think of her*
> *Music, Maestro, please"*

"Well done, Will. You *are* good. Isn't he good, everyone?"

> *"Tonight, tonight I must forget*
> *How much I need her.*
> *Oh Mr. Lieder, play a simple melody,*
> *Ragtime, jazztime, swing,*
> *Any old thing to ease the pain*
> *That solitude can bring."*

"That that Flanagan again?"

"Flanagan and Allen, Raoul."

"Uh-huh. Seems I know it from somewhere." He hummed along, even remembering some of the words. Patrick, Teddy, Marie, the babies, and I swayed and clapped our hands to what was, after all, a sad song:

> *"She used to like waltzes*
> *So please don't play a waltz.*
> *She danced divinely and I loved her so*
> *But there I go—"*

Of all the times, all good times, I don't remember
ever seeing Laura happier than that night, accompanied
in that happiness by the rest of us. Much later, when I
was nearly asleep, she crashed into my cabin telling herself to *"Shhh shhh, pull yourself together girl.* Robs, you
awake? *Bugger what was that? What's that suitcase doing
there?"*

"It's on its rack where it belongs. Turn the light on
before you smash up the room."

"No. No, it's fine. I just wanted to say, Robs, that I was
wrong. That it *is* all right. It *is* all like it was before.
Nothing's changed. Everything's going to be lovely forever. 'Night. Goodnight."

VIII

ESTHER

Esther didn't return with me. Through the early months of the following year I worked on my house, repainting the sitting room, laying tiles in the kitchen. That's what I was doing when I recalled the way she had touched my arm in the airport, and I sat back on my heels fitting together images and the glue dried out on the floor around me. I bought a greenhouse, prepared the foundations and erected it at the end of the garden with help from the man down the road, the one with "the roses on his front." Laura and me teasing Esther about the things she said. That was the kind of memory that made me miss them and reach for the telephone.

I was ready for a gradual return to work, just the Tuesday-evening practice to begin with. By March I was full-time again and glad of it. April was nearly gone before I stopped to think it was spring—the weather was giving nothing away. Sam sent me a letter telling me that life was kind and good where he was in Arles, and why didn't I visit him soon? So I wrote back suggesting some dates, told him I intended to drive there.

It was a Tuesday night and I returned late and exhausted from the surgery, having left home shortly before seven that morning. I had forgotten to check my messages, was nearly asleep before I remembered and decided to leave them until morning. The decision kept me awake. In the early hours I stood barefoot and irritable in my unlit sitting room, rewinding the tape and watching a delicate disturbance at the base of the curtain as a mouse scuttled back under the skirting board. Raoul's voice on the machine was a pleasant shock. *Robbie, you hearing me? You sleeping? Please call. Guess it's seven-thirty your time, morning, that is.* He must have rung during the previous night, *his* night, that is. The second message was also from him, followed by a third and a fourth. *It's nine your time and I'd like you to call me, please, Robbie.*

Me again, I'm waiting on your call now. This damn thing working anyway?

Nearly twelve hours since I first rang. You gone away? Jesus, get back to me, will you? All I can do is keep on calling.

Whether it was the chill of the dove-dark room I don't know, but I was aware of something altering in me, beginning with the way I breathed. I watched myself dialing that number I knew so well, counting the infinite pauses between clicks down the siffling lines, bringing closer that place, that place. "Uh-huh, Janvier," on the very first ring.

"Raoul?"

"Where've you been?"

"What is it?"

"It's your mama, Robbie. Come on over, Darling."

"What? *What then?*"

"Shh, she's alive. Hear me? Being taken care of at Oschner. A stroke, last night. Our old friend the stroke, hey? Come on over just as soon as you can and take it easy now. She's in good hands."

"You *must* tell me more—" To let go of the receiver was to let go of Esther, let go of as near as it was possible to be right then. If my body could reach where my voice was, all I'd have to do was fly down the steps of Janvier and drive north up Interstate 10 towards New Orleans.

This was a death I'd been preparing for since I was ten and the Crohn's disease struck Esther. Her weight had fallen to five stone. The first suspicion had been cancer. Test followed test and we spent hours on hard chairs in hospital corridors waiting for her name to be shouted at the rows of patients in what was then St. George's Hospital at Hyde Park corner. I would watch her—bare feet pushed back into her walking shoes—following meekly in the wake of yet another brisk nurse for a further test, and I'd cover my eyes from her nakedness through the untied back of a green gown. As soon as she was out of sight I tried to feel what it was going to be like, the world without Esther—where had Laura been then? Several months had elapsed before they'd prescribed cortisone and Esther had soared back to an imitation of health. A part of me, forever ten years old, had never stopped rehearsing for this event, rehearsing the unthinkable loss. Now, unable to replace the receiver—*Put it down Darling and get moving, okay?*—I realized it was unrehearsable.

Throughout the journey with its connections and delays, and waits in places with an atmosphere not unlike those hospital corridors, I tired to register a particular silence. I believed that that was how I would know Esther was gone—I would register a private silence.

Patrick met me. His face was haggard. "No bags?"

"No. How far?"

"No way at all. I booked you a room in Brent House so's you can stay nearby as long as you have to."

I couldn't speak in the car. He reached his hand towards mine but closed his fist instead, returned it to his lap. "You're not too late, Robbie."

It was dim in her room, dim as it had been in my own sitting room as I listened Raoul's voice, as it had been on the ride to Heathrow, and in all the planes and airports since. Or was something failing in me? Esther lay on her back, arms at her sides on the cover. Sleeping, just sleeping. A doctor was writing something on a pad at the foot of the bed. A nurse adjusted a monitor beside it and called softly at Esther's face, "Mrs. Heath, your daughter's here," and turned to me with a pessimistic smile.

I knelt close, slid my hand beneath hers, pressed lightly with my thumb. "Esther? Please? Please?"

The nurse touched my shoulder. "Easy, Honey."

"Mummy?"

"Gently now."

Don't go away, Mummy, don't leave me. Don't go. Esther's lids parted on the lands of her eyes lit by duty and concern. They searched my face until—it was there again, that baffled regret I knew from a long time ago. "Hellooo Baby." Behind me the nurse breathed. "Well, I'll be."

After a rush of tests and checks, finally the nurse leaned over her. "You want some juice now, Honey? Mmm? I'm sorry, that *yes* you're saying?"

"She'd like a cup of tea," I informed from across the room where I had been sent. While the nurse was fetching it I reclaimed my place beside Esther. "Well, you did a good job surprising them, didn't you? I think they'd written you off."

She made a chuckle that didn't leave her throat, her mouth twitched, a tremor ran through the fingers of her left hand, which lay between mine. "You're going to be all right now, Esther, aren't you?" Those signals again but weaker.

The doctor led Patrick and me to a windowless office where he sat with his face close to a file on the desk in front of him. The lamp shone into his thinning hair, left us in shadow. "Amazing," he said, "all it took was the right voice to call her back. Wouldn't come for anyone else. She's your mother, right?"

"Yes."

"I have to tell you, Miss Heath, that your mother has had a massive stroke. A stroke is when—"

"I know."

"Of course. I'm sorry. Mr. Janvier told me you're a physical therapist. Took care of Mr. Patout once he left here, I understand? Boy, we won't forget him in a hurry. Miss Heath, I don't have to tell you, then, that your mother could have another cerebral hemorrhage at any time. She's in a very frail state. On the other hand, we saw something remarkable this night, didn't we? So why don't you get some rest now and let's see what tomorrow brings?"

Night again. It seemed to have been night forever. Below my window, river traffic passed through ruby neon melting in black water. "What time is it?"

"Twelve-thirty. Too late for dinner, I guess. Should I order you up a sandwich? No? Then how about a sip of this? Bought it while I was waiting for your plane."

Clutching a bottle of vodka by its neck, he waved it at the wall and I was reminded of another scene. "Where's Laura, for Christ's sake?" He found two glasses and ice in the minibar. "Patrick?"

"Tonic?"

"Straight."

"Wasn't that the darnedest thing? I mean I talked and talked to Esther. Theresa did too for three hours this afternoon. Your voice is what turned the trick."

"What about Laura's voice? Why isn't she here?"

He set his glass down, pushed up his shirtsleeves and they fell right back. "I guess she's scared, Robbie, that's all. Some of us are at such times."

"Yes but—"

"I know. I know. She'll be fine when she knows your mama's come 'round. It happened after supper. Esther rose to go to bed, kind of coughed and seemed to be having a dizzy spell. I helped her down the stairs 'cause that's what she wanted, to lie down in her own bed. Theresa came on out to help, Charles too. She couldn't hardly walk and I carried her. Called the medical helicopter from her cabin just like that time with her leg. I'll never forget that night." He returned to the window, placed his hand on the unopenable pane. "Oh no, I'll never forget it." And he wasn't remembering Esther or the accident but things I would never know for sure. "Same river, Robbie. Same river passing as passes Janvier. The Mississippi. It was all so fast. When I got back up Laura was still standing right where she'd been when Esther came on faint. By the door, she was, standing there rubbing her arm like that"—rubbing his own arm, he stared at the floor. *"Copter'll be here in a minute, I told her. You want to ride in with her?* She just shook her head, didn't move. I looked in her face. I've never seen such an expression of, well, terror? Terror? I don't know. Wouldn't speak. Only by then the 'copter had arrived and I didn't want Esther to travel in alone just in case, well, who'd want to be alone at a time like that, among strangers? I hate to think how it would be with Laura if Esther didn't pull through. But never mind, 'cause she has, hasn't she? Let's call, shall we? Give them the good news?"

"You heard the doctor. Esther isn't going to be okay."

"Hell, she came 'round. She spoke to you. It's something good. We can tell them that much."

I stared through the window again, hearing him

speaking with Raoul, "—an hour ago? Guess it's better not to disturb her then. I'm staying on over in the office tonight. I can't not be there tomorrow, we're in court at eleven."

He stood with his hands in his pockets. I asked, "Well? What's she doing?"

"Asleep. Raoul said he found her in with Will. Better she comes on out in the morning, right? Robbie, there's a meeting I can't miss tomorrow. I've been away from the office so much and it's a bad time."

"I understand," and I told him what he wanted to hear, and what was true, that he couldn't have done more had he been Esther's own son. The limited dialogue of drama.

The following morning there was a stranger in Esther's sunlit room, propped up in bed, immobile. Someone shriveled and vacant with a gray plait of hair snaked around her shoulder and old, old, old. "Esther?" She didn't respond. I approached and saw she wasn't completely immobile, that her eyes were frantically scanning above, below, as far left, as far right as they could reach without movement in the rest of her body. They searched the ceiling, pausing with suspicion on the light, traversed to the monitor on a trolley nearby and blinked in time with the pulsing green light before sweeping past my invisible presence over to the window, where they rested, and the trauma in those washed-out sentries turned to yearning.

"Mummy?"

Her eyebrows jerked high, half her mouth lifted, and her eyes found me. She burbled a collection of noises that made, "Hellooo Dear," and the tone was the one I'd always known. I found her hands, and her reassuring noises broke into something more. She waited for an answer, tried again, at last I understood: "How's my lavender?"

I talked about the lady at the cleaner's who often asked after her and the man with the roses on his front who helped me with the greenhouse and gave me more cuttings and, "I've any number of seeds coming on in there. I can't wait for you to see it."

"Lovely." I knew—only I would have known—that this was what she had said.

If I stopped speaking, despite my sheltering arm, her eyes took up their search again. *What is it, Esther? Tell me why you're frightened?* I released the loathsome plait, so favored by nurses in England too, and rearranged her hair. Then I rang Janvier from beside her bed. "Raoul?"

"Good morning. How goes it with Esther today?"

"Good. She's right here next to me. I'm going to start some gentle treatment."

"Then she has my sympathy."

"I'll tell her. Where's Laura?"

"Down by the water with the children. I'll have Charles fetch her. Theresa's already on her way to you. Wants to sit by Esther too. Laura'll call you right back."

"Laura'll be here soon," I told Esther.

Another series of sounds: "—busy, happy girl, good girl."

Half an hour passed. I rang back. "Is she there?"

"She's not come up to the house, Robbie. Should I—"

"Leave it. It's all right."

Esther watched with detached interest, vaguely impressed, as I lifted her left arm, her right arm, lifted them to my shoulders, supported them there. I wondered if she knew it wasn't treatment at all, that I wanted to feel her hold me. "Clever girl, clever girl" was the meaning of the sounds she made, and soon I was hearing no impediment. We talked about any number of things, whether they had finished the work at the end of my road, if the rose was climbing into the apple tree, was the mortgage too much after all? Not once did we mention where she was, or why.

I was feeding her lunch when Theresa arrived. "May I, please? Can I feed your mama? I so want to do something, please Miss Robbie?"

As I left the room she was stroking Esther's face, tears flowing free down her own. "You're my friend, Esther, you *can't just can't go,* you hear now? Huh?" And Esther returned distorted laughter and the same reassuring noises she made for me.

I rented a car and drove out to Janvier. Raoul was walking towards me on the drive as I arrived. "Leaving home?"

"Waiting for you, young lady. Guessed you'd be out here soon enough."

"Are the children around?"

"At school. Laura's upstairs with the youngsters. You go on now, I'll be in my room."

From outside the playroom door I heard Laura singing.

"*. . . She cried so when I left her*
It like to broke my heart
And if I ever find her
We never more will part.
She's the sweetest Rose of summer
This fellow ever knew . . ."

Flooded in all the pastel colors of the windowpanes, she was all but lost in an armchair with its back to the door. Two tiny, succulent feet dangled from one side of it and a small dark head lolled at the other. They hadn't heard me enter.

"Your turn, Sarah, go on. *There's a . . .*"

"*There's a yellow rose of Texas that, that . . .*"

"*That I'm going to see.*"

"Look Mama, Charlie's waking."

"Then he can sing too. Go on now."

"Laura?"

The top of her head jerked a degree towards the sound of my voice. Sarah's lime green eyes rose over the back of the chair. "Can I come in?"

With one foot to the floor, Laura swiveled the chair around to face me, both babies collected in her lap. "Is she dead?"

I ran forward, embraced them all. "Hi everyone."

"Well?"

"No, Laura, she's not. Come on, there's nothing to be frightened of. She's still Esther. I've been with her all morning. We've been talking and—"

"Talking? What about? What've you been talking about?"

"Just things, you know."

"Just things," she spat.

"What else would we talk about? Come on." Although I didn't understand yet what I was encouraging her to come on from.

"She's going to, though, isn't she? She's going to die any minute."

"She could. Don't say it like that in front of the children."

"I see. You're getting like her, Robs. Don't say this and don't say that, don't talk about it and it'll all go away. All the horrid things." She resettled Sarah and Charlie on the floor. Charlie chugged off on his hands and knees while Sarah remained clutching the arm of the chair, pushing her smock into her mouth. Laura lit a cigarette.

"I didn't think you smoked up here with the children."

"My children, right? My playroom?"

I sank onto the huge yellow sofa, covered my face. So tired.

"What?" Laura said. I looked up. "Did you say you were tired? Jet lag, I guess. Your cabin's made up like it always is. Why don't you sleep?"

"I'm going back to Esther and I want you to come."

"What for?" Persistent barking reached us from outside. "I hear Miss Moley, Baby." Laura crouched in front of Sarah. "She's shut in somewhere. Shall we go find her? Hey Charlie, you want to come find Miss Moley?" And in the same breath, "No need to cry, Robs, and not in front of the children, please."

"Fine. But smoking's okay?"

"Come on, Sarah, leave your smock alone, Angel." She

hoisted the little ones on either hip, turned to me from the doorway. 'So. See you, then."

"Wait."

"What for?"

"Just, just wait a second. You don't understand, I mean you're right, she could go any minute. You have to come."

"Why? She never came to me."

"When? She's been with you constantly."

"Not when it mattered. Where was she then?"

Only the dog barking and barking. "Not now, Laura, for God's sake. Not after all this time."

"Like I said, see you."

I crossed to the window and waited until she emerged on the steps below, her hands linked with the children's. Then she raised Charlie high to fly him and ran with Sarah, rolling on the grass while the two of them clambered over her. I watched them through pink, yellow, green, through all the colored glass.

"Come in, Robbie, take your chair. That's right, now. Can I get you something?"

I closed my arms around the patient Virgin, rested my head against her. "What's happening in this house, Raoul?"

"Moving on, I guess, the way things always do, like it or not."

"Laura's changed."

He picked a string of amber beads from the edge of the mantelpiece, ran them around his hands. "I've seen it. Since Christmas your mama's gotten weaker bit by bit, the way we old people do. Nothing unusual in that. Only it's made Laura mad."

"Mad?"

"Impatient. Instead of that kindness we all take for granted in your sister, she's been harsh with Esther. Even Patrick's had occasion to step to remind her that's her mama she's speaking to."

I let go of the Virgin. "Poor Esther."

"Is that what you think? I believe she understands. She merely smiles that way she always does, utters pleasantries. Myself, I'd say, *Out with it, young lady, what's your beef?*—English phrase, that, isn't it, *what's your beef,* I like it. And you know I've watched Laura of late, hanging around her mama, kind of weighty and expectant, giving her these long looks I wouldn't care to describe much less receive from a child of my own. That's what Laura'd been doing the other night when Esther was taken so bad. Even from the card table I could see Laura staring dark and hard as if to draw the soul right out of her. I wasn't the least surprised when she stood up and reeled that way, passed clean out into Pat's arms."

"I have to get back. She mustn't be alone."

"Uh-huh."

"What do you mean *uh-huh,* like that?"

He laughed with his mouth closed. "Do you really blame Laura?"

"Her timing's off."

"That so? She knows what's coming and I guess there's things she'd like to understand, be freed. I remember those days when you too—it's not too much to ask at such a time."

"Then she should come, shouldn't she? How can she ask if she's not there to do it?"

"Ohhh, Miss Robbie."

"Don't start, Raoul. When I heard your voice on my machine I hoped it was to say you were coming over for a visit. And now—"

"And I will. I see myself dining at the Savoy with you. I take it the Savoy still stands?"

"Still standing."

He held me awhile and we parted. Only after I'd slammed the door of my car did I see Will staring after me from just beyond the oak grove, Miss Moley spilling from his arms, Miss Moley almost as large as he was. He watched me climb out again, cross to him, crouch down for our eyes to be level, only they weren't. His brown ones, tender as earth can be, were lowered on mine. "Aunt Robbie? Is Granny dying?"

"She may be."

"Mummy says she is."

"Yes."

"I've done her a picture." After a search of many pockets he pulled an envelope from the back of his jeans.

Laura's voice came jagged from the house. "Will? Where are you? What are you doing?"

He pushed it into my hand and ran off.

Only Esther's head was visible there on the pillow. So diminished, so left-behind, unwanted even by the rest of her body. Such an inadequate target for anger. There was no point in remaining beside her, yet I couldn't remove myself from the submarine quality of nighttime hospital, bubbles of magified sound floating from unlikely directions, a greeting truncated by the closing of a door, the thin whine of an electric cart.

Some days later Esther was strong enough to lie on a day bed by the window. The same river view as from my window in Brent House. We ranged the usual topics, although it was becoming harder. We would fall silent. Not once had she asked for Laura. Patrick visited every day and Theresa too, bringing always more drawings from Will, notes from Teddy and Marie. Esther seemed to be satisfied picturing Laura among her little ones, happy in her life. "She'll be giving them their lunch any minute now." "Rest time for the babies, she can rest too. She gets so tired. Having babies makes you tired."

A barrier was wearing thin and I couldn't trust myself not to break the last threads. I didn't like what I was feeling. I would turn away but was forced to look at her again, to find out if she was troubled too. No, apparently she wasn't. So long as she faced out the window she was calm, her expression benign, without expectation.

"Esther?" I watched her profile from deep in the room. Her eyebrows lifted, her mouth made that vestigial smile, but she kept her gaze away from me.

"Esther can I"—*Don't*—"Can I just ask"—*Don't, don't*—"Why did you always send us back to Matthew's house?"

I hadn't bargained on any instant reply, any reply at all, was still dizzy from my own asking when—with a trace of that petulance that had always trivialized her anger, but also as if she had been poised for this question for years—"I had to. He was your father."

I was searching for myself, for a way out of what I had

begun here, when she added so quietly in her buckled voice that I might not have been intended to hear it, "*You* didn't always go."

I stood next to her at the window to share the distraction of the river. She turned her head to me, waiting for me to meet her eyes and understand, and know, this very important thing she was going to explain for the first and only time. I saw the expression I'd perceived, possibly, at my own birth, and on occasions throughout my life—hurt, humiliated, angry, unassuageable. "Someone had to see she didn't get it all her own way."

"Who?"

She let go the short-lived courage that had allowed her eyes to meet mine, nodded at the river as though the answer were there for me to see. "The woman Jane, of course."

"Only, Esther, I was thinking—I mean, I'd like to know, did you ever wonder—did you ever—that things happened to Laura, and—and to Laura, to me, there, that shouldn't have—shouldn't have happened?"

We watched a crane lowering on the far key—I think she was watching that. A great iron hook came down to rest against a crate, then, as if caressing it, searched for the loop by which to yank it from the ground.

"Dirty things, Robbie?" Esther lifted her chin as best she could to gain view of something passing, "I thought as much," lifted her chin to gain view, "Is that a steamboat, do you think?"

There's a flower shop on Bourbon. They have all kinds of flowers I wouldn't imagine. In season, out of

season. I don't know how they do it. I wanted mimosa.
"Sorry, no mimosa. But if it's yellow you want—"
"Yes."
"Got cute daffodils. Miniature kind."

When I returned to Oschner there was a commotion outside Esther's room. Thinking back, trying actually to picture it, all I really saw was the doctor's white coat, one trousered leg disappearing through the door. So it was something about the urgency of his movement then. In any case, before I reached there I knew. He must have sensed my approach, backed out of the room again. "Miss Heath, it's good you've arrived, been calling your room. Your mother's having trouble with," and he gave me information I couldn't take in, "causing very severe pain through her right arm to the"—not a stroke then, not the big one anticipated, something else was going on, her body shutting off, a gradual closing—"the most effective way to ease it would be with morphine, which is what I'd like to administer now. Of course you know that from then on she won't be so lucid and,"

What? What? My hearing wasn't right. "Will you let me through please?" I think I pushed him. He could talk all he liked, vouching safe information he might never have done to a layman as he prepared a syringe at the trolley the nurse had brought in. My knowledge of medicine and the human body, my experience of the process of dying, were of no service to Esther now, no shelter for me. Useless, useless. I reached her just as she was gripped by a spasm that doubled her, left her gasping. It subsided and her eyes floated back, found mine. "Robbie, you're there, Dear. Good girl. Always a good girl. What's happening to me? I don't understand."

You do, Esther, you do, don't let's pretend anymore.

"Do you know what she's saying?" the doctor inquired softly at my side, and I nodded. "So should I continue?" And I nodded again.

She was calm very soon after that, secured into a pain-free sleep. I would bring a cup with a straw to her lips and she drank, never failing to utter some syllable of gratitude, and I would whisper, "Is it a lovely sleep?"— careful with my voice that it should contain no plea to summon her—and she murmured, "Lovely, lovely."

I set the single bunch of daffodils in a vase on the floor, returned to my place beside her, waiting for her to wake. She'd only have to open her eyes to see them. But she didn't open her eyes—

from behind the house a bank of cloud advances on the sun, which is slipping, stretching its light further across the red carpet inside, sliding it to the left, leaving the mimosa out of frame. The car is still not in sight. I go in, close the window behind me, and relay, yet again, the scores of fronds in the new oblong of sunlight, setting each one with such care that not a green stem shows, only a mass of yellow flower, the filaments on each round head responding to an unfelt draft so the whole is minutely quivering, seeming to breathe. If she does not arrive soon those clouds will cover the sun, then it will set behind them and leave my offering pointless.

Esther lay on her side, my arm lightly resting on her

shoulder. I felt her stir, saw her face at the moment her eyes opened and seemed to see the flowers. I don't know. She murmured, "Clever girl."

She didn't speak again. She took a week to die.

"Nothing? Not a single word?"

"She said nothing." It was sometime in the night. I was leaving in the morning.

"So that's how she goes then, without explanation. Just like always." Laura was sitting on the bed in my cabin with her back to me, lighting a cigarette while another still burned in the ashtray. "Why can't you stay awhile, Robs. Spring's so beautiful here."

"I remember."

"You will come later, though, in the summer?"

"Not this year."

"Why not this year?"

"Because I want something different just this once, Laura. I've been here enough this year."

"You weren't *here*. You were *there*, with *her*. That's not *here*, is it? Don't you like Janvier anymore?"

"You know I love it."

"So do it. Stay forever. What's there to go back for anyway? Stay here with me. And with Raoul. He's always liked you better than me."

"Don't be silly."

"I don't mind. Wouldn't stop me wanting you to live here. Please?" She had asked a dozen times already. I'd stopped trying to explain. She said, "So that's it, then, isn't it? That's it. There's nothing safe anymore." She crushed the half-finished cigarette and lit another—as if that mangling of the source of her pleasure, or whatever it was that smoking gave Laura, were as essential as actually smoking. "Robs?"

"What?"

"Sorry but, can you just tell me again, did you say— you *were* there with her—yes, right, sorry. But did you say it was daylight? I can't remember."

"It was daylight."

She was parting the curtains with her bony fingers light upon them—life infinitely repeating itself, I'd seen all this before. And from the beginning, it seems to me now, we were speaking at windows, through windows, and never really to each other. "I wouldn't have wanted her to die in the dark. Have I told you my theory about souls—"

"Getting lost in the dark. You were standing by a window the way you are now. You'd arrived in the middle of the night with Will in your arms."

"I did that a lot, didn't I? Sorry. There's nowhere anymore. We're alone now, Robs."

"You're not."

"Oh yes. Except for you."

"Patrick?"

"You know what I mean."

"Can I ask: Do you talk to him, you know?"

She swung around, stared at my offering hand, saw the past poised there as it always was when either of us held a hand in just that way. "Are you crazy?"

"Why not?"

"And foul him? Foul this place? Shut up, Robbie, shut up, *shut up.*"

I waited. "Only, I don't know—you *know* I don't

know—but it seems to me that I couldn't allow myself to love someone, not fully, unless they knew me, everything. I'd still be alone. I wouldn't feel safe."

"That's it. You have it." We remained with that sad understanding until she added, "So what we have to do, Robs, is find the strength to be what they believe we are, fall in with their fantasy of us, and we'll be all right. And no one will hurt us anymore. Then there's loving going on, you see. And people are happy. Isn't that better than having them know and be repulsed? Turn on you?"

"Sam didn't. He knew and never turned."

"Sam." She recalled his name, marking it, honoring it, leaving it. "We'll be all right, Robs. I'll look after you, I promise."

"You don't have to. I'm fine."

She sat on the bed again to shake her hair free of its pins, sweep it back up, tighter, muttering, "Bloody stuff, bloody stuff."

"You couldn't have more, Laura. I mean, Patrick and the children, the people here, this place. Life couldn't offer more."

"I know that."

"And you've succeeded with your loving theory, haven't you? You've made the joy. They all say that, Patrick and Raoul. Even Allie said it to me once."

She wasn't listening but concentrated on some internal thing, following its course, frowning, assessing. "It's very near," she whispered, then she looked at me. "It's coming near, Robs."

"Why wouldn't you come to Esther, not even once? And didn't let the children?"

"To punish her. And don't look at me that way. I'm not sorry. I'll never be sorry."

"Punish her for what?"

"For leaving us in the dark."

There was movement outside, a knock on the door, and Patrick leaned in, uncertain of a welcome. He need not have been. "Darling, Darling, I'm sorry." Laura flung her arms around his neck, kissed him, gathered his hands and drew him inside. "Here's Robs and me banging on about all kinds of nonsense. Sit down here, I want you very close." She climbed onto his lap ludicrously long-legged and gangling—not unlike Miss Moley spilling from Will's arms that afternoon only days before. She kept slipping and hauling herself back onto his knee. "No, hold me, hold me properly or I'll fall, look, I'm falling off—"

"You big kid." Patrick laughed. And I laughed too. Both of us terribly glad to be laughing.

I arrived home to Laura's voice on the machine. *Hi, Robs, call me when you get in, would you?*

"*Laura?*"

"You're back, then. You're safe?"

"Yes. What is it? Is everything all right?"

"Fine. I just wanted to know you were okay."

"I was going to ring you in the morning."

"What are you doing tomorrow?"

"Don't know yet."

"Will you ring me?"

"Sure."

I sorted through Esther's belongings. Clutches of photographs were slipped into envelopes marked *The Girls, Laura*—this included some ragged press cuttings and a glossy publicity shot she'd had taken when she was seventeen. One marked *Family* contained images of people I had never met. Groups of dour-looking women in pointed shoes, ankle-length skirts, and deep-crowned hats—*The Aunts* was scribbled on the back of this one, in Esther's hand. The only color snaps were of her brother—dead Uncle Philip—out in South Africa. There was one very small, deckled-edged shot of a neat old lady griping a handbag to her breast, squinting against the sun to keep an eye on the camera, *Great-Aunt Violet.* She'd taken care of us, Laura and me. She'd been there when we were little. Esther had never mentioned her death to Laura or me.

The boxes of *Panorama* magazine, the bags of clothing, the burned saucepans, a pillowcase filled with wire hangers—a new one on me, I had found it under her bed—I stacked all this outside my gate without sadness or regret and moved fast enough not to examine the kernel of my energy, something like spite, something like revenge. The dustmen came and heaved the whole lot into the back of the cart and it moaned away, mashing its contents. I spun the car tire into a rubbish bin and hawked the mahogany lavatory seat and Bud Flanagan's stools to a junk shop off the New King's Road. It crossed my mind to tell the man, as I was walking out, "Those are Bud Flanagan's stools"—he was old enough to know the name—had turned with my mouth open to speak and he was ready to listen. But no. Not for an instant during any of this—the lugging, the hauling, the giving away—did I feel the presence of Esther, nor did I sense that forlorn animation with which these possessions of hers had maintained their space in my home—in my various homes—throughout my adult life. The rest of the day was taken up with cleaning my house. My house, which was already clean. I was asleep when the telephone rang.

"Robs? You're there. You promised you'd call."

"Sorry, I forgot."

"You forgot? Oh—oh—well. Never mind. What did you do today?"

"Nothing much. You?"

"I want to talk about you. I want to picture you in your house. Talk to me."

And Laura rang again first thing in the morning— it would have been two or three A.M. her time. "Robs? What are you doing?" She continued this way, sometimes ringing almost every hour, never less than four or five times a day, never wishing to speak about herself, nor hardly the children, but pressing for every dull detail of my life. She knew my habits precisely: when to find me in. If I had been out of the house for any length of time, my machine would be choked with silences—no, it was something more than silence: the sound of Laura listening.

Then there was the business of my holiday. I hadn't

intended to deceive her. I can't believe I didn't tell her I would be away two weeks. But she insisted I hadn't— *You told me a few days, Robs. I counted, I counted. I thought you were dead*—there was no point in reasoning with her—*Why are you hiding things? Why have you changed? You're different. Everyone changes. Why don't people stay the same?*

By autumn her calls had begun to be from noisy places, shouting and music all around. "*Robs? Hi? It's me*—"

"Where are you?"

"*Don't know the name of it. What are you doing?*"

"Go home, Laura."

Go home, Laura. I lost count of how often I told her that. Once, after she'd rung me, very drunk, a man yelling her name close by, I dialed Janvier and Patrick answered, "Hey Robbie, great to hear you. *Kids, it's Aunt Robbie. You can all speak in a moment. Me first.* Only it's Laura you'll want and she's not here right now."

"Where is she?"

"Dallas. Christmas shopping. So she says."

"How is she, Patrick?"

"Wait a minute. *Say, kids, go fix your Uncle Raoul one of those bone-shaking cocktails he likes and shut the door.* That's got rid of them. She's not good. I say she's in Dallas but I don't know for sure where she is. I'm losing patience here, you know that? I'm here with five kids and where's their mother, I'd like to know? I been patient since Esther died and God knows Laura's tried it.

She's changed. Sweet as ever with the children, but with me? Cold, unreasonable. She never speaks of Esther. We do. And that makes her mad. She's said some nasty things. You know what? Her voice is changed. Can't say how exactly. Guess I shouldn't talk this way, Robbie, but you caught me at a bad moment. I've just about had enough of Laura's—jeesum what more can a man do? And she's—" His voice faded and I knew how he'd be sitting then, leaning forward, elbows on knees, massaging his forehead with one finger.

"She's what?"

"I came home the other night and she'd cut her hair clean off. I was tired and it was a shock seeing it all over the bathroom floor and her just standing with these little scissors still in her hand. Nail scissors, can you imagine? And her head like, like a victim of—well, I lost it and said a lot of stuff. Told her she needed a shrink. That did it."

"What did she say?"

"Quite a lot. *Asshole* figured frequently among other things."

"It would."

"We never fought before, not really. And she was violent, Robbie, boy. Sure, she's troubled. I know that, damn it. Always did. But she won't talk to me. Won't let the slightest chink. I can't get in there. She's pushing me too far, you hear? Too far—*shut up, in there, I said I'm coming*. Gotta go. We missed you in the summer. You are coming Christmastime, aren't you? Like you always do? You can't not. You've got to come Christmastime."

IX

THE WOMAN JANE

I stoked the fire, swept sparks from the scorched robes of the Virgin, shifted her forward from the blaze. "Don't you mind the back of her getting ruined like that?"

"Warming her ass at my fire's the only excitement my Virgin gets. Leave her be. Your sister needs help, Robbie. I'd speak myself, only what could I say? For all I respect her, and have come to love her, we've never talked. Not the way you and I talk. She doesn't invite it. And Patrick, why the poor man is—"

"Is letting her fall to pieces before his eyes."

"That's not true and I won't have you speaking of Patrick that way. What should he do? What do you recommend, because I believe you're familiar with Laura this way. More familiar than you'd have had us believe.

Pat's behaving the way his daddy did when Pat's mother's health, state of mind, failed her. He's stood by, wanting her to know that he'll always be there, not requiring her to explain or justify herself. It's a valid form of loving, Robbie. Only he's nearly run out. Since your mother died, Laura's different. Bitter. And of late she's taken to making some excuse about staying with a friend or shopping in Dallas then disappears a whole day, a night. What manner of friend is that? You saw her."

Yes. I'd seen her. As soon as I pushed through the doors from the verandah out of the violet Louisiana evening and there they all were: Patrick and Raoul, Will, Teddy, Marie, the babies, in a chaos of Christmas decorations. Everything begun, nothing finished, and something missing, a vitality only Laura could give, and she wasn't there to give it. Nowhere to be seen. Patrick climbed down from a stepladder beside the tree—a far older man than in the previous springtime. "*Robbie*. I wasn't expecting you till—or was I? Did I forget? Jesus, did I forget to meet you?"

"Nope. Surprise. Got an early standby."

Patrick embraced me so hard I knew not to ask anything, but to combine with them in creating the missing spirit. Raoul marshaled us all. "You're balls, Marie. Will, you're lametta, and Teddy, you can do those fairy folk that hang around the base. Only take care 'cause they're even older than I am." There was a whisper of Laura's organizing facility in the tease of his voice. He had watched her and listened and understood. Of course he had. It didn't quite work. The children were surly. Miss Moley choked herself and nearly toppled the tree when she caught her neck in tinsel. Charlie cut his hand on some crushed ornament, and Sarah fell off the ladder having struggled there with the tree-top fairy in her teeth. She screamed and screamed for her mother. "Will someone call Theresa *please*," Patrick shouted, angry as I'd ever heard him as he bent over Sarah in Marie's lap and Marie rocked her. "It's okay, Daddy. I got her. I got her. C'mon, Sarah, Mama's busy right now—"

Then Laura *was* there, listing in the doorway, her weight on the handle, taking stock of the scene. Even Sarah shut her mouth. Patrick said, "Hey, home at last, eh? Well, close the door, Laura, the tree'll keel over." And I felt them watching me, Raoul and Patrick and Will too—Will's brown eyes too—to have confirmed in my expression what they had witnessed coming about over the past eight months. Laura had lost more than a stone in weight, that ragged mess of hair, which had worked, somehow, when she was younger, but not now with her face so gaunt and lined. There was a fresh cut in her eyebrow. "You better get some Dr. Tichenor for your brow." No one asked where she had been.

It seemed to take a long time, this silent presentation of herself, before she inhaled audibly and became Laura. "Robs, Robs, Darling, I've been at the airport for hours and hours, waiting for you." The lie was embarrassing. I said, "Oh. Sorry."

She held me hard, just as Patrick had, and she wouldn't let go. I directed her attention to the children, who were watching us in silence, and to Sarah in particular, who was especially alert.

"Hey." Laura flung her arms high and collected Sarah, as well as delivering a kiss to Marie and examining the minute cut on Charlie's palm. "Now, it's Christmas, right? Come on, everybody. Will, where's that disc with the carols we like, you know the one? Marie, what about the mince pies? We got to have mince pies while we fix the tree or we'll *starve*. Go ask Theresa, Sweetheart, she'll have some hot. Hey Patrick, no cocktails? No cheer to help us along? Raoul, got the kids all organized, I see. Thanks. Sorry I'm late"—to him she said that, *Sorry I'm late,*—"But I got things. Look"—and handed carrier bags for the children to sort. She issued commands as to where everything should go, the kitchen, the playroom: "No, no, don't touch that one, that's a *big* surprise."

So we joined in her frenetic celebrations. If her attention strayed away from us, we were all ready to prompt with the next ritual, all of which had been established by Laura herself over the past four years—"Hey, chestnut time. Let's roast chestnuts—" "Laura? Laura? Will you come and listen, please? The babies've got a carol for you. They've been working on it. I helped."

Marie stood Charlie and Sarah beside the tree and knelt in front of them to prompt as they sang "Away in a Manger." Will accompanied them on his guitar. I turned to wink at Teddy—who would be finding it embarrassing, everything embarrassed him then—and saw Laura. She watched Charlie and Sarah, sad lines chiseled deep on either side of her mouth. Patrick was too close to her to see what I could. He was smiling and charmed and ready to believe in all of this. She clutched his arm. "Our babies, Darling, our babies," Laura said. The quality of her voice made him pull back, and he saw what was there in her face and took it between his hands and kissed it. "That's right, Laura, our babies. Everything's going to be fine. You'll see." She continued to clutch him, wouldn't let go.

"All right then, how *did* your face get that way? No one else is going to ask." Because there was more than just the cut. Ghosts of bruises had surfaced wherever her makeup had worn thin over the following days. I would have liked to believe it was just the drink—because there *was* that—that she had banged herself on those occasions away from her home, out of sight of her family, when she was drop-down drunk. I'd found her the day after Christmas, scuttled under straw at the back of a stall already occupied by a mule—"You're crazy, you could've been kicked"—then I found something had kicked her unconscious. Not the mule but a pint of whiskey, the bottle gripped fast between her legs. I plunged her head in the trough out back of the barn, hauled her to my cabin, chatting and laughing all the way like a fool, to have anyone who saw us stay away, keep clear, believe we were in exclusive sisterly dialogue. I knew she'd been up to something because until then she had insisted on my accompanying her every moment, just as she had with Esther the Christmas before—"Robs? Where are you going?" if I so much as crossed the room.

If I wanted to be alone with Raoul to give him a treatment or simply to talk, I had to disengage myself from Laura as if from a child, asking her to promise not to disturb us, explained how much Raoul and I valued these times. Even then she usually interrupted, having paced noisily outside the door, entering on any excuse, at the crescendo of our laughter. "I can't bear it out there anymore, what are you both laughing at? Go on, tell. *Do* tell."

I could have left it. I could have pretended not to have noticed her bruises the way Laura would have preferred—the way Esther would have done. "So how did your face get that way?"

"Is there anything to drink in here?"

"You've had enough already. If you aren't going to answer me then I'd quite like to sleep."

"I don't know how they got there. Fell over. I fell over. Look what I found"—pulled a bottle of vodka from the cupboard, poured, could have been drinking water.

"All right, all right. I'll join you." I sat opposite her at the table. We liked to have a table between us when we talked—we always had, Esther, Laura, and me. Then just Laura and me.

She steadied herself. "Thanks Robs. Here. And, sorry. You know. Sorry. But I don't know what's happening anymore. There's no one, is there?"

"You keep saying that and it's wrong. You have a whole world. Why can't you see it?"

"I *know*. I see it and it scares me that I could lose it."

"You could."

I *know*—I know. Don't. But there's something—not this"—she kneaded the air, shot glances around the cabin, encompassing more, everything beyond it, and everyone that was Janvier—"There's something pulling at me. It pulls me, Robs. Won't leave me alone, something digging in right under here"—fingertips buried under her rib cage. "I can't forget anymore. Things. I keep asking and asking why Esther let them happen, and trying to understand all the things I knew, just a chink. That's all. The things you knew too. And it's too late now. She's gone. There's no one anymore. She's left us in the dark forever."

"You have to let it go. We must think of ways, Laura. Remember you said to me once there's only the present and future tenses? That was wise."

"I've tried people, you know. Don't tell Patrick. But I've been to people. Professionals. Fucking shrinks. Cruel and cold. Kinky voyeurs. Fifty minutes and they shove you out, don't care what they've unearthed and leave you alone to handle. All they want is to have you dependent and to *tell*. To *tell tell*. They're as bad as them, those other ones. I see my children's faces. I know I scare them sometimes, how I look. I can't help me anymore, Robs— help me—help me—" Her head hit the table, her eyes, her mouth, her nose, all running, draining. "She shouldn't have gone like that, should she? She shouldn't have left me. Us. And never explain all those things. And pretend. And then just go away forever."

"She was an old lady. She did the best she could when she was alive."

"You reckon?"

"Yes. She wasn't brave. She was frightened of things she didn't understand. That's all. There's nothing more useful than that to say."

"*Well there should be, there fucking should be.* Sorry, sorry. I won't shout anymore. Don't leave me, Robs. I can be brave when you're there."

"There's nothing to be brave for anymore. You're safe. Live for Patrick and the children like you did until Esther died."

"I want to live for you. I want to look after you and make sure that—"

"I live for myself. You don't have to make sure of anything for me because all that's over. It was over a long time ago."

"Not for me it's not. No one can see in and know what it's like. Not if you can't. Stay here with me, Robs. Live with us all here and we'll all be happy and safe and I'll take care of you."

"I can't do that. It wouldn't help. I've got my work. My life."

"You always say that."

"Because it's true. So have you. And you're hurting your children, have you thought of that? What seeing you go down this way could—"

"Don't—you're right. I must hide myself, they mustn't see—"

"That's the wrong way. You must work through it and let Patrick help you, even the children want to help."

"Hide myself—"

"Stop it."

How that particular evening closed I don't precisely recall because there were so many times, so many talks in my cabin.

Marie conducted me to the place they had chosen— the children and Patrick alone, without Laura—for a memorial to Esther. Esther had wanted to be cremated and to have no headstone. We had always known this, never questioned it. Marie led me back towards the house, down the bank of magnolia, alongside the barn, over the earth yard to that melancholy tomb containing the remains of so many Janviers. I hope not, I was thinking, I hope she's not in there. Esther so disliked the proximity of strangers. And she wasn't. On a sandstone plinth at the end of a newly planted avenue of poplar was a bird of bronze, soaring free. I touched the place where her name was engraved, ESTHER, nothing more. No date.

"Daddy guessed that's how she'd like it. He says times and dates weren't a thing with her." We rested on a stone seat nearby. "I come here sometimes and I think about Granny Esther, make like we're having a talk like we did. I miss her. Is Laura sick?"

"I don't think so"—I didn't think so, I didn't think so—"but she's sad and it hurts her and confuses her. Sadness can do that."

"I know."

I was in my cabin. It wasn't yet dark. I heard voices, soft laughter, and went to see something I hadn't seen in a long time. Theresa was pulling open the door of the pigeonnier and the pigeons were strutting out. Charles was nearby throwing his hand. "I ain't never seen the like of that before"—laughing and laughing, slapping his thigh, before walking off, scanning the pines, and Theresa ran to catch him up and have his free arm flung around her shoulders while she touched her hair.

I refused Patrick's offer and drove myself to the airport. "It's better you're here when she wakes." Because Laura never woke before midday anymore. She knew I was leaving.

On the flight back I thought of Will, how he'd draw close to Laura without speaking, seeming to require nothing for himself, but wanting only to feed back some of the root-deep certainty she had given him. His guitar was always with him, kicked about, dragged, constantly played.

I telephoned as soon as I arrived in my house and spoke to Patrick, told him I was safe. Laura was asleep. "Tell her I rang, won't you? You won't forget?" She didn't return my call. I thought that was a good sign.

In February I was offered the chance to head up the physiotherapy department of a new private hospital not far from London. The cottage that went with the job was beautiful, the pay was good. I liked the directors who'd interviewed me. I would be allowed to appoint my own team, and the treatment rooms would be state-of-the-art. The downside was that there would be more administration than I was used to.

I wrote to Raoul for his advice on whether or not I should accept the job. His reply was enigmatic, vaguely piqued, he gave me no direction. I would have asked Laura, only she never came to the telephone anymore, hadn't spoken to me since the night before I left Janvier. No point in sending a letter. She had never answered a letter in her life. Most of my connections in the medical world thought I should accept. When Sam told me over the telephone that of course I should, I drafted the letter, left it unposted. I don't know why I didn't ask Patrick. He rang me once a week—"Just to say hi, Robbie, and how are you, we're all fine just fine. Laura sends her love, she's staying over with Daithan/she's in Dallas/she's asleep. We're all fine, just fine—" I couldn't ask Patrick.

The children had also begun to telephone me. First it was Marie to inquire how *I* was, what was *I* doing, and to ask about my patients, and the progress of my garden, which wasn't great. Whenever Teddy rang it was at precisely the same time in the evening, once, twice a week. His talk was matter-of-fact: "We painted the barn, same color of course. An inch of rain Tuesday, then another inch Saturday night." I don't know if any knew the others were ringing. I think not.

Will's calls were the hardest to manage.

"Aunt Robbie?"

"Hello Will. What are you up to then?"

"Aunt Robbie?"

"Can you hear me?"

"Yes."

"How are you? Will?"

"We're going to clip Miss Moley when the weather turns real hot."

"That's a good idea. She'll be glad about that."

"Aunt Robbie?"

"It's all right, Darling."

I redrafted the letter, declined the job. Visions of Laura kept me awake. When I did sleep, the same visions woke me. Laura searching for the light and her voice telling me there's no one anymore.

Mrs. Hester, Carol Hester, was a woman in her seventies whom I'd been treating at the Tuesday-night surgery since my return to work. Her hands were severely arthritic and we worked to keep them mobile until her name came up for the knuckle-replacement operation. I had never seen such a serene, unlined face in a woman of her age. "You have wonderful hands, Miss Heath," she told me out of the blue after I don't know how many treatments. "Healing hands. I have often wanted to ask you, only it seems a little silly—after all, yours is not an uncommon name—but were you related to a Matthew Heath? A man I knew a long time ago. He was a healer."

I lay her hand in her lap. "That's it for now, then"— my closing signal to her—"He was my father."

"Ah. I'm not surprised. He died quite suddenly, didn't he? You must have been very young."

"Ten."

"I suppose you know what a remarkable man he was. He could heal. My word, what a man. I could hardly raise my arms at all when I first went to him. I'd tried everything. A deformity from birth. He taught me to move. And now you. Isn't that a strange coincidence?"

"I can't heal you. I can only relieve your pain."

"And you do. Thank you, Miss Heath."

"Hello? Hello, seven-three-double-five." The woman Jane's voice was unaltered after all this time. "Who's there?" A rich voice, sure, the voice of a woman not easily rattled. "Who *are* you?" I always wonder at those who address silent callers, at their impotent insistence. "Why don't you ever speak?" As if she suspected there

might be someone with good reason to behave this way. "It's you again, isn't it? Speak to me—"

"I'm Robbie Heath." Quite suddenly I remembered how her nostrils quivered when she was stressed, how they'd be quivering now. "I'm Matthew Heath's—"

"I know who you are"—without surprise or hesitation. "What do you want?"

"I want to see you."

"What for?"

"To ask you things, Miss Johnson."

"What things? There's nothing I can tell you."

"It won't take long."

"I'm very busy."

"Nevertheless." I could press because behind her confidence was a colder tenor. The woman Jane was frightened of me.

"When would you want to come?"

"I'm coming this afternoon."

"You don't know where I live. You couldn't get here."

"I know exactly where you are."

I parked my car outside my old front door. From there I chose a memory to accompany me and walked at Esther's pace as far as the point where she had stopped that night to confirm the name of the side street—*"That woman—she took a place down that way—one, two, then there would be the crescent with the church—four, five roads down—a ground-floor flat in a corner house—bewitched him—her with her arms crossed—giving him courage to turn us out*

At that side street I abandoned my image of Esther

and proceeded alone, at my own speed, turning around once, twice. There could have been a figure back at the corner watching after me. A still April afternoon but cold. No one. No one to know where I was going. There was a telephone booth. I had a longing to ring Laura, had even entered the foul-smelling space but no card, no change. Besides—

Three more crossroads, the crescent, the church, a communal garden to my left, densely green and deserted. Deserted as I felt the whole city to be. One more road to cross. Here was the street with the big houses. There's the one on the corner. Five steps up, the line of bells, the names, J. JOHNSON nearly rubbed away. Moments after I rang there were sounds from inside. The heavy door— which I was gripping as though to hold it shut—was pulled away from me. Wearing moccasins and, always, those trousers, that shirt—his still? his?—the sapless fig- ure of the woman Jane stood, so much lower than I that she was forced to throw her head back, revealing dug-out cheeks and a gap, like Esther's, between her two front teeth. Not allowing her eyes to meet mine, she said, "I saw you coming—towards me. I wasn't going to answer but then—my word, I'd have known you. I would have known your face." As she led the way through to a ground-floor flat, she kept turning to scan my features, avoiding my eyes.

A clutch of dogs, nondescript creatures with mange, rounded on me barking, growling, sniffing at my ankles as I entered. We passed through a cramped hallway into a large room with a bay window overlooking the street. Set in the bay was a grand piano covered with a paisley shawl, stacked with sheet music, books, a vase of dead chrysanthemums. In the corner to my right, behind a studded-leather screen, was a single bed and a washbowl. The air was rank with the odor of the four—no, six—dogs.

"Sit down." She indicated an unsprung sofa. "That's better." The dogs ranged around, snappy and uncertain, glancing at their mistress for signals of my status. She was keeping her distance over by the piano. "Well?" she asked.

"You haven't changed. I'd have known you too."

"No. You were nothing more than a child. But, you, you have his face. It's extraordinary—"

"Not really."

"Why have you come?"

"To remember."

"What? To remember what? There's nothing to remember but him. You never knew him. No one did, except me. We were one. No one else, nothing else mattered." Backlit by the last of the afternoon, she moved to the front of the piano and reached, without looking, to lift the lid. I couldn't see her clearly any longer but felt she was looking at me as she said, "When I saw you out there just now I could almost believe that he—" She interrupted herself to glance over her shoulder, alert as she gave the length of the keyboard her attention. I heard her intake of breath coming, apparently, with understanding or enlightenment. Laying her left hand upon the keys, she released a single note and I was small again, an infant, without language. She sat on the piano stool and brought her right hand to join her left, following them with her ear.

I knew the melody that evolved from that note. I'd

heard it played behind a shut door, the handle of which I couldn't reach. And I'd heard Laura sing it—Laura dressed in black, wet through, pacing in my flat—*What is that tune, Robs? Where's it from?*

"Schubert. I haven't attempted this impromptu for years. Not since the day I heard Matthew was dead. And it comes to my fingers—" She continued to play, watching her hands as though they belonged to another while she murmured. "It all comes back, it's all there, just waiting." She raised her voice to me, "I played this for him so often. It's a call in the wilderness. Hear? Archetypal, archaic. Now this, this"—the music swelled—"It's closer now. More passionate, personal. Matthew took my pain away. I was in a train crash when I was a girl. My pelvis was crushed, my insides destroyed. The surgeons couldn't do the things they can now. My young life was passed in abominable pain. Pain was all I knew until I met Matthew. He freed me. Healed me. And I became a healer too. That was his gift to me. And I freed him from his own weakness. Because he *was* a weak man. Does it surprise you I can say that about him? I wonder if you're familiar with the seductive power of weak men, with their viciousness and their tears? A woman could waste a lifetime, a lifetime—only mine wasn't wasted on him. He was only weak with life beyond his work. The petty demands of others. And with women, of course. But brilliant men often are. As a healer he was supreme and that, that power, is what I loved him for. What I protected and nurtured in him. We worked together. We lived for each other and our work. I'm glad you've come, after all. I want to talk about him, I find I want to."

"But he stopped loving you," I called out, called above the sound of the piano, towards her face, unseeable in the play of the light.

"What?" She subsided as the notes died under her fingers.

"I said, *he* stopped loving *you*. He turned you out the way you and he turned Esther out."

"Esther. Esther. What of *Esther?*"

"She died last year."

"I see." The woman Jane left the piano, came towards me, looked into my eyes for the first time, seized them in her gaze, and repeated, "I *see*, Robbie."

I turned away from her. She approached the back of an armchair—the only thing between us—her eyes lowered now on her own long hands smoothing it. "That's why you've come, then. Death does that. It makes you want to look back. Well, well, so Esther died. And I'm the only one now, am I? She was a timid woman. Frigid too. Not her fault, I suppose, but all wrong for Matthew. She drained him with her insipid neediness. With the whining baby and clutter of prams and high chairs. Domesticity. Still, I did used to wonder, sometimes, how she fared."

I could do this. I could pretend for Esther. "She had a wonderful life, and a happy one. She was loved by everyone. And she died surrounded by her five grandchildren and me. And Laura too."

Her eyes peeled in their hollows at the name—

Then she sees me, the woman Jane. She's never caught me waiting for Laura before. "So it's prying little you, is it? Very well then, miss." She leans down, hoists me to my feet, and Laura keels backwards, does nothing to stop herself, her head bangs the wall, she does not cry though. She is suspended only by her knees between the arm and body of the woman Jane, who has released me long enough to pluck Laura upright by the neck of her nightie and grab my wrist again to drag me, arm-stretched, toe-brushing, to the top of the stairs—

"It was you ringing all those times, wasn't it? You ringing and not speaking. What of Laura, then?"

"She's married, has five children. Two of them are steps. They live in a beautiful place in Louisiana. She's very happy."

"But?"

"There's no *but.*"

"I think so, Robbie. That's why you've come. And I can't help you, you see. I don't know anything. I don't remember anything. I'm an old lady now."

I was tired. I couldn't see well anymore. Her voice was very close, though I knew she hadn't moved, couldn't know of my private failing of the light. I must get out, find that telephone booth. A dog had crept up beside me. "Look"—her voice, her voice—"he's accepted you. Stroke him. Go on, Robbie, do as I tell you. He'd like that. He'd be your friend if you were nice to him. No? Don't want to? Now tell about Laura."

Light was returning. "She's had her problems but she's all right now."

Her interest was ignited. "Problems? That's right, she would have." She circled the chair, sat down, craned forward. "Alcoholic, is she?" Then improved her statement to herself, keen to be accurate. "Drugs, nowadays, I suppose. Drugs, Robbie, is that one of her problems?"

"No. Never. There are no problems anymore. I don't know why I said that." My weakness had passed. I'd give nothing away now.

"I know why you said it." Her gaze drifted. "She was difficult." Emotions I couldn't determine were vying in her eyes.

"Why?"

"Because, well, my goodness."

"What?"

"Mmm?"

"You said *my goodness?*"

"Oh, she was destroyed. Destroyed." Arrogance and satisfaction were what had vied in her eyes with prudence a few moments ago, and won. Now the woman Jane was smiling, kind of vacant, kind of smug, not really at me, hardly there with me at all.

"How did you destroy her?"

She came to her senses, watched me, her expression empty now except for cool judgment. "What are you getting at? I didn't say *I*, or anyone, destroyed her. Just that she *was*. Broken family, that's all. Happens all the time."

A different air in the room. "And me?"

"What about you?"

"Was I—destroyed?"

"*You?* You were all right. You were a survivor. We could all see that."

"Who is *we?*"

"I mean *I* could see it. What are you getting at, anyway? I've told you I'm old now. Nothing's clear anymore. I'm a different person. I don't remember."

"You wanted to destroy her, and me as well, didn't

you? We were the only things left in his life not part of you. And you couldn't bear that. Well, Laura's fine, and beautiful, and she's happy. Her husband adores her, and her children, everyone does. She brings joy into people's lives."

"So what are you doing here?" She didn't look at me to ask it.

"I wanted to see your face."

"That's all? And what does it tell you?"

"What I wanted to know."

She didn't ask me what that was. I would have told her I was glad to see evil had not nourished her. And that, for all she denied it, she had guilt, and that she was lonely, and that she suffered in her own unsatisfactory way. She suffered. What I discovered for myself was that Laura had been right all along, there was nothing to be done about the past, or to be gained in searching through it.

"Where are you going?" The woman Jane came after me to the door. "You're not leaving? Don't leave. There's something I want to tell you. Your father came in here with you. His spirit is here now. I haven't felt it for years. I did for a while after he died but it faded. Now he's back. Don't leave now. Don't take him away again. Stay. We were just beginning, you and me. It matters. We could be friends. Wait. Do you know you look like him? Yes, yes, I told you. Of course. Very like. You always did. More so than Laura. I sense you have his powers. We would have got back together, Matthew and me. There's never been anyone else. Please don't go."

On the way back, I stopped outside the same call box

again, almost entered, until I remembered: no card, no coins. No point.

The children telephoned me most days, one or another of them. Patrick would ring on Sunday nights, a habit now. I'd wait in for the call.

"Hi Robbie, on the dot, right?"

"How is she? Is she better?"

"We're all fine, just fine."

"Don't do that. Tell me how things are."

"Not good, in truth. I'm thinking maybe this hasn't worked. That maybe there's nothing I can do for her and maybe, I'm sorry to say this, but that maybe she's not good for the children unless, unless—"

"Patrick?"

"Yes, Robbie, what? Ask me anything?"

"Would you like it if I came over, just for a while? Till she's on her feet again?"

"Would you? Would you *really?* Could you do that?"

Two weeks later I was disengaged from all my commitments. This time I was severing ties. The hospital, the Tuesday-night surgery, a number of my private patients told me they would not have me back. Not with my broken record.

X

WE DON'T DO
TEATIME ANYMORE

From my first sight of it, Janvier had repre-
sented peace and continuity. If ever, back home, I was
disappointed or sad, I could think of the house and its
people, its buildings, trees, the river, the bayou, and be
sure it would hold me again, restore me whenever I
chose to return. But not when I arrived that Maytime. I
had been ready to cope with the kind of depressed chaos
that I'd found there at Christmas. I wasn't prepared for
quiet, listless order, as if the spirit of the house itself had
quit.

It was a Thursday afternoon. There would normally
have been activity, noise—there had been that since the
day Teddy and Marie had raced over the grass towards
us, towards Raoul and me by the bayou. People were

moving about, speaking, it's true: Charlie and Sarah were playing in the oak grove with Lenny's wife, Phoebe, whom I hardly knew, kneeling close by with her own tiny baby in her arms. I could see back there to the left, Theresa hanging over the bridge between the dependency and house, Charles on the ground below with his arms high, hands cupped to receive on his fingertips the bucket she was lowering. And there was Marie, now, walking towards me, maybe her hand was raised, perhaps she was calling. A muffled, slow-motion lassitude enveloped the scene, enveloped me.

"Hi Robbie."

"Why aren't you at school? I was going to pick you up."

"I'm doing a home project. I don't have to go, if I don't want. Teddy neither. Will's there. You can pick *him* up."

"Home project?"

"Uh-huh. Laura's asleep. She'll be up later, I guess." There was a harshness in her manner. Helping me to unpack, she found the photographs I hadn't brought with me since my first trip. Those strangers' faces that had so fascinated her then, and that had become family. They fascinated her again. She stood in the doorway for more light on them, on us, on Esther, Laura, and me in Trafalgar Square, and on Esther in the one where she looks like a forties film star, Laura holding Will on his fourth birthday. Marie studied them for a long time before placing them precisely where they had stood four years before, and turned her back on them, crossing her arms. "So?"

"So shall I make tea?"

"We don't do tea anymore, Robbie. It kind of faded out."

"Well, I'm fading it back in."

I prepared the table on the verandah before fetching Will from school and would have asked him, *How's Mummy*, but he blocked me with talk about a musical the school was preparing, and how he was composing some of the music. His manner was lighter than Marie's or Teddy's. Even the little ones—two and three years old then—seemed to have had drained from them their plump and golden satisfaction with life. They whined and were restless at the table while Phoebe sat with her attention sprung as though waiting for the outcome of our pantomime. She didn't know about teatime.

Two hands came to rest on my shoulders. "I heard your voice." Raoul's caftan didn't disguise the weight he'd gained, any more than it had the very first time I met him. Only now the gain was greater still. He shuffled around the table to take a seat. "Why, teatime again. Now, I like teatime. It's civilized."

I tried to talk about the flight over, life in England, anything, anything, and failed. There were silences. The worst kind, occupied with noisy feeding.

"Hi Robs," from behind me. Laura, in her dressing gown, slouched to an armchair back in the shadow, sheltered her face.

"Guess I'll go fix my bike." Teddy scraped his chair and left. Raoul joined him.

"Can I take the children to watch TV now?" Phoebe asked me. *Me*.

"Like I told you, Robbie," Marie was gathering the

plates, "we don't do tea anymore. Will? Will?" He had curled into the swing with his guitar. "Don't just play that thing, help me clear all this."

Laura seemed not to hear or just not to mind this slipping, slipping. Will helped Marie load two trays, carry them out to the kitchen.

"Do grown-ups not bother to dress around here anymore?"

"I guess I will. In a minute. No one said you were coming, Robs." She allowed me to see her face, tired, vacant, but no cuts, no bruises. "You come to see us through?" Her voice without impetus was altered. "Did Patrick ask you, or Raoul? Suppose it was Raoul. He would. Maybe the children did, is that it?" None of this as though an answer mattered.

"I invited myself."

"Good. Have you come forever? That would be so nice."

"Will Patrick be home tonight?"

"Yes. He comes home every night. He never fails and it can be a long drive when the traffic's bad, you know that. Mmmm. He gets so tired too. Isn't he kind? Robs?"

"Yes."

"Yes. It is kind. He is kind."

"We're going to fix you up, Laura, we're going to get you better."

"Thanks"—possibly just for the ashtray I was offering. I leaned down with it and saw she was crying. "Robs, come to my room. I got to tell you something."

The few steps back there exhausted her and she sank, gasping, onto her bed. To prevent her sleeping away the rest of the evening I offered to help her bathe—*Oh, Robs, would you? Thank you, thank you so much*—and as I ran the bath and helped her in, drew the flannel over her arms, legs—Do you ever eat, Laura?—and washed the ragged tufts of her hair, she resurrected her *Sorry, Robs, sorry-sorry-sorry.* What shakes me now is that I could have touched her body so, been that close, yet sense nothing of what was really happening to her. And they called me a healer.

"What was it you had to tell me?"

She was half-dressed, standing by the window. "Patrick'll be home soon." Shut the curtains. "They say I should be in a clinic. Patrick and the doctor, to stop me drinking and smoking and thinking."

"And what do you say?"

She came close, drew her index finger down my cheek, discovering if it was really me. "Robs?" Her voice was pleading, uncomprehending. "Robs, no? Don't ask me what do I say. You don't have to ask me that. Not you. We said we'd never leave each other. We promised. Don't pretend you've forgotten. They'll shut me up in the dark and they'll tell me there's no one anymore. You haven't forgotten what happens."

"It wouldn't be like that and I'd come with you, be there all the time."

"They wouldn't let you. You know how they don't let you."

"Laura, you're confused. No one would hurt you. I'd be with you—" As I said that I doubted the truth of it. Even the most compassionate psychiatric clinic has its rules and views about which well-meaning souls represent the enemy.

Laura said, "So you want me to go too. I was right. There really is no one."

Will walked into the room and right up to her, guitar in hand—knocking on doors has never featured with him. "Listen to this, Mummy, I think it's nearly right." He settled cross-legged, oblivious to her nakedness, her gaunt features damp-eyed and sick. He saw nothing other than her true value. And right then she was aware of only him, nothing else in her own mind or in the world at all. He struck his first chord.

"Wait, hang on, Darling." She lifted the guitar from his hands and frowned, held her ear close to the strings while she tuned it, handed it back. "There, that's better. You were a little out. I can't believe you didn't hear that, Will?"

"No, well, I did. Well, I didn't really but . . ."

She ruffled his head. He ruffled hers. Her turmoil existed on a different plane from the one they shared. And although over the following three weeks I did see her weaken and grow more distant, whenever her eyes rested on Will she rallied. If he spoke to her she was Laura again. Laura as they all—as we all—knew her.

He finished the short piece. She said, "That's excellent, Darling. You're nearly there. Isn't he good, Robs? It's for the school musical."

As soon as he shut the door behind him I shook her arm to retain her attention, not have her retreat. "You can do that for *him.* You were bright, alert. You could stay that way. Do it for the others too. Don't they matter?"

She pushed my hand off her, rubbed the place where my fingers had pressed.

"You know they do. And Patrick. And you matter."

She lowered herself into a chair, holding on to the arms, frail, something of Esther as she had been towards the end. Her voice was quiet and certain. "But, Robs, I have no more to give. It's all used up. The children sense it and resent it. You must have noticed how changed Marie and Teddy are. They believe I've failed them and they're right. I'm no longer delivering. The little ones cleave to the one who does for them. Little ones always do. That's Phoebe now and she's very good. I hear them laughing with her, playing games. Don't think I don't wish it was me, but I can't."

"Why?"

"Because. It's only Will who never changes, is always himself and loves me, I hope."

"Of course."

"Yes. When I was still very young. Back then. You know—" the palm, the offering palm.

"I know."

"You were three, the age Sarah is now. I would have been seven. I made myself into what they wanted so that everything would be all right. So they would like me, or might be kind. Most of all so they wouldn't hurt me. Isn't that despicable? And, Robs, are you listening? I shouldn't have done that. I didn't understand then that there was no one, and I thought I'd find someone that way. By abandoning the little girl I used to be. I knew what I was doing. And I don't know if this makes sense to you, but she wants me back. And I want to meet her and be what she would have become, an honest person and not this cheap one who sniffs out the need in others, and supplies it to make them like her, and take care of her, and not hurt her. I feel like a building that begins on the second floor, no basement, no first. You've got a basement, Robs, and all the floors above. You go straight up. Still, I do wonder—"

"What do you wonder?"

"If anyone's in. Ha."

"Thanks. Very funny."

"Pleasure. Tell me I'm mad."

"You're mad."

"Then you're mad too."

"Then we're all mad." And we laughed to keep tradition.

"You can't go back, Laura. Nobody can. There's nothing there. I tried. What would you say if I told you I went to see the woman Jane?"

Laura pushed me aside, tramped small circles clutching her head. "I'd tell you to shut up, to shut up—*shut up.*"

I did shut up until, still clutching her head, she asked. "So?"

"She's pathetic."

"Cool."

"I know. I nearly rang to tell you. Then I didn't. Plays the piano quite well."

"I remember. What else?"

"Nothing much. Sad. Lonely. Commonplace. Bit mad."

"Bloody right." She scratched the air with her fingernail, scoring out the invisible. "I've got to get back, Robs, and make it all right. She needs me."

"Who, for God's sake?"

"The one I used to be." She dropped her hands and

swept the world clean with her smile. "Robs, would you rub my back? Click it or something?"

"*Click* it? Bloody hell, I'm a physio and you ask me to *click* your back. Do you really, after all this time, not understand what—"

"Sorry-sorry-sorry"—nearly laughing for real this time. "I mean *treat* it, is that better? Only I've got this pain right here, there, that's it, up a bit. There."

She lay down and I gave her the gentlest massage. Something to soothe her.

It was after two on the same night and I was with Raoul, having our State of the Union, and the state wasn't good. Patrick opened the door—*May I?* and *Oh, Pat my boy, my boy.* Raoul crossed the room to conduct him in but held him in his arms instead. Patrick swayed, drawing strength from him, allowing this old man to support his weight. His appearance was terrible. There was no one in the household who wasn't changed. He wouldn't sit down but leaned against the mantelpiece with his head on his arm and said, "Your face, Robbie, your face. You think I failed your sister, don't you? But she won't take help. I took her to a doctor. To a man I trust. He told her she smoked too much, drank too much, and that she needs the kind of care to be had in a clinic. She won't have that."

"I know."

"Could you persuade her?"

"No."

"I tell you something: If it doesn't work with you here

then—I must think of the children, you see. I'll be asking Laura to—"

"Don't say it."

"But now you're here and now you've seen what you've seen, you'll stay to see us through?" She'd said that too, *Have you come to see us through?*

"I'll stay."

Raoul sighed and turned his face away, placating the air with his hand, settling his emotion. Patrick lay down on Raoul's bed. We thought he was asleep.

The evening before, Laura had eventually dressed, but only once she heard Patrick's car outside. We had dined without the children. Phoebe had settled the little ones in bed and the others found what they wanted in the kitchen. I learned there were no "home projects" for Marie and Teddy, it was their word for truancy. Not once did I see a glass touch Laura's lips, not so much as water, but she became gradually less coherent and at around eleven-thirty she passed clean out. Patrick carried her to bed. Later I found the empty vodka bottle. None of us understood, not even Laura herself. My aim, I suppose, during the short period—was to restore her confidence and enough well-being to make her want to accept help. There would have been ways without her being shut away. I spent time investigating that. I was ready with any number of remedies and plans. Doll-like, Laura allowed me to take over, attempting to imitate what it was she had given to her family, and now withdrawn. I didn't succeed. Marie took pity on me and became her tranquil and wise self again. We would talk alone in my cabin. The first time she arrived that way she said, "I'm sorry for how I was, for being tough. So's Teddy. Only, can we not do teatime? It's not like it was anymore."

So we gave up teatime and settled on supper early enough for Charlie and Sarah, late enough for Patrick to have returned from the city. We all made an effort, Laura too. It was very hard. Raoul and I took up our afternoon walks and I supervised exercises, adjusted his diet to help him lose some weight. He entered into all of it, including tantrums, so we could make believe it was that first summer and start again from there.

Laura found me giving him a treatment and it was the first time she lost her temper. She kicked open his bedroom door. Instinctively I reached for the quilt to cover him but she stormed over, dragged it off him, leaving him unprotected. "See? See? You treat *him*, don't you? But not *me*. You don't care about me. You're not making *me* better. Why not? You don't care about the pain in my back. I'm hurting, can't you understand?"

I had never known her so violent. It was ugly and terrible but didn't last because her strength gave out. Soon all of us had experienced from her something like this, at least once. No professional physiotherapist would treat an unspecific pain without an X ray, I told her that, and offered to go with her to Oschner to have one. But Laura wouldn't leave Janvier. We were getting nowhere. Until the last week of May, when she came to my cabin before eight one morning, all dressed and neat in one of those box-jacketed, gold-buttoned suits she would have rather died than wear a few years earlier. It astonished me that she even owned one.

"It's my grown-up suit. I'm playing people today." She

wouldn't tell me where she was going. "But I promise I'll be back tonight." She was more purposeful and lucid than she had been since our talk on the day I arrived. She was Laura again. The one we'd been coaxing back had come at last and now was leaving. I said, "Wait, let me come too. I want to talk. We haven't talked for days."

She was already in her car with the engine running and pushed her arm out of the window to encircle my neck, pull me close. "It's not what you think, Robs. I'm not leaving you and I *will* be back tonight. And we'll talk and talk and talk and everything'll be like before. I'm going to make it, you see if I don't. Watch me. I can do it. I can, can't I?"

"Yes you can."

I passed the day dreading that anyone should ask where she was—no one did, not even Will—or that Patrick should return from the city to find Laura not there. He wouldn't believe I could have allowed her to go anywhere alone. Alone again. I could not believe it myself.

She didn't make me suffer long. She was home just after dark. I was walking the drive for the fifth time with Miss Moley when her headlights splashed the night behind us. She slowed down. "Naughty, naughty, checking up on big sister, are we?"

"Would I?"

"Quick, Robs, get in. I've got loads of lovely things."

She insisted on showing me her purchases inside the car, couldn't wait to bring them up to the house. Presents for the children, another camera for Patrick—*another camera?—But this one's special, Robs, it does things—*presents for every one of us. We unloaded and the children came rushing to help. How was it that the air danced to Laura's tunes? High and light and fine when she was. No one needed telling that Laura was back. The news was passed in the vibrating atmosphere so that Theresa came from the kitchen and Charles too—they came to admire the glass-globed candles and slipperware plates she had bought.

"The girl who made these is a genius, Robs, a friend of mine. Each one's got a different animal on it, see? Will, this is yours, you're the cockerel. Teddy, you have to be the bear, don't you? Marie, you're the lioness. Charlie, this is a little piglet, that's you, see? Carefully now, set it down on the table, there you go, Darling. Sarah, see what this is? It's a sweet-faced monkey, that's you."

A feast is what we were to have. The table arranged and glowing in time for Patrick's return. There was time enough for Teddy and Will, with Lenny's help, and Raoul's, to build a small bonfire while Laura and I unpacked the unlikely things she had bought to eat.

"You're such a kid, Laura. Is this what you've been doing all day? I could have come."

"Almost all day. Not quite. Love you, Robs." That last, sailing from nowhere like a chip off a meteorite. She deliberately faced me to say it, to show there was nothing to be hidden. "All right? I meant what I said this morning, still do. It'll be fine now."

"Laura?" Patrick sounded tentative.

She swung around and would have rushed to him but raised her arms instead to show she was herself, that's all. Herself again. And that she would have him come to her if he wished to do that after so much. Patrick stayed where he was in the kitchen doorway. "Laura?" He wasn't like us. He couldn't glide between wind and water. She drew him by the hand. "Come and see your present." He glanced back at me and I gave him the thumbs-up. His mouth altered as the decision was made. "A present? For me? Oh boy, I'm right behind you." And I heard them laughing and talking as they crossed the bridge back into the house.

The meal was probably no more elated than many we had shared. The thing being that it was the same again. Laura was showing us that we could go back to where we had once been. I remember her face in the light of her new candles telling each of the children what she thought they would be. "Marie, you'll be a scientist, I bet."

"You think? I want to be. My grades are good."

"Well, you have your namesake, Darling, don't you? And your mom thinks you will. And she knows things, your mom does. Teddy, I think—"

"No, no, not me. I want to be a slob like Great-Uncle Raoul."

"You're too kind, Teddy boy. Too kind. Nice to know I'm appreciated."

"We know about Will, don't we? Do we, Darling? Am I right?"

"Don't know, but Mummy can I play you this thing I did today?" His guitar was hanging on the back of his seat.

So we listened to his new tune and tried to make up words for it. Patrick took a picture of us all with his new camera. I have it right here, the way we were then. Teddy brought his blaster from his room and filled the bonfire-night with music, and the children all linked hands and danced around the embers.

"Hey listen, it's 'Jambalaya,' " Laura said to no one in particular, not to Patrick, not to Raoul, not to me. "Come on, Patrick, let's join them."

Raoul and I watched them down the steps. She held the rail on one side, his hand on the other. She didn't plane down to the water with the children streaming behind her.

Patrick hated having to go to work the next day. I watched Laura seeing him away in his car, wagging her finger and teasing him. One last kiss. He called back, "See you tonight." She stood waving for quite a while.

I drove Teddy and Marie to school. Will wasn't going that day. I didn't know why. I spent the morning with Raoul. We didn't refer to the change. Better not. The sound of Will's guitar, his pennywhistle, and his and Laura's singing and talk reached us from somewhere near the bayou. I believe it was Laura singing too, but I wasn't sure. I hadn't heard her singing for a long time. I saw them later on, as well, up on the levee, walking hand in hand. Neither was around when I left to collect Teddy and Marie. I guessed Laura was sleeping. We could see about that weakness soon. Have her strong again in no time.

Will was waiting for us when we returned from school. He asked if Teddy and Marie would go swimming with him. They raced to the river with Sarah and Charlie on their shoulders, having promised to be vigilant. "Are you sure, now? I better come too," I said. What I really wanted was to go to Laura or at least be nearby when she woke.

"We're fine, Aunt Robbie, you know we'll take care of them, won't we, Teddy? Marie, won't we?"

"Sure thing, Robbie. Anyway, if you stretch out on the swing you can see us all from there."

So I did that. And fell asleep. When I woke it was cool on the verandah and the sun was low over where the bayou ends, towards Pointe Coupee. I maintained momentum with one foot to the floor and shut my eyes to marry the textures of warm wood and the rattan weave pressing into the back of my neck, down the side of my body. There was the smell of creosote but faint, faint, its usefulness long gone, and Theresa's stew cooking over in the dependency. The closest sounds were the creak of that rattan and the chain suspending the seat grinding in hooks fixed to the rafters way above. The voices of the children reached me from the levee where they were still lolling and bathing, livelier with the coming of evening.

I bent forward to view down the steps and saw they were returning—Will, Sarah, Charlie, Teddy, and Marie, all safe—their shadows leading over the grass. Marie was making believe she had a ball to tease Miss Moley, who was jumping, walking backwards on her hind legs with excitement. Gauging some direction from the circling arm, she ran off barking, seeking, then stood forlorn and confused in her failure, watching the figures, drawn close and talking, walking away from her towards the house.

I called, "Miss Moley, poor Miss Moley. Come on, Baby, are they teasing you?"

My call arrested the four of them. They halted in a line, eyes directed towards me. I hadn't moved. I still had my hand raised in a wave to where the dog had been, although she had trotted right up to me.

"Do that again, Robbie?" Marie took the steps in twos. Still I hadn't moved, had stayed just that way, hand up. "You sounded exactly like Granny Esther."

"That was the darnedest thing," Teddy said, his arm sticky with sun oil around my shoulders.

They clustered, amused, interested, smelling of bubble gum, sneaked cigarettes, and the uncomplicated sweat of youth.

"Did you mean to, Aunt Robbie?" Will's brown eyes roamed mine. "Or not?"—with the trace of a frown. I shook my head. He knew it. "So say something else. Speak to us again, please," his soft voice urged. The others became differently attentive.

I felt as if I had been asked to sing, which I couldn't, had never been able to.

"Please," Will whispered, and the others murmured it too, *"Please," "Please,"* courteous in the way they would have been with Esther.

I opened my mouth not knowing, not trying for anything to happen. "Hellooo Babies, there we are then." Esther's voice from my mouth.

"Esther," they said, the four of them, "Grandma," "Granny Esther," "The GrandEst," charmed, uncertain, embarrassed. They settled close to me, behind, beside, at my feet, touching me, a knee, a hand, an ankle. Miss Moley was there too and we stayed, content to be that way, not speaking anymore until the descending night was complete.

I heard Patrick's car. "Look at the time. I must wake Laura."

"Teddy and I'll put Sarah and Charlie to bed." Marie hoisted Charlie up just the way Laura did, had done.

"Not yet," I said. "Supper first. All together like we do."

"Don't worry, we'll fix them something, won't we Teddy?"

"Sure thing." And the four of them were gone.

"I'll go and wake Laura."

"Wait, Aunt Robbie."

Patrick ran up the verandah steps. "Hi, where's Laura?"

Will squeezed the wrist of his stiff right arm, stepped back from Patrick and me. Never had he looked more like Laura, lean, tall for his age. His face was slightly averted but his eyes met ours to inform us that she had gone away on a trip. *On a trip*, he quoted it, like that, giving as precisely as he could her tone of voice when she'd told him that, before his face knotted and he buried his head into my stomach, the cloth of my dress stifling his sobbing, the sobbing he'd kept at bay all afternoon but that had now broken through and wasn't going to abate for a long, long time. When he came into my cabin during the night, climbed into my bed, I tried to tell him that Laura knew best, she would come back when she was better. And although he seemed to agree, it didn't assuage him, really, didn't assuage him at all. After the long crying he was unspeaking, and went without food, and wandered the garden, the banks, and the levee, dragging his guitar, never playing it and refusing company. Only he wasn't truly alone. I couldn't let him be and I watched him all the time. Even after nightfall I watched his shape moving in the darkness. It wasn't hard to see him. My eyes became accustomed.

XI

FREEDOM FIELDS

I hated her. I hated her. Never again would I take on her dished-up life. I promised myself that and more on the flight back to England.

Will had continued as I described, except that after three days he allowed me to walk beside him. We didn't speak. He stayed back from school. He was still not eating. About the same time that he allowed me to walk beside him, he also began playing his guitar again. Then—from nowhere, or, rather, from his own solitary place—Will asked Patrick if he might have piano lessons. Patrick's expression when Will walked up and asked that—*Excuse me, Patrick, but might I, do you think, please*—Patrick staring out from the verandah rail, rigid there for hours, startled from his thoughts, turned first his shoulders, inclined his head down to Will beside him—*I'm sorry?*—and Will repeated his request. It was as if Will had spoken softly—always so softly—in a foreign language. Gradually something took flight from him, from Patrick, it lifted away, and I realised only then that whatever it was had been on him since he had first walked out of the shadow bearing his resemblance to Laura—it could even have been her there concentrating on something in her hand. *Why, Will, you can have all the piano lessons you want—*

Will collected his guitar from the seat where he'd laid it and crouched on the bottom step to play awhile. Patrick snatched my wrist and pulled me after him inside the house. "You listen to me, right"—his face full of hate, as full of hate as it had been with love in that moment when he had understood Will's request. "You go find your sister, Robbie. Because she's in England. I believe so, don't you? You find her and tell her she has no more place in my life. I never want to see her again. If she wants Will I'll send him. I can't withdraw my love from him. Unfortunately I'm not made that way. But I can from her and I have. And she's never seeing our little ones again. I'll make sure of that. She's not fit to be a mother and you tell her—" clenching his fists against his chest, tearing at it as if he'd empty it right there if he could. "Oh, *go to hell*—"

I expected to find her in my house. Where else could she go? There was nowhere else. I opened my front door wearing, no doubt, the same expression as when I'd arrived in my flat to find Esther and her belongings and

Laura installed. Would it never end? But the house was empty. No sign of the break-in I'd so clearly pictured: glass on the floor from the broken pane and a note, *Sorry, Robs, I'll get it fixed, promise, xxx, L.* I tried to telephone Sam in Arles and they told me he was away, didn't know when he would be returning. The whole world was on the move. And so I had no track of her, any more than anyone else in her life. I mattered as little as that. I hated her. I hated her. Two weeks passed. I spoke to Patrick every day, to Teddy and Marie. Not to Will, who remained mostly silent, they told me. "He ate a burger yesterday," Marie told me. "He threw it up."

Then Sam rang.

"Where are you, Sam? I've so much to tell you. I really need to talk. Laura's missing. We don't know what's happened to her—"

"It's all right, Love. She's with me—Robbie, no—no listen, don't, Robbie, stop it, listen, just listen can't you—"

"No I won't listen. You tell her that's *it.* You tell her she's right: There's *no one.* There's sure as hell not me. She's left her children, Sam. You like that? You like that kind of woman? Well fine. Have her."

"She's sick, Robbie."

"You're telling me she's sick. Well good. That's all. *Good.*"

"It's lung cancer and she hasn't got long."

"Good. Good." I slammed down the receiver.

It wouldn't hold in my head, refused to form as certainty or take on any reality. I didn't tell Patrick. Wouldn't tell Raoul. There was no one.

I had no number for Sam and stalked the café I used

to go to for two days before I found someone who knew Dan, the Rastafarian, and I waited outside his house until one evening he returned. He knew where Sam was. Laura had been to him for Sam's number in France. Sam had come back and he and Laura had stayed with Dan a night or two before leaving for Sam's mother's place in Plymouth. When he heard my voice, Sam said, "Robbie, Love, I'm so glad you've rung. Will you come and see her soon?"

He explained how the tumor exposed by the X ray at Oschner, taken the day before she left Janvier, was inoperable. She had already been through two sessions of radiotherapy. Neither had reduced it. She was supposed to have been beginning chemotherapy but there had been a misunderstanding. The doctors seemed to have thought she had some principle against it—*They were wrong, Robbie, she* wants *to live, she'll try anything.* This confused me until a long time afterward. Such misunderstandings so rarely occur. *It might only be six months, Robbie, a year, two years even, and like my mum says, like we're all saying now, miracles happen all the time, don't they? Come soon—*

"Sam, I'll call Patrick and explain everything."

"Don't do that, Rob. It'll make him come and she couldn't handle it, not just now. I suggested it myself. I swear I did. I'm not that possessive, you know that. I thought he should know. But she won't have it. Just let it be, eh. Let her have it her way."

But I did call him and of course he wanted to come right away. "Please, Patrick," I used Sam's phrase, "let her have it her way," and added, "for now. I'll keep you posted. They say six months, so there's time yet. And you never know, it could be longer. I mean—"

I wanted to say that it could be a year, two even. I wanted to say miracles do happen, and if they happened to anyone they happened to Laura. It was almost peaceful to have a reason for her having left Janvier, to have a perspective. Patrick was unspeaking, although I knew he did not want to end the call. Neither did I. Eventually he said, "You still there, Robbie?"

"Of course."

"Please tell her—and I want you to know as well— that I know I should have spoken more, asked more, that not to was a form of cowardice. I knew it then too. I wouldn't be that way again. If I had another chance I'd speak. I wouldn't leave her alone in silence. I'll never leave anyone alone in silence again."

I can't explain why I didn't rush down to Plymouth except that I was paralysed. It was dusk in my brain, there was no retreating to afternoon, I knew that, but at least I might stay still awhile. And so I did, until Sam rang on a Thursday night. He was crying. "Robbie? Are you there? Hello, Love. She's got five days, that's all. *Please* come now."

Freedom Fields used to be the main hospital of Plymouth. Now there are just two wards in the whole building, and the radiotherapy unit. The inspiring name isn't reflected by the building, five floors of shabby concrete in a short derelict street of one-story houses, a sad park at the end. Sam, who'd been squatting on the steps outside, supporting his head in his hands, nearly pulled me over in his effort to rise. He kissed me on either cheek before stepping back to show his face and tell it without words and I heard "Ah Sam" come out of me like a cough.

"I know." Taking time to adjust, he added, "She's on the top floor, end bed on the left"—thumbed towards the doors behind him without attempting to move. "Lovely weather."

"Yes. 'Specially here with the breeze from the sea." You could smell the sea from there.

"Good journey?"

"Hardly any traffic."

"Surprising really, that A303 can be a shocker. 'Specially in June. Is it holiday time? I don't know."

"Sort of."

He pulled out a handkerchief, blew his nose. "There's a little park at the top there. Found it yesterday. Had a bit of a sit."

"Are you coming back up?"

"Oh yeah"—staring towards the park.

"Shall we go then?"

He shuffled ahead to where the lift was obscurely situated, pressed the button, and leaned with palms pressed against the wall. We listened as it ground down towards us, stopped at the floor above, moaned up, away again. Content to be waiting, Sam nodded. "Bit slow sometimes, comes in the end."

Well, I couldn't wait for the end. "I'll take the stairs. See you up there." But he followed me, hanging on to the rail, laboring at every step. Two nurses going off duty passed me, came to him five steps behind. The dark-haired one patted his shoulder. "You all right, Sam? Take it easy, Love." She smiled up at me about him, about his fortitude.

There was a sign outside Ward 23, UNRESTRICTED VIS-ITING. PLEASE ENTER. It chilled me. Once through into the stifling heat of the unaired ward, Sam assumed his familiar cocksure bounce to proceed down the aisle of beds occupied by women, all of them well over seventy. "Hello, Alice. See your old man's in, then? Keep an eye on her, George, she's hiding her toy-boy under the bed there." George saluted from his visitor's chair and lifted the banter from out of the air, pocketed it, before continuing to bathe his wife's face. Sam stopped at the foot of another bed. "Oi, Rene, you got those dirty mags again? I'll tell matron."

"Knitting patterns, Saucy. This Laura's sister?"

"Yeah. It's Robbie."

I was looking for Laura, for the end bed on the left. It was empty, freshly made. I gripped Sam's sleeve. *"She's not there."*

"Yes she is Rob, look."

A figure was sitting up in the chair on the far side of the bed, eagerly observing our approach. Sam strode ahead, perched himself on the arm of the chair, gestured towards me to announce, "Here she is, then, here's our Robbie."

I stopped.

Laura's head was swollen to twice its natural size. There was no definition where it met her neck, and almost none where her neck met her shoulders. Her skin was tight, tight to bursting, bluish, transparent. Holding on to Sam's hand, she rose, swamped in a pair of striped pajamas. "Robs?" She stood steady, giving me time, lowered her eyes to Sam, and he winked at her. "Robs?" she said, her head on one side, and it was her old smile in that massive face—already becoming less strange. Laura shining through. "This isn't me, Robs. I'm not what you see here"—denting her cheek with her finger—"This is just, just—" She twisted her mouth in that way she always had and she could have been twelve, or seventeen, or twenty-four. "Aren't I right, Sam?"

"Yes, Love. Just your little chrysalis."

She was pleased with that, repeated, "Just my chrysalis, Robs." Then my weak arms held her. Hers were strong. "Sorry-sorry-sorry," she was saying into me, and from our embrace I had a dissolving view of Sam pressing the heels of his hands hard against his eyes. I'd seen him do that before too, a long time ago, when he'd lost Laura. Could it be true that this was the three of us here?

"It's all right," she was telling me. "Come on now, it's all right," and, "Here, now you sit in the chair." She settled on the side of the bed and I did too. "The chair's lovely, really. I wish you would."

"I'll get a couple more." Sam made off down the ward.

"We'd better ask first, Sam. There's Debbie. Debbie, sorry?"

The nurse finished adjusting a drip feed leading to, to—all you could see was a web of yellowed hair on the pillow, the faintest outline beneath the sheet. She came, deftly catching up Laura's wrist with one hand, reading the watch pinned to her lapel with the other and asking, "Hello my girl, how's tricks?"

"Is it all right if Sam gets some chairs?" Although Sam was already back with two. There was something of Esther visiting here in this meekness that Laura displayed to this nurse and others.

"Course, silly." Debbie chucked Laura's chin. "So this is Robbie, is it?" leaning around her, "Hello, Robbie. Can I get you anything. Cup of coffee? Sam? Coffee?"

"Have a cup of tea, Robs, the coffee's filthy. Oh sorry, Debs, but, you know. Sam likes the coffee. You'll have a coffee, won't you Sam? Robbie and I'll have tea if that's all right?" She might have been hosting a garden party at Janvier. Until Debbie stood up to go, that is, and Laura clutched her arm with both hands.

"So how's work then, Robbie?" Sam called loud, although he was close enough to hold my shoulder. I was watching Laura. He pulled at me. "Robbie?" To prevent me from seeing, hearing.

Laura's voice was savage and strained and her words worked out from rigid lips. "How much longer?"

Debbie stroked her back. "Forty minutes, Love."

"Forty? *Forty?* It can't be."

"Is it very bad?"

"Uh-huh." Breaking on the highest note.

"I'll speak to the doctor."

"No. No. Sorry, sorry, be all right. Must try."

"'Tea along in a minute, then." Debbie's eyes moved to Sam, delivered Laura back to him.

"Come and sit here, Laura. You like it here, that's right, there you go, that's the way." Sam helped her sink into the armchair she'd offered me, her mouth gaping, eyes given up to pain. And as she sat, as she sat I saw her feet, noticed them for the first time, blue-white, massively swollen like her head, great veins riding on them and I couldn't, not any more, a minute, just a minute please, felt eyes on me as I groped my way back towards the doors.

Outside in the passage Debbie asked, "Would you like to sit in the office a minute? Sure? Take your time then, just take it easy." Take it easy. They knew about *take it easy* and now I did too, knew where all Sam's strength had gone and why he'd needed to be outside discussing traffic and the weather.

Tea had arrived when I returned and Sam produced a packet of Hobnobs. "Here, Robbie, have one. We love them, don't we Laura?"

"Yup, but you prefer the milk ones, don't you, Sam. I like these. Robs?" Setting aside her plate. "Poor Robs, I'm so sorry, but listen . . ." Cup in hand, Sam wandered purposefully away towards Rene with her knitting patterns. Laura leaned forward. "Look at him, isn't he wonderful? He knows most of them on the ward, makes us all laugh." She reached to touch my face, but something was making me angry and I wouldn't let her. She sank back. "I'm sorry, Robs. I don't know what to say to make it better for you. But I am all right, if that's any help. I'm glad I was told, in case you were wondering. Do you know I feel less lost now, more myself than in the whole of my life. Isn't that funny? Who was she, that mad girl, that Laura? I'm real, Robs, this is me, inside, I mean."

"I spoke to Patrick."

"You weren't meant to, Robs. I don't want him to see me this way and I can't talk to him, it's too late. And I don't have the strength. It doesn't matter anyway. I've written him a long, long letter. Tried to make up for a lifetime." She tried to laugh. "I explained as much as I could so he'll understand. And he will, really. I know what they must all be thinking. But, Robs, I couldn't have them suffer more on my account. Not the little ones. Not Will. Listen"—she reached out to have me face her—"they've lost no one of any substance. We know that, don't we? And it *was* lovely, wasn't it, what Patrick and I created? Our life there and everything? Five minutes of perfection?"

"*You* made it. Patrick says that, Raoul too."

"And I was on course to destroy it. Would have too. You know that, don't you? See? You're not arguing." And I wasn't. "But I made it good for a while. And Patrick liked the way I was?"

"Loved, Silly."

"Yes. I couldn't let them see me this way, not after everything else I'd put them through. That got to be bad enough. I'm ashamed, don't think I'm not. But they'll forget all that, won't they? And remember me like I wanted to be? You won't have to explain anything. Do you like my pajamas? They're Sam's. Slippers too, only they don't fit." Rocking forward to glimpse her poor feet. "*Feet's too big.* Remember that? Fats Waller? They told me there was a chapel in the hospital, the other place I was in before this, Derriford, before they sent me here. I walked about one night looking for it. They let you do that, walk about if you want to. That's good, isn't it? Found it in the end. It was nice, except I thought I'd have some *experience*, you know, that now of all times if there is someone, something, they might put in an appearance." Attempting a dismissive laugh, she was overtaken by violent coughing fit to split her head, then resumed where she'd left off, as if the raking her body had taken was nothing to do with her. "Anyway, it was tranquil in the chapel, helped me to think a bit, and I see it differently, the way it's all been——" It wasn't the cancer or what the drugs had done to her body, it was her acceptance of it all that was carrying her away from me.

"Hey, Robs, no, don't look away, look, *look*, Robs." Her hands were raised to pinch an imaginary cloth before her face. "It's very easy when you know it's got to be. Honestly. All you have to do is this"—she opened her fingers and blew—"Is to let go, just like that." Her eyes were wide. There was wonder in them for the first time that I'd ever seen.

Sam returned at the moment the light shut out in her face and she threw her head back, her mouth a rictus, fingers splayed flat on the arms of the chair. He lunged past me to the oxygen cylinder, she grabbed the cup from him with both hands, and as she fought for air against pain, her eyes fixed on me, telling me things I'll never forget.

Sam said, "Get the nurse, Robbie. Quick." Only the nurse was already there and we stood back. Viewing it all now, it seems to me that Laura was the one who knew her part and played it well. Sam and I were the shuffling amateurs, more often in the way than not. There was nothing to do but watch until the spasm subsided enough for the nurse to tip some pills from a plastic cup and pour water to help Laura swallow them. "Is that all," I hissed at him, "is that all they can do?" He squeezed my elbow. Soon after, she was dazed, calm again. Sam arranged a pillow on the floor, tenderly raising her left then her right foot, to rest on it. He placed another pillow so her head couldn't fall. "There you are, Love. Have a snooze now. Robbie and I are off for a bite to eat, all right?"

She started forward. "Sam? Sam?"

"We'll be back very soon. Take a nap and keep an eye on my bongos." He nestled them in her lap, set her hands around them.

"Will you bring some cigs? I've only got two left."

He rooted in his own pack, tucked the last three in her breast pocket. "I won't forget."

"I don't believe about five days. How can they know? She's so strong, her voice and the grip in her arms and hands. She's hardly like a sick person at all."

Sam listened. We'd found somewhere on the harbor front open to the pavement, crowds pressing by. Such a hot day. "Busy sort of a spot," he said, pushing aside a menu and a bottle of tomato sauce.

"And she's not even in bed, Sam, or lying down."

"Hasn't been to bed since she was diagnosed back in the States. Sat up in a chair every night at Dan's place before I came, he told me. Took her down to my mum's as soon as I got back. Toddled along to the doctor, signed on. Good old National Health. Square-one stuff, made out she didn't know. They had her in for X ray straight-off. Didn't let her out again till she'd had the first lot of radiation. Didn't make so much as a blip on the tumor.

'Inoperable.' And I'm thinking—like I told you on the phone—all right but it could be a year or two, suddenly even six months was a lifetime ahead. Funny little plans entered my mind. Places to live. How it could be. She sat up all the time back at my mum's, easier to breathe, much as anything. You won't go, Robbie, will you?"

"Where?"

"Anywhere. You won't leave?"

Leave? Leave? There was no other world but this. "What did she say when she was told about five days?"

He lit a cigarette. The waitress arrived. We dutifully ordered fish and chips, two pints of beer. Several times he attempted to answer my question, left it. "Nice to have the sunshine." Esther. Esther about. Thank God she was gone, not to have to suffer this. Our order was dumped before us. "Lovely," Sam said and drank half his pint in one. "I wasn't there when they told her, see. Only I asked the lady, a counselor. She was the one who did it, uninvited. Told me she'd been talking to Laura on and off—well, I knew that—and she said to me that the moment came she 'saw a window,' fuck her. Like you, I wanted to know what Laura said. Quite happy to describe it, she was. 'Spect she's asked that all the time. She, the lady, was sitting on the bed, Laura in her chair like she always is. She takes Laura's hands to tell her, both of them, like that, and Laura listens. Drops her head, grips tight. Doesn't say a word. Just goes on gripping. Five minutes, more. She told me, this lady, that she, she was the one to pull away first, *before my back gave out* was what she said." Sam blew his nose, lit another cigarette, considered it there between his fingers. "Funny how they let them smoke on the ward. Only why bloody not? Christ, Robbie"—his words almost sung in the effort for control—"glad you're here, girl."

The waitress wanted to know if there was something wrong with the food and I told her we'd changed our minds, weren't hungry. I think she thought we were lovers.

"I knew already, see?" he said. "They'd told me yesterday morning, right before I rang you. Would've talked it over when you got here, what to say and all. Only in the afternoon she'd been in first, this counselor person. Can't help wondering if it's right. She's got this proprietary air about death, like she holds the ticket, password, whatever. Sodding know-all. Only Laura thinks she's great. And she may well be. I don't know if I'd have had the courage, don't want to think."

No.

Laura was different when we returned. The wonder, the inexplicable energy, the tensile strength: all gone. No partying now, no courtesy or small talk. We were dumb visitors on chairs drawn close as could be to a young woman heaving for oxygen through the mask she kept clamped to her face, removed, anonymous in her sickness, not Laura anymore. Not until suddenly she lowered the mask. "Did you get my cigarettes?"

Sam gaped first at her, then me. "Christ. *Christ.* I forgot."

"Sam, Sam, you didn't?" Tears blotting out her eyes.

"I'll go right now, right away. Won't be a sec."

"No, it's all right." She tried to mean it, only you could see it wasn't all right, and he was already on his way.

"Robs, got, letters, there, take, them"—stuttered between gasps from the cup and pointing an undirected finger. In the bedside cupboard I found three letters. One each for Patrick and Will, another for Teddy and Marie. "Give, later, whenever, not, yet."

When Sam came with the cigarettes, he lit one and passed it to her. She was too weak to take it and he held it to her lips. She drew slightly, turned her head away, closed her eyes. A different nurse came and sat on the bed. "Hello, Laura, I'm Jill, here for the next three nights. I'm just going to give you a little injection, all right?" Sam and I moved aside. Laura was barely conscious when we sat down again. Soon after Sam rose to leave, and I followed, only I didn't want to go. "I don't want to go, Sam."

He told me, outside, waiting for the lift, "Stay if you want, but I've tried it. There's a different world beginning in there, their night world. Starts when they bring the trays around. The nurses, the patients, doctor doing his rounds, quite late sometimes. Same things as during the day when they're only too glad for you to lend a hand. But at night it's more exclusive, like a club you're not a member of. Try if you like, so you'll know."

I didn't. I could have stayed with Sam at his mother's house but preferred to be alone and he understood. He helped me find a B&B three streets away. I was hungry and couldn't eat, restless but without the will to move away from the questions to which Laura was finding answers. I'd seen them, untranslatable, in her eyes. I had no more reserves or rules to guide me through this terrible limbering for an event that wasn't yet, but was promised and still inconceivable. And I can admit now to another element in my anguish: something like impatience. As if this moment we were waiting on, knew about—a moment as impenetrable as infinity—would be an inspiration, a letting-go, an unraveling, not just for Laura but for me as well.

Somewhere around three in the morning I telephoned the ward and discovered even from a distance that Sam had been right. A male nurse answered and told me that of course I could speak to her, that they'd been sitting in the dayroom playing Scrabble, we could talk while he made her a hot drink. "Hang on a sec, I'll get her." I heard the receiver containing me being placed on a table, his footsteps going away, a trolley clank, voices coupled in laughter, a door close, and Laura's cough before I was collected up again. "Hi Robs. That was Steve you were talking to. I've been playing Scrabble with him and Jill."

"Am I disturbing you?"

"No, course not." But yes. There was something intangibly businesslike in her voice.

"How do you feel?" Bloody silly, really.

"They're getting something to help me sleep."

"Laura?"

"So I better not stay long, you see."

Sam came around first thing to say we couldn't visit until after lunch because due to staff shortage they were moving the occupants of Ward 23 downstairs to Ward 22 for the weekend. He said it was mayhem there. I mentioned my telephone call and how well she'd sounded. He nodded like he knew and how little it meant, which annoyed me because he shouldn't give up, he shouldn't. Except he was right again. I'd thought we might play Scrabble with her too in the afternoon, like they did in the night. It wasn't that way. The ward—so cramped that six beds were arranged lengthwise down the center aisle—was filled with the noises of the sick and the all-too-well. Those who couldn't visit during the week were here now—babies, children, friends, and relatives distant in every sense, they'd all come, as though for a good day out, because not everyone here was dying. My guess, you understand, but there was a hearty interchange taking place all around that wasn't like that between the living and the dying, when, as one of the living, I was becoming impressively redundant.

It took us a while to find Laura. When we did, she'd slipped sideways in the bedside chair, unable to right herself, head sunk, face lost behind the mask, behind her hands. She withdrew it long enough to grasp the nearest of us, which was Sam. "They don't come anymore, get them, *please, please, please.*" Her words dragged down into the coughing that yanked her forward, and she dropped her precious cup, flailed for it, and we knocked into each other, Sam and I, in our effort to reach it. I went one way, Sam the other, to find a frantic nurse simultaneously ministering to a patient and fielding inquiries from visitors. We were told to bear with them, please, they'd be along as soon as they could. At last I cornered the matron in the office next to the ward. "My sister," I said, "my sister," was all I could say.

"Is that Miss Heath, Laura Heath?" She'd never been anyone else, after all. "We're moving her to the side ward any minute. I'm just waiting for another nurse."

"Side ward?"

"Over there"—pointing across the passage. "She'll have it to herself."

I entered. Very clean and ready. A bed, a basin, and a great big window with a view of that park at the end of the street and beyond it a space of green, a cliff, I think, so the sea would be after that.

"Sam, they're giving her a room, I've seen it. It's lovely. Laura? Laura? They're giving you a room all to yourself."

Sam tried to console with his expression for her lack of response. They preferred we should leave when they came to move her. That was Saturday. I can't think how the rest of it passed.

On Sunday I was woken by my mobile ringing under the pillow, infiltrating something not sufficiently removed from reality to be called a dream. "I promised my mum I'd take her over to her cousin Betsie's. I'll be back by lunchtime. Will you go in, and I'll meet you there as soon as I can?"

After the previous evening, I was sure I'd find Laura weaker still and lying in that ready-bed. Wrong. Reclining in a chair—electric head- and footrest this time— bathed, dressed in fresh pajamas, her hair fluffy from a wash, she was watching the door and chattering the instant she saw me. "Robs, Sam just called, said you were on your way. Look at my room. I've got my own basin, look. And the window. It's huge. I was wondering, is that Plymouth Hoe, that green over there? Come and sit down. I've got a plan."

There were two chairs that hadn't been there the previous day, but no space for me on either side of her, squeezed as she was between the bed and the window. "I want to go out, Robs."

"Where?"

"Anywhere. It was so exciting yesterday going down in the lift, when they moved us all. I want to do something else. It's such a beautiful day. What about that park Sam mentioned? Matron said I can. She's got a chair. You don't want to, do you? I can see you don't."

I was terrified, that's all. I'd done as much for others who'd been far weaker than Laura was then, handled their limbs with perfect confidence, insouciance. Where was that woman now? When the matron arrived I said, "Laura wants to go out," certain, hoping even, she'd forbit it. "And why not" was what she said. Like the unrestricted visiting, the smoking, *Why not?* They provided an antiquated chair, four wheels with minds of their own. As I helped Laura into it, she clasped me around my neck and her cry of pain was so close it could have been my own. The matron must have heard, returned. "Are you sure about this, Laura?" And she was, but with less strength to show it.

When we were waiting for the lift, Laura began a childlike commentary on things she saw. "The lift," she said as the doors opened and I pushed her chair forward. "The hall, the doors, that's a ramp"—collecting these things as if learning the language, or recording the images to examine later. It required all my concentration to maneuver the chair. There was no one on duty in the hall, the building being almost vacant but for the two top floors. The front doors were padlocked. A back door was open. Out in that street, deserted and run-down, we passed a corner shop. It was boarded over and Laura said, "Oh look, they've closed the shop," as if it were known to her and a special place.

"Have you been there before?"

"No. Look, Robs, can you see the trees?"

It was a long time after that I understood she was seeing the world anew. The drugs maybe, or her simple joy in being out. I leaned hard to keep the cumbersome chair propelled forward, the top of her head below my eyes—not a fleck of gray in the black hair—vulnerable, innocent even, in the way it moved from left to right to see everything, miss nothing. A man passed us on his way out of the park. He smiled down at Laura, then at me, and quickly averted his eyes from the tears streaming down my face.

All the years of her existence, through the beatings and the rows, the days of her dashed hopes, the times she sheltered with me, and even when I abandoned her to find my freedom at Janvier—and then me unable to take that freedom, so she did—through all of this I was drawing strength from Laura, given by the simple fact of her existence. My sister, there in the world before me, and now here I was pushing her dying body ahead of me in the saddest park in the world. A couple of bleak acres set on a hill, the path-side lamps all smashed, a breeze-block hut smattered with graffiti, reeking of piss. Lonely people, Sunday people, walked there with us. A woman passed, her dog a long way behind. He slowed as he saw the chair. "A dog, a dog." I thought Laura was still noting things, didn't hear the fear in her voice as it approached and stiffened, its eyes on line with hers. "Hello boy," I said, then Laura uttered a strange sound, she was shaking. I placed myself between the dog and Laura. "Get on boy." He didn't move. I yelled "Call him" to the owner and she did, displeased.

"I know what, let's sit down." Laura seemed to be with me again.

There was a bench ahead. We stopped there. She surveyed the pathetic park, all scant grass and dog turds and signs telling you what wasn't allowed. I knelt to arrange her blanket, saw her face. It was radiant. "Robs, this is so beautiful. Thank you. Thank you. Look at the trees. The air, smell the air blowing up right off the sea. Can you hear all those birds?"

So I used her eyes. The trees were young, bending with, whispering to, the wind, the air was crystalline, the fast-moving clouds pale gold, and Laura was right. I wanted to talk so much and say important things but nothing came. When I looked at her again she held her palm open. Our signal. The open palm with the past poised there. "Robs?" She waited to be sure I was listening, then she was distracted by something the distance held, and her voice was so vague she might even have forgotten me. "Let all that go with me, Robs. Let it go when I do." Shortly after, she asked to return to Freedom Fields.

The chair stuck on the very last curb before the hospital steps. No matter what, I couldn't move it. My cussing aroused Laura, and she became bright and attentive and began to laugh. And for once no cough curtailed it. "I'll get up, wait, let me"—raising herself.

"Don't you dare get up. Get up and I'll kill you."

"Thanks a lot"—completely overcome with laughter now and me too.

A woman was passing with a baby in a pushchair. She grinned at us. "Want a hand?" Together we lifted the chair with Laura in it. The wheels unlocked, and all the way up to her room Laura repeated, "That was *so* kind, aren't people kind, people are so kind——"

I was elated, triumphant, when we arrived back. It *was* such a beautiful day. The most beautiful I could remember. And the window there. And this room to herself. And everything was going to be all right. Laura rose unaided from the wheelchair, all ready to laugh some more. "I must have a pee."

"I'll get a bedpan."

"Ergghh. Robs, please. I use the lavatory out there. Always do, if you don't mind."

A doctor appeared while she was away. A short man, very young, Indian. I told him where Laura was and he smiled, shook his head.

"Hi Doc." Laura breezed halfway across the room, where she froze and let out a cry, not loud but horrible. Together we caught her as she fell forward, helped her to the bed, where she refused to lie, remained upright. "Okay now, okay now." But it came out of her again, that sound that I'll hear forever.

The doctor stood in front of her. "You're very brave," he said and watched her. "Would you like the shunt now, Laura? Do you think you're ready now?"

A discussion well-worn between them—nothing I knew anything about—to and fro they must have been, something in the offing that Laura had resisted until now. A nurse came to help him strap a box low on her stomach while she held her pajama top high, winking at me above it. Resettled in her chair once more, she was intrigued by the sky. "Can we open the window, Robs? Wider, wider. That's great. Isn't that great?" Then she drifted. I sat well back in the room, feeling like an intruder. Minutes passed, suddenly she jumped. "Oh Robs, you're there. Sorry, sorry. Have you been waiting? Do you want to leave?"

"No. I'll never leave you."

Shortly she jumped again, came to as before and found me there, although I believe her sight was failing. "So lovely, the air. Glad about the window. Robs?" I held her hand. "Robs—would you—don't be cross—but would you mind going, please. I just want to—mustn't mind. See you later. Sorry, sorry."

Sam told me he'd arrived not half an hour after I left and found her scarcely conscious, and he told me that he too had felt as I did, he had felt in the way. He rang me at four-fourteen the following morning. "I'm with her. Come on over, Robbie, quick."

She was dead when I arrived. Lying in the bed, but she'd died in her chair, a hemorrhage brought on through coughing. Sam was on the far side, his head sunk on the bed. Blood was congealing on her wristwatch. Sam had been there. "It wasn't minutes ago." He encouraged me with his eyes to look on her dear face.

Four days, not five.

XII

YOU CAN'T GET TO
HEAVEN WITHOUT PASSING
THROUGH ATLANTA

I had seen. I did not believe. I saw her face as she lay there, still warm, already set in death. And again later in the mortuary, hard, cold to my touch. Gone out of my life forever. I had seen. I did not believe. There was no such thing as the world without Laura.

Sam and I returned to London together. I telephoned Patrick and straight-away he said, "You don't have to tell me. She's gone. I know it. I just know it."

"She has."

"I have her letter. She sent me a letter. Never had a letter from her before. She let me understand everything so carefully, why she ran, wouldn't let me see her go down. Such a letter. I wish I could have, though, seen her." There was a long pause. I didn't try to speak—he would have been seated on that straight chair by the telephone, doubled over, forehead touching his knees, clasping the receiver with both hands. Curious, really, that I should have been so certain of the image. "Robbie?"—his voice in pieces. "I'd be different, another time. I'd do better. I never really spoke to her or encouraged her to speak to me. That was wrong. Leaving her alone in silence that way. I know it, only I didn't know how. I still don't, but I would learn. I want to."

"So do I, Patrick. How's Will?"

"You can imagine. It's going to take time."

"Yes."

Sam remained with me. We saw no one, turned the bell off the telephone, rarely left the house, and lived with recurring pictures like cuts from a movie—and he had so many more than I—clips of Laura's suffering, vivid enough to halt us. We were fit to be with no one but each other.

Two, three weeks passed until I arrived down one morning and found Sam preparing to leave. "I'll be off today, Love. You be all right?"

"Back to Arles?"

"Yeah. Love it there. You? Don't tell me, back to work, right?"

" 'Spect so."

I learned something about myself during those days with Laura, observing the nurses who cared for her. I learned about my coldness, about something inside me left for dead a long time ago. Something that had been barely formed and easily overlooked ever since. I doubted that I could ever be close to suffering again because I knew it now. My capacity for it was like a worn balloon, too easily inflated. A child crying in the street, homeless sheltering in doorways, lovers turning from each other outside an unlit house, a book on sale—a copy of which Laura had once given me—anything, anything brought tears to my eyes. I wasn't safe to be out. I could even have—didn't, but could have—turned to a stranger on a bus and told them, *Laura, my sister, she's dead, you know. She died.*

That was how it was for a long time, living alone, registering such events as the beating of my heart, the silence between breaths, whether I blinked or for how long I could bear the light scalding my uncovered eyes. The only truth left was Laura's truth, There's no one.

I already knew the dead have gifts to bestow. After all, hadn't I received Esther's voice, that afternoon at Janvier, and all the children heard it. Possibly I was waiting for Laura's gift.

The first sign of any willingness to go on somehow must have been when I played back the messages on my machine. There were only two, both from Raoul. *Robbie? You hearing me? Come on back, won't you?* And the second said, *This damned machine working anyway, talking to myself, am I? I don't think so. Come back, Robbie, come on back where you belong.*

You can't get to heaven without passing through Atlanta, they say that around here. They're not referring to the city but the vast airport, a changing point to so many places throughout the United States and the rest of the world. My flights had always touched down there, picked up another on to New Orleans.

When I asked the cabdriver to take me out to nearby Dawson Switch he slammed off the meter, twisted around with fine drama, stretching his arm along the front seat. "Dawson Switch? Sure, I know where it is, ma'am, but it'll cost you."

Leaving the airport—I think it was midday, daylight at any rate—through the back window I saw a little girl in a yellow skirt on the island between the terminal and parking lot. She was quite alone and the traffic was hurtling around her. She was waving at me. Without losing sight of her I reached to touch the driver, have him stop, but before speaking I looked harder. Waving, waving she was. Then I understood she wasn't waving for me to return. And she wasn't waving Goodbye. She was waving *Go on, go on*—and I laughed. Laura's laugh from my throat. In the rearview mirror I saw the driver's smile.

They still come to me unexpectedly, Esther's voice and Laura's laugh, when I'm wholly involved with the moment of my own life.

XIII

SNAPSHOT

It won't always hurt like this. Time will pass and it'll be different and you will still be here with all of us. With me. I know it and you don't—Patrick is telling me, telling it without speaking—*You would know it too if only you looked at me for long enough*—making this known to me while my face is averted to where Miss Moley is pressed against the screen door, following the passage of moths on the other side with her paw, like a short-sighted person reading small print. Darkness surrounds where our two faces are candlelit at the supper table. The children have left us for the cool of the verandah steps, the heavy air bringing back the sound of their talk and Will's guitar. It is a composite picture of how our lives have been for a few months now, and of how they could be for all time if only I look and see what he is telling me, and cover his hands, resting together before him on the table, cover them with my own.